Pam & P

Enjoy !

BLUE LOCUSTS

BLUE
LOCUSTS

AND OTHER WORKS BY
MARION BLACKWELL JR.

DEEDS PUBLISHING

Published in the United States of America
Published by Deeds Publishing, Marietta, GA
www.deedspublishing.com

Library of Congress Cataloging-in-Publications Data is available upon request.

ISBN 978-0-9834105-5-3

Books are available in quantity for promotional or premium use. For information, write Deeds Publishing, PO Box 682212, Marietta, GA 30068 or info@deedspublishing.com.

First Edition, 2011

DEDICATION

This book is dedicated to my precious, sweet wife, and in-house editor, Terry Christian Blackwell.

Terry is not only a wonderful wife and sweetheart, she is also a professional editor. Before moving to Atlanta, Terry was editor of several magazines in Tampa. She decided to become a psychological counselor, so she resigned her editorial positions and moved to Atlanta so that she could earn a master's degree in psychological counseling from Georgia State University.

While attending Georgia State she held a position as editor of a magazine, *Pulse*, published by *Atlanta Journal-Constitution* for the health care profession.

With beach sand still between her toes, she wrote and published a book on Atlanta restaurants and tourist attractions.

Terry has served as a Psychological Counselor at the Centers for Disease Control and Prevention during the past eleven years and remains in an on-call position at the CDC's request.

Her part-time job, which was trying at times, was editing this book for me. She spotted errors which I had read over three times, and patiently shot down my arguments as to why my way was right.

She is, I am certain, the sweetest, most unselfish, cutest, and most loving person in the world, and I am also certain that without her guidance this book never would have become a reality.

So, I thank you with all my heart, Miss QTPi.

M.B.

CONTENTS

Blue Locusts

November, 1864

Atlanta was destroyed and abandoned by the Confederate and the United States Armies. A United States army of 62,000 battle-hardened veterans, divided into three long columns, began its March to the Sea – to Savannah. The force included 218 regiments of infantry and artillery, a few thousand cavalry, and a wagon train several miles long of supplies. The objective was to devastate a swathe through the Confederacy, crippling their war effort, and, most important of all, breaking the will of the people to continue the war. It was harvest time, and the invading army did its best to live off the land. The only forces in their way were a few teen-aged cadets from Georgia military academies, some poorly trained and poorly armed "home guards" made up of old men and young boys, and a tired force of cavalry on worn-out horses. General William T. Sherman vowed to "make Georgia howl," and he did.

* * *

Sounds of tramping boots, shouted commands, jangling harnesses, rumbling wagon and cannon wheels had wakened the General at first light. Stretching on his cot, he waited until the smell of hot coffee and bacon simmering on a wood fire aroused his senses before sitting up and pulling on his boots. Orderlies immediately started taking down the tent and handed the General his breakfast. "Good morning, Sir," a Major greeted, stepping back from the fire.

"Good morning, Major. Looks like another delightful day. I had no idea that autumn in Georgia could be so crisp and invigorating."

"Yes, sir. Maybe we can come back some day under more pleasant circumstances."

"I would like that," the General agreed as the Major unrolled a hand-drawn map. "What's ahead of us today?"

"We are about here," the Major pointed as the General held one corner of the map. "No towns today. We should reach Sandersville tomorrow. Scouts report that the country ahead appears to be more of what we have seen since we left Atlanta, a few large plantations and a mixture of small farms and woods. No major concentrations of rebels and no large rivers, so it should be a pretty easy day."

"Any dispatches from General Sherman?"

"No, sir. And no rebel activity around our camps during the night."

"So unless we meet some unexpected resistance we should be in Savannah by early December along with the other columns."

"Yes, sir. There's a small reb cavalry detachment on our tail, and yesterday a bushwhacker took one shot at a forager's wagon and missed. Lt. Terrell's cavalry scouts are in our immediate front today. We are moving along at a good pace."

A sergeant held the General's horse as he swung into the saddle. "Well, then, let's just enjoy our ride through the Georgia countryside. Some of these plantations are quite impressive. Let's try to keep the men under control and hold down vandalism as much as possible… and mis-treatment of civilians."

The General admired the column moving by his camp site… infantry, artillery, cavalry, and the endless train of supply wagons. "Look at that, Major. My river of warriors flowing to Savannah."

* * *

Liz Williamson put aside the corn she was shucking and stood up to see who was galloping down Sandersville Road in such a hurry. Darius, from the Butler plantation up the road, was screaming at his mule, trying to turn in the Williamson farm lane, but the mule had built up a good head of steam and would not slow down until he had passed the gate. Finally getting the mule under control, Darius thundered up the lane at such a pace that Liz thought he might run right up on the porch.

"They's comin', Miz Lizzy, they's comin!" screamed Darius, using both hands to hold the excited mule.

"Slow down, Darius. Who's coming?" asked the startled Liz.

"The Yankees, tha's who," shouted Darius. "They's on our place right now and comin' this-a-way. Marse Butler, he say you better git on out of here." With that, the mule spun around and galloped off with Darius still screaming unintelligible warnings.

Some of the Williamson field hands heard the commotion and came running around from behind the house and from the fields, their eyes growing big with excitement as Darius screamed of the Yankees.

Mattie Williamson, thirteen years old and definitely the second in command on the Williamson farm, called to the hands from behind her mother, "It's nothing to worry about. Let's just get on about our business."

John Williamson, just turned ten and eager to assume his father's responsibilities, came quickly to his mother's side. "Do you think Darius knows what he's talking about?" he asked. "I didn't think the Yankees were coming this way."

"Look, Mother!" Mattie pointed out across the wide corn field. In the edge of the woods Liz could make out five horsemen. They had stopped to study the house. Then there were more, many more. Liz guessed twenty or thirty, obviously Yankee cavalry.

"Momma!" shouted John. "On the road!"

Coming down Sandersville Road was a column of Federal cavalry, riding two by two, easing its way toward the Williamson farm. At the same time, several dismounted troopers, with rifles at the ready, began walking cautiously through the dry corn stalks toward the house.

Liz pulled her two young ones to her side. "Be calm, children. Let's just wait and see what our guests are up to."

The column on the road stopped, and Liz witnessed the military precision and quickness with which they formed in groups of four, with three men dismounting and the fourth holding all four horses. Liz counted a dozen troopers approaching from the road, and another dozen through the corn field. At a signal all of them stopped within rifle range of the house, and then dropped to one knee, observing the house and barns intently.

A young officer and a sergeant rode up the lane toward the house, both watching the windows. The sergeant held his Spencer carbine in his left hand ready for quick use. The officer untied the flap on his holster.

Stopping at the porch stairs, directly in front of the Williamson family, the officer touched the rim of his black hat. "Good morning, m'am. Are there any men around the place?"

"We have five field hands out working," answered Liz.

"Slaves?"

"Yes."

"Any white men?"

"Just my son John, here." John puffed up at being considered a man.

"Mind if we look around?" he asked, at the same time motioning his troopers forward.

Liz looked him squarely in the eyes. "Looks like I don't have much choice."

Three soldiers entered the house, and three went around each side toward the barns and outbuildings. John spun away from his mother's side and followed the soldiers inside. "John! Come back!" she ordered.

"I just want to keep an eye on them," he called back and was gone.

The officer and the sergeant watched the procedure as all rooms in the house and all the farm buildings were checked. By this time there was a circle of dismounted cavalry around the whole place, with more still mounted waiting at a distance.

"Nobody inside," a soldier called out from a front window.

"All clear out back," called another, coming around the side of the house.

The officer retied his holster and the sergeant slid the Spencer into its scabbard. The other troopers relaxed on seeing this. The horsemen waiting in the woods rode toward the house, bringing the led horses with them.

Liz stood up to observe all the blue uniforms around her house, more people than had ever been on the Williamson farm at one time.

The officer watched her appreciatively for a moment, allowing her to absorb the power of his force on her farm. "M'am," he commented more politely this time, "I'm Lieutenant Terrell. Me and my boys here, we're from Ohio."

Liz nodded, unsmiling. "Pleased to meet you, Lieutenant Terrell. I am Mrs. Bentley Williamson. These are my children, Mattie and John. We are Georgians, and have always lived right here on this place."

"Might I ask, where is Mr. Williamson?" ask the Lieutenant.

"Major Bentley Williamson is somewhere in Virginia, doing all he can to help General Lee obstruct your General Grant as he tries to invade our country."

"I see." Lt. Terrell watched a moment as the sergeant posted pickets around the buildings, sentries to give an early warning in the event of a surprise movement by rebel forces. He studied the well-built, well-kept Williamson home. It was not as large as some of the plantation mansions he had visited this November since the army left Atlanta, but looked clean and comfortable. Fields and fences were well cared for and all the necessary farm buildings, barns, stables, corn crib, smoke house, tool shed, slave cabins, and wagon shed were a credit to their owners and their workers. He looked at Liz and Mattie. "My sincere best wishes for his safe return." Then after a brief pause, "May my men fill their canteens from your well?"

"Yes," said Liz a little too abruptly, taken aback by his sudden politeness.

The necessary orders were given and the soldiers went about the business of drawing buckets of cool water, filling canteens, adjusting saddles, and checking ammunition.

Lt. Terrell handed his canteen to the sergeant and swung off the left side of his mount, which immediately started grazing on the grass around the front porch. "We're going to give the horses a short rest. What are you going to do, Ms. Williamson?"

"What do you mean?"

"Well, you're not going to stay here, are you?

"Why not," asked the puzzled Liz.

Lt. Terrell removed his hat and studied her carefully. So pretty. So vulnerable.

"Ms. Williamson, we are scouts. We go in front of the main army to be sure that your boys don't surprise our boys, and to be sure that the army can get through. We report what we find back to our commanding officers. Do you know how big General Sherman's army is?"

"I don't have any idea."

"Well, it's about 60,000 men. Sixty thousand, Ms. Williamson. That's probably more people than you have ever seen in your whole life. It's divided into several columns, I don't know the whole picture. There are about 12,000 in our section, and they are all coming right down that road in front of your house, which I believe is the Sandersville Road."

Liz's mouth hung open in surprise. "But I thought Sherman was heading for Macon?"

"No, m'am, we're heading for Savannah. That move toward Macon was what we call a 'feint.' "

"Savannah!" exclaimed Liz. "We don't get much news out here, Lieutenant. Lots of rumors, but not much news. Wounded soldiers bring us information, and sometimes someone visits

Atlanta or Macon and brings us the latest news, then that gets spread from neighbor to neighbor, and often gets distorted in the spreading."

Liz looked at the troopers, many of whom were watching her. "Do? What could I do? What should I do, Lieutenant? Now that you have searched our home and farm, surely your army will have no concern for us, and will just march on by."

In addition to attractive and vulnerable, Terrell thought, how naive.

"What you see here, m'am, is about half of my scouts. There are 120 of us all together, all cavalry. Our other half is on the other side of the road. We straddle the roads, and move ahead of the main body of the army. In a few minutes we will be gone on down the road, and you will scarcely know we've been here.

"Now, right behind us will come a rough and rowdy bunch we call the pioneers. Their job is to see to it that the road is wide enough and good enough for the army to move through. They will take down all your fences along the road... yes, m'am, every bit of it... and throw the rails back away from the road. They will cut down any trees in the way, which will get some of your apple trees, and tear down any buildings too close to the road, which you don't have to worry about. Then will come the soldiers. Tired, mean, hungry, and angry. They are mad at you, and some of them will try to punish you. It's not personal, they just don't like rebels. Ms. Williamson, they will come through your farm like a swarm of blue locusts. We try to control them, but you cannot control 12,000 angry, tired men. They will go through your house, take what they want, eat all your food, and probably destroy what they can't eat or carry. If they don't like the way you act, they will burn your buildings, including this fine home. And, heaven forbid, they may abuse you and the children."

Liz felt back for the chair and sank down.

"Right behind them will come more cavalry, I think about 2,500. Then a very, very long line of infantry. Then our artillery, you'll see about 12 guns, cannons, with their limbers and caissons. Then more infantry, followed by our supply train, which will be more wagons and mules than you might see in a year. Then the rear guard, even more cavalry and infantry.

"As this force passes, your slaves will try to join them. We try to run them off, but they will not go. There are several hundred followers now, and they may or may not cause you some trouble.

"I hate to tell you this, m'am, but that is not the worst of it, as far as you are concerned. There is always a bunch of stragglers, you call them bummers, who can't keep up, or won't keep up. They are completely lawless, and won't hesitate to harm you if you try to keep them from taking your jewelry, watches, silverware, or anything else of value which the main column may have missed. Then they will eat or destroy any food which may be still around.

"As if that is not bad enough, probably mixed in with the stragglers and bummers, will come your own rebel cavalry. It's a small force which is there just to harass our rear and prey on stragglers. They are much hungrier and more poorly equipped than we are. If you have anything else at all left, they will take it, especially livestock."

"Our own men? Certainly not!" exclaimed Liz.

"Yes, m'am, I'm afraid so. Then, after your boys, more stragglers might keep on coming by for several days, seeing what they can find, taking what they want, and making all kinds of mischief."

The sergeant rode up. "All ready to move out, Lieutenant."

Lieutenant Terrell mounted. "I'm sorry to be the bearer of such unpleasant information. We will leave very quickly now to keep your people from following us."

Terrell spun his horse around, and with a command from the sergeant, the cavalry scouts trotted away from the Williamson farm.

Liz looked back down the road toward the Butler plantation. She heard the bite of an ax, saw a tall pine tree lean and fall away from the road, and saw a plume of smoke rising into the still fresh morning from the direction of Solomon Butler's home.

Other sounds came nearer – axes chopping, trees falling, men shouting. Life here will never be the same, she realized. Never again. Life on the Williamson farm will be changed forever.

Mattie and John watched their mother, trying to understand, waiting for a sign from her. Liz's attention snapped back to them, to the farm, to the urgency of the situation. Waves of emotions swept over her – fear for her future, pity for her children, concern for the future of their two families of slaves, and anger toward the Yankees for disrupting the lives of so many people. And then there was Bentley in Virginia – what would be here for him when he came home? The weight of these unknowns fell upon her like a smothering cloud, almost forcing her to her knees, almost bringing tears of resignation to a situation over which she had no control.

Almost, but not quite. She recalled one of Bentley's favorite axioms, "Don't just stand there, do something, even if it's wrong."

Grabbing the children, she held them to her tightly, then at arm's length. "Very quickly," she instructed, "we must get all our people to the front. Mattie, get everyone from the cabins and the house. John, bring in those still in the fields. Quickly! Now!" Without a question the two children sped away, sensing the urgency of the situation. Now alone for a moment, Liz sat down on the top step and closed her eyes, but she could not shut out the sounds of axes and shouting, and now the smell of wood smoke from the Butler plantation.

Soon the crew of black farm hands began to appear around the corners of the house, men and boys from the fields moping sweat and dust from their brows, two women leading children, all wide-eyed with concern and fear of the unknown. The two slave families on the Williamson farm were the Greens and the Harpers. Alonzo and Mary Green had three boys in their teens, all valuable parts of the team which kept the farm producing. "Big Joe" and Samantha Harper had a boy and a girl, both too young to be field hands, but still eager to be helpful. They all watched Liz with questioning eyes, eager to have the situation explained to them.

Liz hugged Mattie and John to her side again and addressed her anxious audience. "We have all been hearing a lot about the war. Some of it has been true, some has not. But one thing we know for sure, the Yankees are here, now." They followed her gaze out toward the road, where the pioneers were coming into view, with infantry skirmishers around them. "You know that one of the things this war is about is your freedom. Even though you have not been free, none of you can say that you have ever been mistreated on this farm. You have been asked to work hard, and you did, but none of you has ever been whipped, and no family has ever been broken up. And we never would. You have been well fed, and your children have been educated along with our own – right along with Mattie and John. But the fact remains, you have not been free. Until now. You would have gotten your freedom anyhow, sooner or later, but those Yankees coming down the road are making it sooner. So, as of now, you are free."

Mary hugged Alonzo and began to sob. The young people looked at each other, wondering what was happening. Big Joe, holding his straw hat across his chest, rubbed one hand across his head. "What we 'spose to do, Miz Liz?"

"Well, Joe, you can do whatever you want to do. Lieutenant Terrell said that a lot of freed people are following the army, but I don't think that's a very good idea. The army doesn't know what to do with you. You can go wherever you want, maybe into town, and find a job, or you can stay here and work the farm with us. We could pay you a salary, but then you would have to pay rent for your houses, and buy your own food and clothing. Maybe we could work out something depending on the crops, you could get a share of what we produce. And an awful lot depends on what the Yankees leave here after they go by."

Joe looked at Alonzo. "What you gon' do, 'Lonzo?"

Alonzo stared at the ground and shook his head. "Lawd, I don't know. I just don't know. I guess I'll just wait and see what the Yankees do. That all right with you, Miz Liz?"

Liz watched the soldiers now in plain view on the road. "You are free, Alonzo. You can do what you want. It's all right with me if you stay."

A zigzag split rail fence separated the farm's peach and apple orchards from the road. Each oak rail had been split by hand by Alonzo, Big Joe, and Bentley, and each mature peach and apple tree had been nursed from a seed to becoming a source of pleasure, nourishment, and income. The Williamson family, the Green family, and the Harper family watched helplessly as some of the trees near the road were cut down, and the rail fence was dismantled and pitched back from the road.

"Hey!" shouted Big Joe. "You can't do that! Them's our trees!" Big Joe started walking toward the soldiers. John started to follow, but Liz caught his shirt and held tightly. A soldier stepped out and lowered his rifle at Joe's chest. Joe stopped, and after exchanging a few words, backed off and shuffled back to the house with head hung low.

"What did he say?" asked John.

"He say they do anything they damn well please. 'Scuse me, Miz Liz." Joe turned and watched the soldiers, with hands on his hips, kicking at the ground.

The pioneers and skirmishers passed on by, and soon the road was covered with cavalry and dusty, blue-clad marching soldiers as far as Liz could see in both directions. Guarding the flanks of the moving army, small scattered groups walked through the orchards, through the fields behind the house, and some even close enough to the three families to nod, grin, and hurry on by, but never spoke. Thousands of feet and hoofs stirred up enough dust to almost obliterate the entire main column. A cacophony of sounds grew louder and louder as commands were shouted, men talked, feet and hooves stamped, wheels groaned, wagons creaked and rattled, canteens and equipment banged against the heavily laden troopers, teamsters and artillerymen yelled at horses and cursed their mules, and heavy artillery pieces rumbled over the rocks and ruts of Sandersville Road. In awe the three little families watched this spectacle seen by few, an army on the move.

After a stream of cavalry and infantry which seemed endless, there came wagons, wagons, and more wagons, each pulled by two, four, or six mules, transporting this moving city's supplies of food, ammunition, clothing, and medicine. The strong smells of droppings, urine, and sweat soon drifted to the house.

These passing sights, sounds, and smells in a density and quantity never before witnessed had an almost hypnotic, overwhelming effect on the families. Samantha clung to her children, Liz clung to hers, and all retreated to the perceived shelter of the porch.

The trance was suddenly broken when three wagons and several horsemen turned away from the passing army and rode up the lane to the house. With only a glance at the civilians in the yard and on the porch, the horsemen kept rifles ready and studied the surrounding farm with vigilance. The third wagon stopped at the orchards. Several soldiers jumped out and started gathering apples, filling bags they had brought. John jumped up defiantly, but Liz pulled him back to her. "Be still, son. Like the man told Big Joe, they are going to do anything they damn well please. Best not to rile them," she warned through gritted teeth.

A wagon stopped at the front of the house, the other continued on around back.

"What they gone' do?" wondered Mary.

"They are stealing our food," answered Liz.

A sergeant who seemed to be in charge jumped off the wagon and started into the house like he owned it, followed by two other soldiers. Liz called to him, "Sir, could you tell us what you are going to do?"

He paused for just a moment. "We are foragers, m'am. Our men have got to eat and we don't carry enough to last all the way to Savannah, so we live off the land. We appreciate you rebs being so generous," he laughed as he went through the door, followed by his two lackeys with "what are you going to do about it" smirks.

Ripe apples disappeared from the trees with military efficiency. She could tell that those Yanks had done it before. A commotion from behind the house told her that the chickens were being chased down, one by one. Pigs squealed in terror as they were run down, caught, and literally hog tied. Laughter and loud talk came from inside the house as every cabinet, closet, cupboard, and pantry was carefully searched and cleaned of its edibles.

Alonzo and his boys walked by close enough to whisper, "We's hid the cows and mules in the woods." But within minutes three soldiers walked by leading two of their cows, and one mule. Alonzo shook his head, "Well, reacon we didn't hide 'em good 'nuff."

The front door banged open and a forager ran out waving a pistol to his friends and shouting, "Look what I found!" The pistol was an antique flintlock muzzle loader with an engraved silver knob on the grip, silver trigger guard, silver inlay on the oak stock, and a silver tip on the ram-rod. Both children looked at Liz, eyes round with helpless dismay. "That was grandpa's, Mother. You can't let them take it."

Liz stood up and faced the forager. "Sir, that is a family heirloom. My father's ancestors brought it from England. It is out-dated as a weapon, would be useless to you, but has a world of sentimental value to us. I beg you, plead with you, please don't take that pistol."

The soldier cocked the hammer, pointed it at Liz's head, and pulled the trigger. The hammer fell with a sharp snap. Liz did not flinch – she knew that the pistol had not been loaded for forty years. "Too bad, lady. That's war. You damn rebs started it," he cackled as he climbed back on a wagon.

The wagons began to leave, loaded with all the corn and other vegetables they could carry, flour, lard, syrup, butter, hams and beef from the smokehouse, squawking chickens and squealing pigs, and anything else which happened to appeal to the foragers.

Liz called, "Please! Leave us something to eat! Do you want us to starve?"

The sergeant called back, "Lady, you rebs should have thought about that when you tried to bust up the country."

The wagons, loaded with the produce of months of hard labor, joined the marching army and soon were gone down Sandersville Road.

Liz sank down on the porch steps with Mattie and John tight beside her. "We did think about it," she sobbed quietly. "We never would have broken the union if you had just left us alone."

She looked up when Alonzo softly called her name.

"Thank you, 'Lonzo, for trying to hide the cows."

Alonzo stared at his feet. "Miz Liz, we goin' with the Yankees."

"You are?"

"Yass'm. We's free now, like you sez, and we wants to see what freedom is. We needs to know what we can take with us, m'am."

Liz held her head in her hands and stared at the porch steps where she sat. "You can take all the clothes and anything in your cabin you can carry. Take some food if they left any, but leave enough for us."

"Thank you, m'am." The Green family hurried to their home and soon returned with their possessions bundled in sheets and quilts.

Alonzo's eyes were moist, but his face showed excitement as the family stopped before Liz. "Thank you, Miz Williamson. You been real good to us. We hopes to see you again some day." The boys mumbled their thanks, and Mary sobbed an emotional good-bye as she and Liz hugged tightly until Alonzo gently pulled her away.

Liz wiped away a tear. "Good luck to all of you. I hope freedom is good to you."

The Green family hurried off down the lane to join the mob of other new freedmen following the army, and was soon swallowed up by the crowd and its dust.

Then the last wagon rumbled past, followed by a rear-guard cavalry detachment, and the road was empty. A gentle wind blew the dust away. For a moment it seemed like a bad dream from which she had just awakened. She could hear birds again, and the normal farm smells of earth and animals and plants returned, but mixed with the stench of droppings and urine from the road. It had been just like the young Yankee lieutenant had said, first the scouts, then the pioneers, then a seemingly endless line of marching soldiers, wagons, artillery, and cavalry. And the foragers... what had they taken, what did they leave? Liz could not force herself to get up from the porch steps and face reality.

She heard John's heavy footsteps running through the house and out the front door, and Samantha's familiar soft tread right behind him. "Well, Mother, they didn't take everything," John informed with an air of responsibility. A quick thought flashed through her mind, you will have to grow up quickly, too quickly, my son.

"Miz Liz," Samantha called, "them Yankees done made a mess of this house. You better git on in here and le's try to straighten things out. I'm 'fraid theys took a bunch of our things. Lawd have mercy, jes look at this parlor!"

John and Samantha's remarks broke the trance and brought her back to the real world, the changed world. Liz sprang to her feet, hugged John, and hurried inside to Samantha. "Sam," she asked, "yall are staying?"

Samantha looked puzzled. "What you mean, Miz Liz?"

"You are not going to follow the army?"

"Lawd have mercy, chile! Aint no way under the sun that me and Joe gon' git out there with all them sorry folks, not with our two babies. No, m'am, we aint. Now, if you wants us to git, then we'll git, but seems to us like you still gon' need some help."

"Oh, Sam, we need you now more than ever. I'm glad you're staying."

"Yass'm. Les' look at the kitchen first, see what them rascals left."

They had not left much. All the corn meal was gone except about enough for a couple of pones. All flour, fresh from the mill, was gone, along with all the vegetables from the safe and cupboard. A cask of molasses had been thrown off the back porch, broken, its precious contents now seeping slowly into the dirt. The root cellar door was torn off its hinges and the cellar cleaned of its preserved fruits and vegetables.

Food was their first concern, and they found just enough to know that they would not starve. A few ears of corn dropped around the corn crib, some un-dug potatoes and turnips still in the fields, and a few overlooked apples would provide sustenance until more food could be found or bought.

Big Joe came across the field from the woods leading a cow. "Them thieves missed this one, Miz Liz, and they's still some mules back in the woods somewhere." All the pigs were gone, the smoke house was empty of its supply of pork and beef, but a few skittish chickens came wandering in from the corn field.

Then it struck her like a lightening jolt – Lt. Terrell had warned of more plagues to follow. But she put this out of her mind as everyone concentrated on restoring order and finding food.

Darkness brought an autumnal chill, matched by the dark moods of the two families. Fatigue and a somber realization of their predicament brought their efforts to a halt. One by one, with very little conversation, they all gathered on the front porch.

"Well," sighed Big Joe, "'least we's done scrounged up 'nuff food to last us a day or two."

After a long silence, Liz asked, "How about chickens? And the mules?"

Samantha's oldest, nine year old Ollie, had taken on himself the responsibility of rounding up as many chickens as he could find. "I think they's twelve."

Big Joe reached out and hugged his son to him. "They's still three mules down in the swamp somewhere. And the cows. They come in when they gits hungry."

Liz stood up slowly. "Let's get some sleep and get an early start in the morning. We don't know who might be out in the woods around us, so we better not light any lamps or fires right now. Joe, do you still have the shotgun?"

"Yass'm. I got it hid real good."

With Mattie and John close behind, Liz turned and entered the dark house, encountering a feeling of gloom which she had never felt before. Sleep that night was fitful at best.

At first dawn, even before the one remaining rooster crowed, the two families were up preparing to meet the day's unknowns. Samantha had a fire started in the black cook-stove and was banging pots and pans. Little Jane Harper and her brother Ollie had found four eggs laid by the scattered chickens. Mattie brought in a pail of milk from the one cow which wandered back. The breakfast they scraped together was adequate and eaten in silence, but was a far cry from their usual fare of hot biscuits dripping with freshly churned butter, crisp bacon, scrambled eggs, syrup, honey, and hot coffee when they could get it.

All eyes looked to Elizabeth for directions. "John, go over to the Butler's and see how they are. Go through the woods, not down the road. Hide if you see anyone. Be very careful. Mattie, you take Jane and Ollie and comb the buildings and fields to see what food you can find. Joe, it might be best just to leave the mules and the other cow hidden for a few days. Would you repair the cellar door and anything else the Yankees tore up?"

Liz watched Mattie and John going about their assignments, and began checking the condition of the cow and the chickens.

My children are losing what was left of their childhood, she thought.

Soon John came running back from the Butlers, taking care to stay on the edge of the corn field and close to the tree line. Liz hurried down the porch steps to meet him. Out of breath, John clung to his mother's shoulder until he could speak. "Mom! Oh, Mom," John was almost sobbing, "they burned it. They burned it down!"

Liz held him to her. "Easy, son. What did they burn down?"

"His house. His big, beautiful house, with all those nice things he had."

"Oh my Lord!" Liz exclaimed. She heard Samantha gasp behind her.

"And that's not all, mom. They burned his big barn and some other buildings, too." John panted, catching his breath now. "And Mr. Butler, he's just sitting on the ground leaning against an oak tree, staring at the ruins. I tried to talk to him, but he would just look at me like he didn't know me, and looked back at the ruins. And all of his people, I guess they left with the Yankees, 'cause there wasn't nobody else there."

Big Joe had come around the corner of the house. "Want me to go git him, Miz Liz?"

"Yes. Better take the buggy... oh, we don't have a horse, do we. Just help him back the best you can. And, Joe,... I hate so much to do this... take John back with you and try to find some food."

Joe and John left at a trot.

They were a long time coming back. "He was done dead, Miz Liz," Joe explained. "Yes, m'am, sittin' up against one of his big oak trees, eyes wide open, just starin' at where his fine house used to be. Sho' was sad. Me and John, we dug a hole and buried him right there, best we could. Guess that's where he would like to be."

"We found some food. Not much," added John. "I carved his name on the tree." Each had a sack which they turned over to Liz and Samantha.

As they always had, the little group quickly resumed their work as a team – two strong women, one strong man, a strong-willed teenage girl, and three willing children, realizing that they must work together to survive in the face of adversity.

Liz and Samantha were in the kitchen garden, surveying the damage done by the foragers, and determining what could be salvaged. They heard Joe exclaim behind them, "Well, now, would you look at that!" Standing in the midst of a corn field, almost a quarter of a mile away, was a mule. He was looking for ears of corn that had been missed, but found few, so he was slowly working his way back to his familiar barn.

Liz clapped her hands with joy. "Our mule is back! Oh, how wonderful! Now we can harrow the fields, plow, plant some greens, put in a new crop this spring, haul fire wood, and haul whatever we might need!"

With a renewed optimism they realized how much their plight had been improved by the appearance of this animal. As ornery as mules could be at times, they were as strong as ten men, and could do the work of twenty when treated right and fed well. They were as essential as people to the southern farm.

Mattie was the acknowledged animal charmer, so they all stepped back as she eased her way across the field to the still skittish animal. A rope halter hung from its neck. The mule watched her, took a step back. My lucky day, thought Mattie, as she found an ear of corn still on the stalk, miraculously missed by the pickers and the foragers. Shucking the dry ear as she walked, she talked softly to the mule, which was watching the ear of corn with great interest. The mule came to her, and she held the ear for him to eat, rotating it for the powerful teeth to clean it down to the cob. Then taking the rope, Mattie led him easily back to the barn.

Liz was watching her daughter with pride, recognizing that this animal could be both a blessing and a burden. A mule could mean the difference between subsistence and poverty, if she could keep it strong and healthy-- and well fed.

Work continued through the afternoon, which had turned into a cool, crisp, autumn day, with darkening clouds moving in from the northwest. Liz and Samantha surveyed the progress and mentally inventoried the food supply. "I think we can make it, Miz Liz," Samantha said as she lowered herself into a kitchen chair. Lawd, I'm tired."

Suddenly they heard footsteps on the back porch, and with surprise looked up to see Alonzo waiting at the door. "Well, I'm back, Miz Liz." They rushed to him. "Alonzo!" shouted Liz. "The prodigal returns."

"Where is everybody else?" asked Mattie.

Alonzo shook his head. "Can I sit down? I done plumb give out." Samantha slid her chair over for him, and they all waited to hear the answer to Mattie's question.

"We followed them Yankees all yesterday," he explained. "Then they stopped and put up their tents and started fixin' their food. We set up near 'em, and asked for something to eat. They say ain't got hardly 'nuff for themselves, and wouldn't give us none. But then one of them took a likin' to Mary, and offered her some. She went off with him and I ain't seen her no more. The boys, they all left and took off through the woods. When the soldiers packed up in the morning, Mary still didn't come back, so I just left and come back here."

Now depressed more than ever, the tired group of farmers bedded down for the night, once again without fire or candle.

Scattered showers during the night left a cold dampness which permeated their clothing and chilled to the bone, spreading a temptation to linger around a roaring wood fire in the kitchen which Joe and Alonzo had started before daylight. But lingering was a luxury they could not afford. The people needed food and shelter, the mule needed fodder.

About midday everyone had gathered in the kitchen for a meager meal when they were startled at the sound of horses – many horses, coming up the lane to the house. Rushing to the front door they found themselves facing a gaunt, ragged troop of Confederate cavalry. They wore no uniforms, each man dressed in strange combinations of CSA butternut, captured Yankee blues, and civilian clothes from home. Men with hollow cheeks and ragged beards sat astride horses and mules which were little more than walking skeletons.

Are these all we have to protect us from the Yankees, Liz thought? "The Yankees have gone. They went that way," she said, addressing a man who appeared to be the leader.

"We need food, mounts, and wagons," he said in a soft voice, avoiding her eyes. A group of horsemen had detached itself from the column and rode toward the barn. The others studied the apple trees and fields for anything the Yankees may have missed. Four soldiers dismounted and brushed past Liz into the house. Without a word to anyone they scooped up the small meal which had just been prepared, searched the pantry and safe for any other food items, and bundled up all they had found in the table cloth. They seemed not to hear the meager pleas.

The first group of troopers came back from the barn leading the mule and wagon with the cow tied behind.

Begging and accusations of cruelty were ignored by the silent, ghostly band. Then the troop was gone as quickly as it came, disappearing like shadows.

Dazed and helpless, the nine weary, hungry farmers stared out into the cold mist.

With a deep sigh, Liz finally broke the silence. "We will just start all over. Joe, Alonzo, John, search the fields for any potatoes, corn, or peanuts which may have been missed."

"We done done that," protested Joe.

"Well, do it again," snapped Liz. Too harsh, she thought. I don't know how much more I can bear.

Other assignments were accepted without enthusiasm, and one by one they dragged themselves to the chores of subsistence.

Dense fog and cold drizzle continued. If it were not for the gnawing pangs of hunger the outside workers would have already sought refuge in front of a good fire.

The fog concealed them, and the wet soil muffled the hoof beats until four horsemen in dirt-smeared blue uniforms were at the porch steps, off their horses, and tracking mud across Liz's good carpet. Kicking the door open they burst into the kitchen. Samantha shouted in surprise, her children screamed, Liz dropped a china bowl and Mattie grabbed her in fear as the four men, pistols and rifles leveled, moved quickly through the room.

"Shut up, women!" shouted the first one, who wore a corporal's stripes. "We got no time to mess with you. Just tell us where it's hidden and you wont get hurt."

Liz clutched Mattie. "You're too late. Your army and ours have stripped this place bare of anything to eat."

"We're not lookin' for food. Where's your jewelry, watches, silver, money, stuff like that?"

"We have nothing of value you would want," Liz replied.

"I'll bet you don't," sneered the corporal. "Search the house, boys." The three soldiers departed and could be heard slamming doors, dumping out drawers, and tearing boards off the wall with their bayonets.

"Where are the men?" the corporal asked Liz.

"In the fields."

Just then the back door flew open and John popped in. The corporal swung his cocked pistol to John, who jumped back in surprise to see a Yankee in his kitchen.

"No!" screamed Liz. "He's just a boy!" John eased over to his mother, big eyes staring at the Yankee.

Soon the other three bummers came in with a pillow case full of their findings, which they dumped on the table.

"Where's the rest of it?" growled the corporal.

Tears came into Liz's eyes as she saw her wedding rings and their few pieces of heirloom jewelry in the pile.

"Where'd you hide the rest of it?" screamed the corporal, threatening to slap Liz.

Liz flinched but stared him straight in the eyes. "We are not rich. That is all of our valuables."

"You're lying to me, bitch. We got ways to find what we want." The corporal pointed at John. "Grab him, Virgil."

Virgil shoved John out the back door and down into the muddy back yard. Liz screamed, "Leave him alone! He's just a boy!" but they ignored her.

Alonzo and Sam came up, but backed off behind the cabins when guns were leveled at them.

A rope was brought from the horses. Liz watched in disbelief as John's hands were tied behind his back, the rope tied around his neck, and the other end thrown over the limb of an oak tree. Speechless with fear, John stared at his mother, expecting help.

"Ready to tell us?" asked the corporal.

One soldier grabbed Liz and held her arms behind her. "You can't do this!" she screamed. Samantha turned away and covered the eyes of her children.

The corporal pulled on the rope and it tightened around John's neck. "Mother!" he shouted.

"You have it all, I swear," Liz screamed, collapsing to her knees. "Let him go!"

The corporal pulled on the rope with both hands until John was touching the ground only with the tips of his toes, coughing and gurgling sounds coming from his stretched throat.

"Ready to tell us now?"

Liz could only scream, "No, no, no. There is nothing else. He's just a boy. Don't hurt him!"

"You're lying, lady." The corporal pulled a little more, and John began kicking wildly as his feet left the ground and the rope tightened around his throat.

Liz fell to her knees in despair, not believing what was happening. She started one last desperate plea when an explosion suddenly ripped the air and the corporal's head disappeared in a cloud of blood and splattering flesh and bone. John hit the ground hard as the rope was released by the lifeless body. Liz heard Samantha scream, "No, Joe!"

Joe had brought the old double barreled shotgun, loaded with buckshot, out from its hiding place in his attic. He came around the corner of his cabin unseen, until he fired both barrels at close range into the Yankee's head.

Startled but battle hardened, the other three bummers turned quickly and fired. Joe fell backward into the mud and never moved again. Samantha and their children fell on Joe's still form with screams of grief and disbelief.

Liz rushed to John and took the rope from his neck and hands. John was coughing, holding his neck with one hand and his ankle with the other.

Virgil shouted, "Let's get out of here. If that rebel cavalry heard those shots they'll be all over us before we know it." As they thundered away the fog and mist swallowed their departure just as it had spewed out their arrival.

With two dead people on the ground and one badly hurt boy, the survivors hardly knew what to do, where to go. Alonzo and Mattie moved back and forth from Samantha to John, helping however they could, and trying to ignore the headless corporal and stay out of the way of his frightened horse still tied to the back porch rail.

Daylight was fading quickly. It was imperative that something be done with the two corpses and the injured John.

"Master John doin' all right?" asked Alonzo.

"His ankle is broken and his throat is injured. How badly I can't tell. We need to get him to a doctor right away."

"They ain't no doctor nowhere around here now, Miz Liz."

Liz realized the truth in what Alonzo said. "Then we will leave at first light and go to Sparta. We must find help for John. We can use that Yankee's horse.

"Yes'm. He's tied to the porch."

Liz nodded approval. "John, I'm going to help Samantha bury Joe. Will you be all right for a while?"

"Bury Joe!" John moaned. "What happened to Big Joe?"

"The yankees shot Joe, son, when he shot the man who was hanging you."

John whimpered and turned away, sobbing in both pain and anguish over the loss of Joe, while Mattie helped Liz move him inside out of the weather.

Joe's body was carried by Alonzo and Samantha, out to a plot which Bentley Williamson had staked off years ago, realizing the need for a family burial ground some day.

"Can't we make a coffin?" sobbed Samantha.

Alonzo rested on his shovel. "Sam, honey, I'm done wore plumb out. It's gon' be all I can do to help dig this grave. We needs to get Joe in the ground tonight. Tomorrow I'm gonna help Miz Liz take John to find a doctor. Let's just wrap him up good in quilts and blankets and I will come back in a few days and make him a proper coffin."

In the light of a lantern the grave was dug, a few words were said, and the soil of the Williamson farm covered its first corpse. Then the lanterns showed the way as the corporal's body became the second, with each person in the burial party harboring mixed feelings about defiling the family plot with the body of a Yankee soldier.

At first light, John was painfully placed on the horse. The drizzle had mercifully stopped, but the chill of the November dawn and a thick fog soaked through to the bone. John swayed in the saddle and almost fell off, so they took him down.

" 'Lonzo, do you know what a travois is?" asked Liz.

"Yes'm, I saw the Indians use them, back when the Creeks was still around. That'll be just the thing for John."

Alonzo cut and trimmed two slim poplar trees and tied their ends across the horse's back, the other two ends trailing behind on the ground. Ropes were looped between the poles, and John was placed on the ropes.

Liz hugged Samantha and the children. "You can stay or come with us."

"We will stay here with Joe and watch after the place for you, Miz Liz."

Alonzo led the horse as Liz and Mattie walked along beside John. As the two trailing ends of the travois bumped through the rough dirt road, badly churned into ruts by hundreds of wagons and cannons and thousands of feet, John cried in pain with each jolt. Finally Liz and Mattie picked up the ends of the poles and carried them, doing their best not to stumble. Samantha sobbed as she watched the little procession struggle away.

* * *

W. T. Sherman's army marched, burned, and pillaged its way through central Georgia, captured Savannah, and gave the city to President Lincoln as a Christmas present. They had accomplished their goal of destroying the will of the Southern people to wage war. The war eventually ground to a close at a small town in Virginia and a railroad crossing in North Carolina. Armies of the Confederate States of America were disbanded, and their tired and broken soldiers worked their way home to find their families and try to put their lives back together.

* * *

Travelers between Savannah and Macon using the Sandersville Road would look with dismay upon the Williamson farm, wondering at the blighted rows of peach and apple trees, the ruins of a burned barn, the sprawling farm home with broken windows and faded, peeling paint, a dead oak tree fallen across the front porch, and vast neglected fields of briars and scrub pines, where a man in a ragged Confederate major's uniform with an empty sleeve gathered twigs for a fire, and occasionally gazed at the road as if watching for someone to come back. One traveler might look at the ruins and desolation and ask, "Who would do such a thing?" Another might ask, "What had these people done that God would punish them so?"

* * *

"Summer in Georgia is certainly much hotter than it was in autumn," said a young man driving a two-horse carriage.

"I agree," added the oldest of the three men. Their coats and ties had been piled on the back seat an hour ago.

The oldest of the three gentlemen had led his troops along this road on their march to Savannah over two years ago, and was now governor of his home state in New England. The other gentleman had served as a Major on the General's headquarters staff and was now representing Iowa in the United States Congress. The young man driving the carriage had been one of his cavalry officers, and was now a newspaper editor in Ohio.

"Didn't we camp here one night?" asked the Governor.

"I believe you're right, General," agreed the Congressman.

Farther down the road the carriage stopped where a long avenue of oaks led to four tall chimneys standing solemnly at the end of the lane.

The Congressman stood up in the carriage. "I remember this place. It was one of those fine plantation homes with those large white columns. I certainly hope our men had nothing to do with its destruction."

The next farm, too small to be called a plantation, appeared to have been abandoned. The young man stopped the carriage, remembering how prosperous it had looked when he first saw it. "I remember this one. Remember it well. There was a pretty, young mother here who had no idea what was happening. We filled our canteens at her well. I've often wondered what happened to her after we left."

They were startled to see that the farm was not abandoned after all, as a one-armed man in a tattered Confederate officer's uniform walked slowly down the lane toward them, stopping a few feet away, studying them carefully. A black man and woman watched from the corner of the house.

"Good day, sir," said the Governor.

The weary Confederate stood up straighter. "Yankees?" he asked.

"Why, yes. Would you be so good as to give us your name, sir?"

"You come through here during the war?"

"Why, yes, we did."

The one-armed man studied the three in the carriage and took a deep breath. "Major Bentley Williamson, CSA Retired."

The young driver of the carriage held out his hand and leaned out of the carriage. "Major Williamson, sir, I am Lt. Terrell. I met your wife here as we passed by."

Bentley Williamson ignored the hand. "Where is she? Where are my children?"

"I don't know, sir. They were here when we left, and I was concerned for their safety. But I had to scout ahead for the main column."

Williamson studied each of the three men carefully. Then he turned and looked at his farm, as if remembering it green and productive as it was when he left for Virginia, and remembering Liz and John and Mattie, and the two families which helped make the farm prosperous and beautiful. Then, bending over slowly, he picked up a rock, about the size of a hen's egg, and with his one good arm, threw it at the former General. They all dodged as the stone flew by their heads.

"What is the meaning of this, sir?" demanded the General.

Without answer, Williamson selected another rock, and rearing back as much as he could, threw it with better aim this time, hitting the General on the shoulder, and before the astonished veterans could react, Bentley, with his one good arm, threw another rock, rendering a stinging blow to the rump of one of the horses, which tried its best to rear up in the harnesses, causing the other horse to start running, whereupon both horses started running full speed with the carriage bouncing through the ruts and rocks behind, with the Yankees holding on for dear life.

The black lady, with white hair bundled in a red turban, walked up behind Bentley Williamson. "Lawd-a-mercy, Mr. Bentley, you sho done run them Yankees off this time."

Major Bentley Williamson, CSA, Retired, looked back toward the battered house with its weed-grown fields and blighted orchards. "I don't think our families are coming back, Samantha, but I will never give up hope. Like a lot of people in that damn war, they are just gone. Their general said, 'war is hell, and there isn't anything we can do to make it better.' He was right. But if they do come back, if they do, we sure don't want them to see it looking like this. Those dead apple trees will make good fire wood."

A noise up the road caught Bentley's attention. The buggy was coming back. Slowly. It stopped out of rock range. Lt. Terrell climbed down and walked with caution toward Bentley, who stood with his arm across his chest, and Samantha, with hands on her hips.

Terrell approached, raising one hand in the peace sign. Bentley stared without a word.

Terrell stopped, not close. "Major Williamson, sir, we were going over to Milledgeville for a short while, and then catch a train back home. But we would like to change our plans, with your consent. We would like to know if we could – if you would be so kind – if you would allow us to help you around here for a few days. The General has offered to take the buggy into

Sparta and buy a saw and some tools, maybe some food. We need the exercise, and would like to help a little, help you get your farm back in shape. We don't know much about farming and carpentry, but we will put ourselves at your disposal, if you agree."

Bentley turned to look at Samantha, who rolled her eyes in surprise, but showed just a slight smile.

He turned back and studied Lt. Terrell for a moment. "The idea of telling a Yankee general and a major and lieutenant what to do, does have a certain appeal."

Terrell held out his hand. Bentley grasped it firmly. Both men smiled as they saw a little mist in each other's eyes.

End

REVENGE OF THE LAUREL

This is a true story. Only the names have been changed to protect the guilty.

A friend of mine, let's call him Ralph, and his wife, Betsy, had a cabin back in the hills of Rabun County, Georgia, next to several thousand acres of woodland known as the Chattahoochee National Forest. Now, one of Ralph's greatest joys, as was mine (and still is, was to fill up his back-pack with water and snacks and spend the day wandering along the trails, creeks, and ridges of these magnificent woods. Occasionally I would hike with him, but not often, because both of us had realized that one of the greatest pleasures of walking in the woods is solitude.

These woods had been cut for timber almost a hundred years ago, and off and on since then, but the only vestige of those ancient attacks was the old logging roads, which had now become interesting hiking trails.

Through the years Ralph covered the area thoroughly, learning where all the creeks flowed, how the old logging roads networked together, which ridges had the best views, where some rusty old moonshine stills were located, where the best huckleberry and blackberry patches grew, when would be the best time to find Joe Pye Weed and other wild plants in full bloom, and where and when to find ripe persimmons on the ground. He even developed a close friendship with a couple of trees, one a hemlock which was so big that Ralph thought of it as the grandfather of all hemlocks in Rabun, and the other was a gigantic pine tree with a crooked, twisted trunk and crooked, twisted limbs, so deformed that the timber cutters had left it standing when its more perfect brothers were turned into 2 X 4's eighty years ago.

Ralph always enjoyed it when Betsy would walk with him, but sweet Betsy did not have the stamina which Ralph had, so she would walk until she was "half tired," as Ralph expressed it, and then turn back while Ralph walked on. Or, if bear tracks had been seen in the trail, or their territorial slash marks spotted on nearby trees, then Ralph would turn back and be her protector.

Some spring days in the mountains were so filled with bird music and wildflower aromas and colors that Ralph often said that it would be sinful not to hike through the hills and soak it all in. It was on just such a day that Ralph came upon one of the most glorious mountain laurel thickets he had ever seen—a profusion of white blossoms as big as a house, and as tall as a young dogwood tree. On closer inspection he found an even greater surprise—an old, overgrown logging road ran right through the middle of the thicket. The laurels had arched over that old road, making Ralph feel like he was walking in a tunnel through a pile of snow.

Well, Ralph could not rest until sweet Betsy saw it. He hurried back to the cabin, calling her name even before he got to the door, "Betsy, put on your boots. There's something out here you've got to see." The snowy laurels were easily within Betsy's "half-tired" range, so Ralph held her hand as they hurried through the woods. "Now, close your eyes and hang on to me," he said as they got closer. Then he stopped. "Now, open your eyes," he whispered. Betsy gasped, speechless with surprise and delight. In silence he led her to the white tunnel, and held her tightly to him as they walked through. Tears trickled down her cheeks. No words were spoken, for each realized that there is nothing a person can say to enhance such a glorious creation.

Ralph and Betsy made a few more visits to their white hill of mountain laurels until finally the heat of summer brought the colors of spring to an end. But the sight of so many plants covered with snowy blossoms, and their white tunnel, was a sight they would never forget.

Later that summer Ralph began to see disturbing signs in that section of the Chattahoochee National Forest, which he had begun to think of as "his." One of the old logging trails had a new layer of gravel. A new culvert had been built where a creek had washed out the old one. Mysterious little flags of red and yellow were tied to tree limbs in various places throughout the woods. Some of the old trails which had not carried a vehicle for forty years were beginning to show tracks of trucks and jeeps, and old trees which had fallen across the trails were being cut back out of the road.

Then one morning Ralph and Betsy were awakened not by the usual chatter of Chickadees, Tit Mice, and Nuthatches, but by the distant roar of diesel engines and chain saws. Ralph was up and quickly out the door with his boots on. He followed the trail from the cabin toward the noise. Less than a half mile away he came upon what looked to him like a herd of yellow monsters attacking the woods. Men with chain saws were toppling trees with rapid efficiency—not just the pines, but also dogwood, poplar, maple, oak, and anything else which had the misfortune to be growing among the pines in this forty-acre patch. Huge yellow machines were picking them up like pencils, shearing off the limbs, cutting them into manageable lengths, and loading them onto trucks. Ralph stormed up to a burly man in a hard hat who appeared to be in charge.

"What's going on here?" he demanded.

The hard hat patiently explained that they were a timber company, that they had a contract with the U. S. Forest Service to "harvest" the pines in this tract, that they were authorized to "clear cut" the 40 acres while they were at it, and that they would be cutting every tree in other sections as soon as this one was finished.

There was nothing Ralph could do to stop this cutting, but he resolved to do whatever he could to stop future cutting. To him, it was nothing short of raping a beautiful woodland.

Later that morning Ralph stopped at the Clayton office of the U. S. Forrest Service to get an explanation. He was politely informed that the Forest Service had the responsibility of "managing" the forests. Their idea of "management" consisted of periodically "harvesting" the sections of the forest which contained mature pine trees, trees large enough to have a good market value when sold for lumber to feed the nationwide construction boom.

Ralph argued, "Cutting pine trees for lumber is one thing, but cutting hardwoods like oak and poplar and maple is a waste." It was an effort to keep his temper under control, but he managed.

Ralph's arguments got nowhere, of course, so he decided to take it to a higher level. He wrote his Representatives and Senators in Washington, D.C., where he was, again, politely, told that the Forest Service was fulfilling its responsibility as manager of the forests, and that there was nothing that they could, or would, do about it.

Ralph did not stop walking through the woods, and on a later hike he discovered another tract, this one about 100 acres, which was also flagged for harvesting, which raised his ire to an even higher level. But it was not until Ralph saw the total process of clear cutting that his ire raised to the top of its capacity, and boiled over.

First, the tract to be clear-cut would be marked. Then every living tree in the tract would be cut down – every living tree. The larger pines would be hauled off to be cut into lumber, and then the maples, oaks, poplar, hickory, dogwood, and all other hardwoods, along with shrubs like wild azalea and mountain laurel within those 100 acres, would be burned. After the burning, the good old Forest Service, the same people who brought us Smokey the Bear, would wait several months to let the clear-cut, burned-off tract start to renew itself with fresh growth, and then they would spray the entire tract with a potent herbicide to kill off every green sprig of every tree and plant which was trying to grow back. Then, they would come back and plant young pine trees, about a foot high, in neat, straight rows over the entire tract. At this point the forest had been successfully converted to a tree farm, or so they thought.

Ralph began seriously contemplating what other courses of action were available to him. He was not a violent man, but he was not above using violence to correct what he considered a diabolical attack on nature.

Later that summer Ralph set out for another all-day walk in his favorite woods. His course would take him by the mountain laurel thicket with its tunnel, and even though all the blossoms were gone for the summer, he still enjoyed walking by to picture the white sight which he and Betsy had so enjoyed. But when he rounded the curve in the trail which approached the thicket he stopped in horror—the mountain laurel thicket was gone. Only remnants of a few trees were left, smoldering. The thicket had been within a tract which was clear-cut and burned the day before.

Ralph hurried back to break the news to Betsy. They held each other with consoling tightness for a long time. Neither cried, but both felt determined to strike back in some way, even if in a very small way.

And so they did.

Ralph continued his long walks, sometimes walking down the old timber trails which had been upgraded to allow 18-wheelers to haul the timber out. Whenever he saw a dead tree small enough for him to handle, he drug it across the road, thinking maybe some truck driver would have to stop to move it.

When Ralph came upon a newly planted field of young pines, if it was late in the day and all the workers had gone home, he walked along the neat rows and pulled up as many trees as he had time to, knowing that hardwoods would naturally take over the space, along with more pines. At least it would be a forest again, and not look like a tree farm.

Sometimes with Betsy, they walked to the site of the new culvert and tried to dam it up with rocks and tree limbs, hoping that a good rain might overflow the road and wash it out, but that never happened.

Once he and Betsy were walking by a site which had been cut, burned, and partially sprayed with herbicide to kill any new sprigs. It was late in the afternoon, and the workers were gone for the day. They had not finished spraying, so their spraying equipment and drums of herbicide were left by the side of the trail. Ralph and Betsy got a great deal of satisfaction out of throwing the spraying equipment into a huge briar patch, and rolling the drums down into a very deep ravine.

The cutting of certain sections continued through the following winter. Later Ralph told me, not long before he died, that the closest he came to serious violence was one cold, stormy winter night. He and Betsy were sitting in front of their blazing fire, enjoying the warmth of their cozy cabin, when he started thinking about those big yellow monsters which at that time were parked at a site not far away, waiting to start clear-cutting the next day. Ralph thought long and hard about taking his .38 revolver, bundling up against the cold and rain, and shooting out the huge tires on the tractors, trucks, and cutting machines. But he didn't.

Not long after that sweet Betsy died, and not long afterwards, Ralph joined her.

That was twenty years ago.

Just a few days ago I decided to go up to Rabun County and walk over those same old trails that Ralph and I had enjoyed so much. I recalled him telling me about the snowy hill of mountain laurel which he and Betsy had so enjoyed, and which had been destroyed and re-planted as a pine tree farm. It was there that I again saw the great power of the earth to defend itself from corruption and violation, and the irresistible force of nature to renew itself.

Several years after the pine tree farm was planted, when young pines had grown to about fifteen feet tall where the white laurels once had bloomed, the north Georgia mountains experienced an attack by a pesky and resilient little critter called the pine beetle, or sometimes pine borer. When these little bugs hit those pine tree farms which the U. S. Forest Service had so carefully planted, the pines were wiped out. Spraying with insecticides had very little effect. The tree farm tracts became nothing but long lines of gray skeletons of former pine trees, with bright green young oaks, poplars, hickories, and dogwoods taking over in their beautiful random fashion. Nature is renewing the space which man had cleared.

I wish Ralph and Betsy could see it, the mountain laurels are coming back with a vengeance.

END

JACK THE YAK

(A story for my grandchildren)

Jack the Yak wanted a new kayak. So he went to the kayak store. Jack said to the person at the kayak store, "My name is Jack and I want a new kayak."

The kayak person said, "Hi. My name is Mack."

Jack and Mack shook hands. "What color do you want?" asked Mack.

"I want a black kayak," said Jack the Yak to Mack.

They looked at red kayaks and yellow kayaks and blue kayaks, and finally found a black kayak.

"That's just fine," said Jack to Mack. "Just put it in my car."

"What kind of car do you have?" asked Mack.

"A Cadillac," answered Jack.

"Where do you want to put it?" asked Mack.

"In the back, Mack," said Jack.

So Jack the Yak and Mack tried to put the black kayak in the back of Jack's black Cadillac, but it would not fit.

"I know what you need," said Mack.

"What?" asked Jack.

"You need a rack on the back of your Cadillac," said Mack.
So Jack the Yak and Mack put the black kayak on the rack on the back of Jack's Cadillac, and Jack drove away.

END

Red '40 Ford Coupe

Whatcha lookin at, kid?

This car, sir.

Yeah. Don't stand too close. Don't scratch it or nothing.

It's the best lookin car on the lot, alright.

Yeah, come back in a few years and I'll sell you one. Don't I hear your mama callin?

It's a 1940 Ford, isn't it?

That's right. You know something about cars?

Yes, sir. '40 Fords mostly. It's the best car ever made. This one is really a beaut.

They're good cars, alright. Not many cars last twenty years like this baby has. That new red paint job sets it off, don't you think?

Yes, sir. Could I just sit in it?

Naw, kid, this car is for sale to serous customers, people with dough, know what I mean? I don't want you scratchin' it up and getting' it dirty.

I'll be careful, and I've got some money. See?

Hell, kid, that ain't near enough. You need a hundred times that much. Get a job, and come back in a few years.

I already got a job. Deliverin' papers. Does it have a four barrel carburetor? Its got duel exhausts – I bet its got a four barrel carb too.

You do know something about cars.

Could we look under the hood, please?

Get outa here, kid. What if a real customer comes along? I ain't foolin' with you.

Please, mister. All my life I been wanting a '40 Ford. A red one. I even dream about it. This is the best lookin' '40 I ever saw.

Kid, if you make me miss a sale, I'm gonna tan your ass. Stand in front while I open it. There... how do you like that?

Oh, wow! Gosh! That engine looks just like new. Not a speck of grease or dirt anywhere.

The original owner took real good care of it, and the guy we got it from spent a lot of time restoring it.

It's just beautiful. I sure would like to hear it run.

Well, I've got better things to do than spend any more time with a kid who isn't old enough to drive. Get on home, kid. Come back in five years. With some bucks.

Does it make that real deep, rumbling noise?

Sure it does. It's better than new.

Some of them don't. Sometimes they just shake and pop and stall.

Trouble with you, kid, is you got no faith, no trust, no confidence. I been sellin' used cars on this lot for three years, almost. People trust me. They keep coming back. If I tell you it's like new, or it runs good, or it makes a damn rumbling noise, then it makes a damn rumbling noise. Now get outta here. Get on home.

You don't have to cuss, mister.

I'll cuss when I damn well please, you little... kid, get on outa here before I lose my temper.

I'm sorry, mister. It just looks so good, so perfect, that I was just hopin' that it would run as good as it looks.

I don't need to prove nothing to you.

I know that. But sometimes they don't get the timing right, or they don't put the mufflers on right, and the whole thing is spoiled.

What do you care? You can't even drive.

But I can dream. And if I dream about it, I want it to be perfect.

Boy, you are wearin' me out.

I don't want to be so much trouble, but I sure would like to hear it run.

Yeah, and I sure would like to sell it to the King of England.

Well, couldn't you let me hear it run just once before he buys it?

You are absolutely drivin' me crazy. No king ain't gonna buy no twenty year old used car.

Why? It sure is pretty enough for a king or a queen or anybody. Would they be afraid to buy it because it doesn't rumble like it oughta?

Hell, it rumbles like thunder! Get back, let me close the hood and I'll show you, damn it.

You don't have to cuss. Can I get in with you?

No, you cannot.

I just want to see the dials and everything, and watch what you do. You must know how to run a car real good.

Oh, Christ! What am I doing?

It ain't good to say it like that, sir.

Don't preach to me, boy.

My pants are clean.

Your shoes will track up the floor mat.

I'll clean them off real good on the grass. I would not get it dirty for anything in the world.

You never give up, do you? All right. Get in. And be careful.

Wow! Thank you. Mom says I'm presistant, or something.

Whatever. Now just listen to this.

What's wrong with it?

It doesn't want to start. How the hell do I know what's wrong?

Please try again, sir. It has to start.

It's cold, kid. Sometimes they just don't start, these old ones.

Just try one more time. Please. You said it's better than new.

You're too much, kid… hey… there she goes!

Listen to that rumble!

Didn't I tell you, kid? Just like thunder!

I bet she will really go.

Hang on, boy. I'll take you around the block.

End

Red '40 Ford Coupe" was written as an exercise in dialogue for a writing class at Georgia State University.

RETURN TO CHICKAMAUGA

Hot dust hung in the air from the horses' hoofs and the carriage wheels. Septembers in Georgia are always hot and dusty. Dust clung to the sweat on the lone passenger's face and on his lone hand, but it bothered him not. It covered his black suit and wide-brimmed gray felt hat, but he did not notice. His attention was focused on the land around him, the rutted dirt road, the cultivated fields of corn and cotton, and the dark, foreboding shade of the forests of oak and pine. Twenty years had passed since two great armies clashed here on the banks of Chickamauga Creek, and the ravaged land still showed many scars of battle.

"Where to, Colonel?" asked the driver. With soft words and gestures the Colonel directed the carriage through twists and turns, standing in the carriage often, searching for the particular site, and finally instructing, "Stop here. This is it."

On the side of the road was an immense corn field with brown stalks eight feet tall and the largest ears of corn he had ever seen. On the far side of the corn field was the forest, with shadows as dark and shrouding as they were on that day when he had led his men here.

Not really men, but boys. Georgia boys, filled with the excitement of war, from towns like Macon, Columbus, Decatur, Marietta, assembled here to stop the invader from the north. It was in the shadows of the woods behind him where he had formed his regiment in line of battle, with bayonets fixed, and it was here where he had exhorted them, "Do not let them spoil this sacred soil of Georgia!"

Where the tall corn now grew was then a meadow of knee-high grass, gleaming in the summer sun, decorated with patches of blue and yellow flowers, deceptive in its tranquility. And it was here that he had commanded them, "Now, here we go, lads. Regiment, forward! For God, for home, for country... give 'em hell!"

But in the darkness of the trees on the far side of the meadow there were other boys, dressed in blue, some kneeling, some standing, with rifles primed, waiting, watching the brown and gray line as it advanced across the contested meadow. The boys in blue heard their leader whisper, "Steady, steady, hold your fire. One good volley, then retire."

With sabers and bayonets gleaming in the sun, regimental colors streaming ahead, the Colonel's regiment advanced rapidly across the glade. Their heads held high, their muskets lowered, their Colonel shouted, "Forward, forward!"

Some heard from the dark woods ahead, the one word – "Fire!"

A brief rattle of muskets was followed quickly by thunder and flame as the entire blue line projected a blizzard of lead and steel to meet the Regiment. A six gun battery of polished brass artillery opened fire with canister, and the Regiment melted into the Georgia soil.

Still standing in the carriage, the Colonel saw it all again, as if it were just now happening. He saw his boys stumble and fall, the Regimental colors fall and not be picked up, and in the space of a gasp he saw his people around him without limbs, without jaws, without heads, without life… enriching the soil with their blood and gore. He remembered the sting when a round of canister carried away his own left arm, to be left upon the field forever. It, too, had eventually disappeared into the soil.

But that was twenty years ago. The left sleeve of the dusty black suit was empty now, and the field of carnage was a field of corn now.

With a loud rustle of dry corn leaves, a farmer, with hoe in hand walked out from between the tall rows and saw the Colonel gazing at the field. Mopping his brow, the farmer addressed the Colonel, "Like my corn, do you? All my neighbors wonder why my corn grows so green and high. Sometimes I wonder why myself."

The Colonel's hand touched the brim of his gray hat, shielding the anguish in his eyes from the farmer's proud stare. The Colonel knew why.

END

"Return to Chickamauga" was originally a poem, but I kept on getting requests to rewrite it as a short story, so I did. It was first published in an anthology, "O Georgia," published by O Georgia Writers Foundation of Cumming, Ga., and a slightly revised versions published in Georgia Backroads magazine. MB

This will be the first chapter of a book I hope to finish someday. It stands alone as a short story.

INJUN JOHN

Kennesaw Mountain threw its shadow closer to the field of dead, brown corn stalks. The soft mist was not quite cold enough to force the two farmers indoors, but when the mountain shadow reached them the mist would turn to snow and the damp chill would end their labors for the day.

Will Barnett set his feet in the muddy stump hole and swung his ax with all his might. Titus Jackson flicked the reins on the mules' rumps and yelled, "Ha Mule, Ha Big Mary," but the stump did not budge.

Will wiped his red nose on his already wet sleeve. "If we had one keg of gun powder we could blow this damn stump out in five minutes."

Titus gripped the reins on the two powerful animals. "While you if'n, if us some hot coffee. Ain't been no coffee naw gun powder 'round here since the war started, 'less you in the army."

Will steadied his feet in the slick Georgia red clay and swung the ax against the stubborn root. Titus kept the mules leaning into the chains, but the stump would not move.

Both men paused to watch a ragged line of Confederate cavalry plod north along Powder Springs Road toward Marietta. Tired, lean horses and slouching, poorly clad soldiers soon vanished into the mist. There were rumors of a Yankee invasion in the spring, but few Georgians believed that the Yankee army was big enough or bold enough to invade Georgia. Will changed his footing to get at the roots at the bottom of the stump and swung his ax with determination. The onerous winter chore of stump clearing was hard on the team of four workers, Will, the farmer, Tutus, the slave, and two powerful animals, Mule and Big Mary.

Titus watched, keeping the chains taught. "I'll swap with you when you ready, Mr. Will."

"Two or three more roots ought to do it," Will replied, feeling the dampness of his sweat inside his coat and the winter's wet chill on his hands and face.

Suddenly Mule made his strange noise which sounded like a cross between a grunt and a whinny, which Will and Titus had come to recognize as Mule's way of calling their attention to something, or that he suspected danger. Both men looked at Mule, then followed his gaze.

A lone rider was coming down the lane toward the houses, leading a pack horse, accompanied by a large gray dog. The rider stopped and held up one hand, a gesture of friendship. Dressed for the winter's dampness, he wore a black felt hat which could have been a Federal cavalry hat. He had long gray hair which hung below his shoulders, a heavy coat made from animal skins, and trousers wrapped in deerskin tucked into high boots. A musket in a deerskin scabbard was held across his saddle.

Will and Titus were uneasy with a stranger between them and their families. The old flintlock shotgun had been left in the house. It was prone to mis-fire in good weather and was next to useless in this dampness. Will climbed out of the stump hole, holding his ax in both hands.

Titus held the mules steady. "Looks like an Indian."

Indians presented little danger now, since most of them had been driven west twenty-five years ago, but it was rare to see one anywhere except in town or on the road.

The rider slid off his horse and tied his musket to the saddle. He stood for a while studying Will's house, Titus' house, enjoying the comforting aroma of oak smoke from the two fireplaces. He gazed for a while at the small gray barn, smokehouse where meat was stored, corn crib, outhouse, and rail fences, then turned and approached through the field of dead corn.

The Indian was a large, strong man, who strode with confident steps. Only his ruddy complexion, high cheek bones, and long hair distinguished him from a Georgia farmer.

Stopping a few paces away, he looked at Will and announced, "I am John McIntosh, of the people you call Cherokee."

Will nodded, "I'm Will Barnett, and this is Titus Jackson."

John McIntosh walked up and held out his hand. Will rubbed the mud off on his pants leg and was treated to a long, pumping, almost ceremonial hand shake.

The Indian then approached Titus, holding out his hand. "I am John McIntosh."

Keeping one eye on the mules, Titus was treated to the same vigorous hand shake. "I am Titus Jackson, of the people you call African."

McIntosh studied Titus. "I thought you people were called Negro."

"Same thing," Titus replied. "Negroes is from Africa."

"Where is this Africa?"

"It's a long way off."

"I have never been there."

"Neither have I."

Suddenly the men were startled by Mule's peculiar sound and a quick stirring of the two animals. The big gray dog had been sniffing around and had gotten too close to suit Mule. Titus grabbed both lines firmly and yelled "Ha, Mule!" Mule appeared to be about to attack the dog, which would have created quite a tumult, considering that Mule was still harnessed to Big Mary and chained to the stump.

McIntosh shouted something to the dog in a language which Will and Titus did not understand, and the dog trotted back toward the horse.

Will crossed his arms, still holding the ax. "We don't need a watchdog around here. We've got a watch mule instead. It don't pay to get around that brown one. He don't take kindly to strangers." Will poked at the stump with the ax. "Can we help you with something, Mr. McIntosh?"

McIntosh studied the farm around him. "I wanted to see this place one more time before I go away. I lived here when I was a boy."

Will was surprised. "You lived here? On this land?"

The Indian nodded yes. "Before we came here this land was the home of a family of the people you call Creeks. They built a good house on the hill, where your house is now. They farmed this land, but there were more trees then. You have cleared much land, Will Burnett, dug up many stumps."

Kicking the rich, muddy soil, McIntosh went on. "A few Creeks were in this land for many seasons. This was our land, Cherokee land, but we did not need it, so we let them stay. Then your people began to come into this country, so the Creeks moved away to the south, where their people were, on the other side of the Chattahoochee.

"Our village was in the mountains, maybe ten days from here. When we heard that the Creeks were gone, some of our people decided to move here. My family found this place, with the good cabin, and some land cleared by the Creeks, so we stayed. I helped my family farm the land and hunt deer, rabbits, possum, and many other good animals. We planted corn, beans, squash. The land and the woods made good food, plenty for us.

"Sometimes I played in that creek. Catch a small fish or a frog. Frog legs are good to eat.

"Then, just before I became a man, the soldiers with blue coats came. They said we would have to move away to a strange land, many days west of here. My father did not want to leave this place, but there were many soldiers. There were too many to fight, my father and uncles said, so we would move. I did not understand why they wanted our land. It seemed like there was plenty of land for everybody."

Titus and Will looked at each other, both thinking of the discovery of gold in north Georgia, then the confiscation of

Cherokee land by the governments, and the forced removal of the Cherokees to lands west of the Mississippi.

"The blue soldiers treated us like cattle, herding us along the roads, then kept us prisoners in a big pen, up near Cumming. Our people began to get sick. The soldiers sent doctors and medicine, but not enough. Many died. One of my uncles and his woman died. I told my father that I wanted to run away, that they would never find one Cherokee in the woods. He said go. So I did. I never saw my family again.

"I lived in the mountains for a long time, then came back to this place, because it is a good place. But white people were already here. I could not stay."

Titus looked at Will. "That must'a been your pa." Will nodded.

"I found a small piece of level land on a creek near what is now Roswell, where I built a cabin and stayed for many years, until now. I helped the white people with their work, and they would pay me a little. People called me 'Injun John.' A Cherokee woman named Nancy lived not far away, and we became good friends, but they made her move off her land. So now I must go away again. You have a good farm, Will Burnett. Thank you, and Titus, for letting me see it again."

McIntosh turned to walk away. "Wait a minute," Will called, "why do you have to go away now?"

For a moment the Indian looked intently at Titus, then at Will. "I am going away because I think there will be much trouble at this place. Your country is now divided like two tribes, and you fight against your brothers. I think the blue soldiers will come here again. There are many more of them than there are your gray soldiers, just as there were more than there were my people. The blue soldiers make war on your towns and destroy them. They will make war on Marietta and Atlanta, and destroy them. I hope the blue soldiers do not come to your farm, Will Burnett, but who can say? There is nothing to keep me here. I can live from what the land gives me, anywhere."

"Where will you go?" asked Titus.

"To the river, and follow it up into the mountains. There is a good place up there called Nacoochee. Some of my people are still there, and the white people are good. Maybe when the blue soldiers go away I will come back. Maybe not. It would be good for you to go away too. It would be good to get out of the path of the blue soldiers."

Will dropped his ax head into the mud and rested on it. "Now, John, that ain't necessarily so. We whipped them Yankees good up at Chickamauga back in October, and sent them running back into Chattanooga, with that old fool General Rosecrans leading the pack."

McIntosh nodded yes. "Some of my people are still in Chattanooga, too. They say more soldiers come almost every day, with many canons, and many wagons and train cars loaded with guns and bullets. In the spring they will come. This will not be a good place to be."

Titus and Will weighed the words of the Cherokee. The war had been far away, but it seemed to be spreading, getting closer. Yankee armies were getting larger, and were winning more battles. Would the war really come again to Georgia? To Marietta? To the Burnett farm?

John McIntosh held up his right hand and spoke to them in Cherokee, which they did not understand, but it seemed to Titus like a blessing. Then he walked away through the dead corn stalks.

Will felt colder. The mist was turning into a light snow. The shadow of Kennesaw Mountain fell across the corn field.

"John," he called, "Wait. Stay the night."

End

THE FOUR NAPOLEONS
OF CEDAR HILL

George Stover put down his dog-eared copy of last week's Mid-Georgia Tribune and stared out the window of Bob Cline's Barber Shop. Saturday was the day that folks, mostly men-folks from around Cedar Hill, convened at Bob's barber shop to swap news, tell stories, and generally get caught up on happenings around the town. Sometimes they might even get a haircut or a shave.

Four barbers worked on Saturdays, and all four chairs were busy. A steady drone of conversation and laughter filled the shop from the assortment of odd seats around the wall, along with the clicks of the clippers and the pops of Joe Lee's shoe-shine rag. A steady flow of customers came in and out, so no one noticed when George Stover got up and walked over to the window and stared out at the town square. This square was much like other small town squares, but Cedar Hill was too small to surround the square with businesses, so the other three sides contained homes, churches, and a house that had been converted to City Hall.

After studying all four corners of the square for several minutes, George Stover turned around and asked no one in particular, "Where'd we get them four cannons?"

The drone of conversation slowed down and came to a halt as people looked at George. "What cannons?" someone asked.

"Them four cannons right there," answered George, pointing out at the square.

The four bronze cannons were mounted on stone pedestals at each corner. Local farmers, bringing in produce to sell from their wagons, would often hitch their mules to the barrels. Traditionally, the local high school would polish the bronze and cut back the weeds as a community service project, once a year.

"They've always been there," volunteered one customer, setting off a steady flow of guesses and opinions.

"Hell, they couldn't have always been there, you dumb nut."

"Yea, cannons don't grow on trees."

"Them growed on those rock stands," was followed by chuckles.

"Maybe the State gave them to us."

"Have you ever heard of the State of Georgia giving away anything?"

"I've been in Cedar Hill since 1890, goin' on thirty years now, and they've always been there"

Bob Cline had put down his clippers and joined his customers at the window when a tall, slim citizen approached the door of his shop. With careful steps, aided by a cane, wearing his customary black suit, white shirt, black wide-brimmed hat, and black string tie, Mr. Henry Hill did not lose an ounce of dignity as he looked with surprise at the faces staring out at him from the barber shop window.

"Here's the man who can tell us," said Cline.

George Stover opened the shop door. "Mr. Henry, how you been doin'?"

"Fair to middlin," smiled the dignified gentleman.

"Good to see you, Henry," welcomed the other old-timers, and "How you been doin, Mr. Hill?" inquired the younger customers.

"Come on in, Henry," welcomed the barber, "we've a puzzle I'll bet you can solve for us."

"I'll sure do my best," said Henry with a friendly smile.

Henry Hill was escorted to a comfortable chair near the middle of the shop. A noisy Model T Ford chugged by causing a few mules and horses to shy away. Bob Cline waited for quiet. "Mr. Henry, we've been wondering about those four cannons out there on the square, and everybody agreed that you would be the man to tell us all about them. Do you have any idea about where they came from, and why they are on our town square?"

Turning to look out the window, Henry Hill put his cane between his legs and pulled himself up to gaze out at the four guns, one by one. Sitting down, he thought for a while, and scratched his short white beard.

"Yes, I can tell you where they came from."

"We'd sure like to hear it."

The stately old man began his tale.

"During the war…"

"Now, which war, Mr. Henry?" Even though The World War had ended only a few years ago, Bob Cline wanted to be sure which war Henry Hill was talking about.

Henry nodded his head in understanding. "The War Between the States. The war that was fought right here in Georgia," he said, tapping his cane on the floor for emphasis.

"During the war, well, actually for about twenty years before the war, there was an old boy named Bing Kates had a mill down on Folsom Creek. It was a fine mill, too. Ole' Bing had built a good dam, backed up a fine mill pond, and always had plenty of water to turn the wheel. Folks around here took their corn or wheat or whatever down to Ole' Bing to grind. He was one smart miller, and could rig his wheel to run a big saw up and down, so he could cut lumber, too.

"Well, Bing had this pretty young daughter named Georgia who was smart as a whip. Helped ole' Bing a lot at the mill, but Bing kept her in school most of the time, 'cause he wanted her to marry as high up as she could.

"Business at the mill got better and better, so finally he had to hire him some help, so he hired this boy whose family needed a little extra income. Now, some of y'all might remember that old road down to the mill. It was a bad one. Narrow, steep, and full of ruts and rocks. It curved around the side of a good-sized hill, and was so steep that most of Bing's customers could not make it back up the hill with a two-mule wagon and a full load. So this boy that Bing hired would take two of Bing's mules and hitch them up to the wagon in front of the customer's mules, and then the four mules could get on up the hill pretty good."

Some of the older men nodded in understanding.

"Once they got to the top, the boy would unhitch old Bing's mules and take them back down to the mill."

A customer leaned forward and said, "Mr. Henry, I'm surprised y'all had any mules left, with the war and all."

Henry Hill nodded. "Yes, that's true. The Yankees had stole just about every animal around here, and the Confederates had what they called "confiscated" all the horses and mules they could. But they knew that they depended on this part of Georgia to grow food, and we sure couldn't grow food without our mules for plowing and hauling, so they left us farmers pretty much alone."

"You can't teach a pig to plow," cracked one customer.

Henry grinned and chuckled with the others at that old saw. "Well, that summer when they were fighting all around Atlanta, and had Atlanta almost surrounded, everybody around here was working as hard as they could to grow food for our families and still have some to sell to the Confederates. At the same time, Yankee and Confederate cavalry was roaming around all over the place, and one was about as bad as the other for taking what they needed, and just generally keeping things stirred up."

The old man paused and stared out the window at the cannons while he rubbed his fingers through his beard, thinking. No one made a sound. "Did any of y'all ever know two old boys who owned farms right next to each other about a mile down south from town, old Ben Norton and Hansel Pulliam?"

A few old-timers nodded in recollection.

"Well, the Pulliams and the Nortons had been fussin' with each other for two or three generations. Had something to do with an old property line dispute between their grandpaws. They were both fine farmers, but never could get along. One time the sheriff had to separate them right here in the middle of town when they started fussin' over who was next at the blacksmith shop."

Bob Cline interrupted, "Now, Mr. Henry, this does have something to do with those cannons, doesn't it?"

"Oh, yes, yes it does," grinned Henry Hill and then went on.

"Hansel Pulliam took a wagon load of corn down to Bing Kates' mill for grinding. When the corn was ground, sacked, and loaded on the wagon, that boy that worked for Mr. Kates brought out his two extra mules I told you about, hitched them to Hansel's wagon, and they started up the hill. That was always a tough job, but it had to be done.

"We'd had some bad rains over the past few days, and that road up the hill, which was narrow and rough anyhow, was about as bad as a hillside road could possibly be. The mules were straining and the wagon was lurching around in the ruts, when who would you guess they saw a-coming down the hill?"

"Ben Norton!" laughed a chorus of customers.

"You got it. Old Ben and Hansel met face to face on a bad, narrow road, where there wasn't no way in the world to turn around. Old man Norton was taking his corn down to be ground, and Hansel was taking his load of corn meal back up."

"Well, sir, as you gentlemen know, one of the hardest things in the world to do is back up a wagon and a team of mules, 'specially on a curvy, hillside road. Ben had one of his farm hands with him to help with the loading and unloading, so that boy held his mules while Ben and Hansel got down and commenced screaming and shouting at each other, making about the worst commotion that anybody ever heard. Hansel screamed that if Ben had any sense at all he would not have been coming down the hill at that particular time, and Ben claimed the down-hill wagon had the rights, and threatened to turn Hansel's wagon over and roll it down the hillside into Folsom Creek.

"About the time when them two men were about to have at it, there was another racket back up the hill, and here come down the hill and around the bend a bunch of Yankee soldiers on horses, then right behind them, as far as you could see up the hill, was a long line of wagons and cannons! It was a whole Yankee artillery battery with cannons, caissons, supply wagons, and I don't know what all, and four or six horses pulling each one!

Henry Hill paused to let the commotion of laughing and knee-slapping die down.

"Now, there was a young lieutenant in charge of the Yanks, and he proceeded to get right in the middle of the fuss between Hansel and Ben. Seems that Yank wanted them both to push their wagons off the road and just let them tumble off down the hill so him and his boys could get by. Naturally, they didn't take too kindly to that idea, and it looked for a while like the Yank was going to have his men start shooting at Ben and Hansel and just push them out of his way.

"That boy that worked at the mill had jumped off his wagon and was about to high-tail it out of there when there was some gunshots somewhere back up the road. Well, the Yanks all got out their guns and was ready for a fight. Seems that they had been caught-up with by some of our cavalry which had been tailing them for a long time, and now had them pretty well pinned down. Our boys had dismounted back in the woods and got the drop on that whole battery, as they called it. But the Yanks didn't want us to get their cannons, so they rolled them off the road and let them just go crashing down that steep hill, through the woods, running into rocks and trees. Wheels came off and them little carts they was hitched to broke all to pieces as that whole battery tumbled down the hill and into the creek."

The barber shop was silent.

"Our boys took charge real good. Their officer decided that it was easier for Hansel to back down the road with their help, so he did. What was left of that Yankee battery was a wreck, so they just unhitched the horses and pushed the rest of it off the road, too."

Henry Hill rested his chin on his walking cane and thought for a moment. The customers made not a sound. He took a deep breath and gazed out the window toward the town square.

"About five years after the war, that boy that worked at the mill got a bunch of his friends together and went back to the creek, near the mill, down the hill from where the big fuss was. They looked and looked for them cannons, but could not find a one. Then that pretty little Georgia Kates came out and showed them right where they was – buried in the sandy bottom of Folsom Creek. The busted wheels and carriages were pretty rotten by then, but the cannons themselves were just like new, except tarnished real bad. So that bunch of young men got their mules and horses together and hauled them up to the square, all four of 'em. People around the town helped and built those rock pedestals. They been there ever since."

The barber shop was very quiet.

The barber finally broke the silence. "That was about 1870 when the cannons were brought up, right, Mr. Henry?"

"That's about right."

"And who was that boy who worked at the mill, the one that had those cannons brought up here and mounted, the one that had an eye on Georgia Kates?"

Henry Hill just smiled and looked at the floor.

George Stover finally spoke. "It was you, wasn't it, Mr. Henry?"

Henry Hill looked up and nodded. "They are called Napoleons. There was a lot of them around when the war started, and both sides used them. It is said that bronze guns like them, Napoleons, were General Robert E. Lee's favorite artillery."

"And whatever happened to Miss Georgia, the miller's daughter?

Henry Hill pulled out a gold pocket watch and glanced at it. "She's at home right now wondering where in the world I am. I better git."

END

WHITED SEPULCHRES

…ye are like unto whited sepulchres, which indeed appear beautiful outward, but are within full of dead men's bones, and of all uncleanness.

-Matthew 23:27, King James version of the Bible

Reverend Verlon Dixon, pastor of Greyson Full Gospel Baptist Church, shaded his eyes from the glaring summer sun. "Now wait a minute here, Ralph. What are we supposed to do with Milton Talley's body?"

Blackrock County Sheriff Ralph Cogburn, red-faced and sweaty, was trying his best to close the door of his cruiser, but the crowd of concerned citizens of Greyson wouldn't let him go. Cogburn pushed hands off his door. His motor rumbled, "Preacher," he growled, "I don't give a god damn what y'all do with that damn body. We got all we could find, which ain't a hell of a lot. Y'all let that GBI agent go back to Atlanta with precious little. Now until we hear from the State about their investigation, or until some of your so-called 'flock' here wants to come forth with what they know, I got more important things to do than to try to find out who bashed in the head of that damn worthless, semi-retired bootlegger, Milton Talley."

Cogburn slipped the white Ford into gear and started easing forward. The crowd stepped back and dodged the gravel which flew as the sheriff careened out of the church parking lot.

Rev. Dixon fingered the stainless steel cross on a string around his neck. His wife, Trixie, took his arm and, with the rest of the crowd, looked up to the minister for leadership.

Dixon pushed his coal-black hair back from his face and glanced around at the group of mountain people, some from his congregation, some not. "Let's get out of this sun," he stated, and led them into the shade of a gigantic red-oak tree in front of his church. In his "uniform" black pants and white shirt he was the only man in the crowd not wearing blue jeans or overalls. Even Trixie wore well fitting faded jeans, much to the quiet approval of the male members of the crowd.

"All right," he said in his sermon voice, "since Milton's body was found in our church, I guess it's our responsibility to handle this thing. I don't want to make a bunch of decisions on my own, so, Bob, I guess we need to have a deacons' meeting. Think we can get everybody together tonight after supper?"

* * *

Bob Dilbeck, Chairman of the Board of Deacons, whose jeans were the cleanest and whose truck was the newest in the lot, was one of the largest land owners in Blackrock County, and made a very nice living farming, selling timber, and speculating in land. His weekly contributions were generous.

Since most of the Board of Deacons were in the crowd, Dilbeck just glanced around, got enough affirmative nods, and agreed, "Right after supper."

Verlon rocked slowly on the back porch of the parsonage, silently contemplating the mountain forest behind his home and the events of the day. Trixie cuddled in his lap, respecting his quiet time. Their bodies always fit together as one, and each served as a consummate tension reliever for the other. Verlon's hand found its way up her blouse and absently stroked her warm, smooth back, the curve of her waist.

" You better stop that if you want to make it to the deacon's meeting," she whispered. "Are you ready for supper? It's almost done."

He kissed her on the neck and gave her an extra hug. "I'm always ready."

"I can vouch for that," Trixie grinned as she pushed up from his lap and straightened her blouse. "The pork chops will be out in ten minutes."

Soon the aroma of pork chops, black eyed peas, cabbage, and corn bread pulled him off his back porch to the kitchen table. As he slid his chair out with one hand he grabbed Trixie around the waist with the other. "All right! There's nothing like a good meal to take a man's mind off his problems." Trixie stiffened and glared at him. "And a good woman," he quickly added. "Hugs from a good woman. A good meal and hugs from a nice, soft, gorgeous woman. Hugs are important. Very important. Very very important."

"You better look out, boy, or you might have to go to that meeting hungry," she chided, joining him at the table.

They held hands as Verlon blessed the meal and asked for God's help in guiding the church through this difficult situation.

After a few minutes of quietly and seriously enjoying the meal, Verlon took a long swig of iced tea and shook his head. "Honey, something is not right. Not only that it's just downright inconceivable that a church member is murdered—has his head bashed in—right there in the church basement, but now nobody want to do anything about it. What's going on here? Did you notice that Bob and Junior and the rest of them were not the ones trying to get old Ralph to stay and help us? I just can't figure this thing out."

"Now, Verlon, you be careful," warned Trixie. "Those good men know best. They will know how to handle things."

Verlon looked out the window toward the church parking lot. "Looks like most of them are there. I'd better get on over."

With a hug and a kiss, the preacher left for his church. Trixie could see the concern and apprehension in his face.

A Baptist Church is one of the most pure democracies in existence- one person, one vote. All major decisions are made by the entire congregation in Church Conference. The congregation elects deacons, to whom they delegate certain responsibilities. The Church Conference could be compared to a stockholders' meeting of a corporation, and the Board of Deacons to a Board of Directors. The deacons then delegate the day-to-day responsibilities of running the church to a business manager, or in many small churches to the pastor. There is no higher body directing the church, unless the church desires to affiliate with some association of Baptist churches. Preachers are hired and fired by the church members.

Most Baptist churches, including Greyson Full Gospel, have 12 deacons, to correspond to the 12 disciples. At Greyson there were four honorary positions held by elderly members who very rarely came to meetings, leaving seven or eight who usually attended meetings. Bob Dilbeck was chairman.

Attending this meeting were the Gazaway brothers, Junior and Jack, who ran Gazaway Garage; Lester Brown who worked at the post office for his wife who was postmistress; attorney Taylor McCoy; farmer Lamar Pennington; elementary school Principal Dean Ledford; Bob Dilbeck, and the preacher, who had no vote.

The meeting commenced in the Adult Men's Sunday School classroom. Dilbeck called on Jack Gazaway to open the meeting with prayer. A short prayer of thanks for blessings, guidance in the matter at hand, and comfort for the bereaved but distant family of Milton Talley was offered, and concluded with a chorus of amens.

Dilbeck looked at the preacher. "Verlon, is the body still up at Jones & Burden?"

The preacher nodded affirmatively.

Dilbeck looked at principal Ledford, who kept records on the church cemetery. "Dean, we've got plenty of room in the cemetery, don't we?"

Ledford sat up straight. "Oh, yes. Actually room for several hundred more graves, and by clearing those pines on the back of the hill…"

"OK, thanks, Dean," interrupted the chairman. "Verlon, you think the family has done all they gonna do?"

"Yes. Everything they can do." Milton Talley had lived alone, and what few relatives he had were of very meager means and of even less interest in Milton.

Dilbeck looked around the table. "Anybody see anything wrong having Jones & Burden bring the body down Sunday, and have a service for him right after church?"

The preacher watched affirmative nods all around.

Dilbeck took a deep breath and looked around the group. "Milton was a good man, a righteous man. He didn't have no money, but he gave his share by hauling coal and firewood, and keeping the grounds clean. The least we can do for him is to buy some nice flowers, and have a monument of some kind put in. And maybe send a hundred dollars to his daughter, if we can find her. This was a terrible thing, but we can put it behind us now and get on with our business… uh, our lives. That OK?"

An obvious consensus approved with nods.

But Verlon, who had no vote, did not move. Dean Ledford, who had been taking copious notes, stopped and looked up. The room was quiet. "Is that all?" Dean asked. "Somebody killed that man. Shouldn't we try to find out more?"

"That is not our business," stated attorney McCoy. "The Georgia Bureau of Investigation could not find anything, our own sheriff could not find anything, so it appears that this will go down in the history of Greyson as our first unsolved murder."

Most heads nodded agreement, but most feet shuffled uncomfortably.

"Is there any other business?" asked Dilbeck.

"Gentlemen," asked the preacher, "may I say a word? Dean may be right. Could we be dismissing this issue too easily? Somewhere out there a murderer is loose. He could be a member of our congregation, God forbid. Also, Milton Talley may not be the last on his list, if he has a list. I think we need to look into this matter more thoroughly. If we can't get the authorities to help, then let's look further ourselves. This board could easily appoint a committee to continue the investigation. Several of you good men right here have the knowledge and ability to see what we can find. Let's not stop too soon."

"I agree," added the principal, and sat back to watch the response.

Chairman Dilbeck studied the preacher and the principal. The other deacons studied their feet or watched Dilbeck. The room became quiet.

Dilbeck looked at the principal. "Dean, how long you been in Greyson? Three years, that about right? This is your first year on the board, and you are very valuable to us. Verlon, you've been with the church a little less than two years." Dilbeck paused and glanced around the group. Verlon followed his gaze and picked up almost imperceptible nods from the Gazaway brothers. Looking back at the preacher, he asked, "Verlon, have you ever seen the furnace?"

"What?" asked Verlon, surprised at the sudden change in direction.

"The furnace. Down in the basement. How 'bout you, Dean, you ever seen the furnace?"

"No," was the puzzled reply.

Dilbeck looked around the group and took a deep breath. "Well come on, boys, let's show 'em the furnace."

The thick canopy of red oak trees deflected what little light the stars and the moon afforded, spreading pit black darkness over the church grounds. Junior Gazaway led the deacons and the preacher around the building and down the outside stairway, carefully feeling for the steps. He fumbled with a ring of keys, trying several until the door finally swung opened into even blacker darkness of the church basement.

"Wait 'till I find the string," he asked. The light came on. "Come on in."

Verlon had never seen the church basement. He had never had any reason to. Milton always kept a good supply of coal or firewood, built a fire in cold weather several hours before services started, and kept the sanctuary at a comfortable temperature.

The furnace stood in the center of the basement, a huge round steel fire box with octopus-like pipes extending up to vents in the floor of the sanctuary. Dean Ledford and Verlon stared at it and at the huge pile of coal, then stole a questioning glance at each other.

"Well, what do you think?" asked Dilbeck.

Verlon shrugged. "I've seen furnaces before, Bob. What's so special about this one?"

No one answered. Verlon wondered, there must be something more, something unusual about this furnace which he and Dean were not seeing.

Dean walked up closer and around to one side of the fire box. "What are these drums for?" A group of six fifty-five gallon drums were connected by pipes, and to the furnace.

No one spoke. Verlon walked up and inspected the drums, then looked questioningly at Dilbeck. "Bob, is this what I think it is?"

"Well, Preacher, if you think it's a still, you'd be about right."

Dean Ledford took a quick jump back as if the octopus were about to grab him. "A still? Right here in our church basement?"

Verlon's mouth hung open as he studied the faces of his Board of Deacons. They avoided his gaze. The principal started easing toward the open basement door, but Taylor McCoy kicked the door closed and stepped in front of it. "Dean, just be patient a minute."

Bob Dilbeck nodded to the lawyer. "Taylor, how about you telling Dean and the preacher what we have here."

* * *

Trixie stood in the dark living room and watched as car lights came on and the deacons drove away. As soon as she heard the screened porch door open she rushed out to meet her man. "Well, what did y'all decide?" Verlon did not answer put plopped down in a rocking chair and started slowly rocking, staring out into the darkness toward the church.

Finally he took a deep breath and looked at Trixie. "Honey, you are absolutely not going to believe what's been going on over there."

"What? Verlon, tell me."

"There's a still in the church basement."

"A moonshine still?"

"A moonshine liquor still."

"Now, come on, Honey. How could a church have a still in the basement?"

"They asked me not to tell you about it. They're afraid you will tell somebody. I told them that I would never keep anything from you and that they would not need to worry about you talking if I asked you not to. They did not like it, but they had already shown it to me and Dean, so there is not much they can do about it."

"Verlon honey, God knows I drank my share of liquor back before I got religion, but how can we stay at a church with a still in its basement?"

"Well, Precious, they explained it like this. You've seen the other two churches here in Greyson, the Methodist church and that little Presbyterian church. The Methodists have not painted their building in probably ten years, I hear the roof leaks, they don't have indoor plumbing, and cars get stuck in the parking lot when it rains. That little Presbyterian building is in awful shape, and they don't meet but once a month. The two of them together don't do half as much good for the community as our Greyson Full Gospel Baptist Church. Now why is there such a big difference? Think about it a minute.

"Our folks are not any richer than the Methodists or those Presbyterians. Our people are mostly farmers, timber cutters, or mill workers, just plain ordinary working people, and most of them don't have any money to spare. So, then, how does our church afford to look—and be—so much better than those others? Our building is freshly painted. We keep plenty of gravel in the parking lot. We have indoor plumbing. Our hymnals aren't ragged or musty from getting rained on, and lots of ours are new. We have this nice parsonage which you and I enjoy. We help out families around the county when somebody loses a job or gets sick. The deacons always take care of the finances, but I can tell you by just observing the collection plates that there isn't a lot of money coming in from the congregation. The difference is the still. The deacons take the profit from the still and spend it on the church and the community. Without the still we would be just like the Methodists."

Verlon rocked and stared out into the darkness. "So the big question is, does the good justify the bad?"

For a long time they both just rocked quietly, listening to the hum and buzz and peeping of cicadas and tree frogs and an occasional owl or whippoorwill, comforting mountain sounds.

"How did Milton tie into this?" Trixie finally asked.

"I seems that good old Milton was a highly experienced moonshiner. A still has to have a fire to cook the mash, so Milton used the church furnace."

"Did the deacons know about that?"

"Oh, yes. They kept him supplied with raw material, and set up a network of drivers to run the "white lightening" into Atlanta. Everything done at night. I never heard or suspected a thing, and I guess you didn't either. All old Milton had to do was cook it- and take care of the church."

"What about the money? I always heard that moonshiners make a lot of money. Do you think the deacons keep any of it for themselves?"

"I asked about that, and I'm not satisfied with the answer. I suspect they might. You're right, moonshining is a highly profitable business, and, as I found out, it's one of the most important industries in these mountains. Including our still— our still! Well, including our still, it seems that there are three families that control the liquor making around here. The deacons think that Milton might have been killed by one of 'our' competitors."

"Oh, Verlon!"

"This whole thing has got me mighty confused, Precious."

Trixie came over and curled up gently into Verlon's lap and hugged him tightly to her breasts. "Do you think we are in any danger too?"

"I hope not. It won't hurt to be careful until we get this thing figured out." He held her tightly as they rocked. The soothing night sounds continued. Then he thought about all those mountain boys, and what excellent shots they were with their deer rifles. "Let's go in, and let's not turn on any lights. Can you find everything in the dark?"

"You know I can find everything in the dark."

* * *

Verlon's sleep was fitful at best. Trixie did not rest much better.

He eased out of bed at first light and tried to dress without disturbing Trixie, but she smiled and waved at him without opening her eyes, then turned over and snuggled under the covers. Mountain nights are cool even when summer days are hot.

Verlon scratched a short love note on a scrap of paper, drew some hearts on it, and left it on the kitchen table.

A heavy dew covered the windshield of the 1947 Plymouth which the church furnished, along with the parsonage. The two-door Plymouth coupe ran well for a five-year-old car, although it tended to over-heat after long drives in hot weather. He was glad it started quickly. Their bedroom window was not far from where the car was parked, and he did not want to disturb Trixie any further. The gravel drive-way crunched a little as he eased out onto Rockmont Road and started the twenty-minute ride to Rockmont, the County Seat of Blackrock County.

An organization know as Blackrock County Men's Breakfast and Discussion Club met the first and third Mondays of each month at 7 AM at the Rockmont Café. The club had no officers, no dues, no roster, no by-laws, and no program. Members were Blackrock County businessmen of one sort or another, except for Verlon and Dean Ledford, the principal of Greyson Elementary School.

The Plymouth cruised smoothly along the winding mountain road. Verlon's mind was on last night's deacons' meeting, but he nervously kept one eye on his rear view mirror. He took a deep breath when a black Ford pickup pulled out of a dirt side-road and closed the gap between them quicker than Verlon would have liked. The low morning sun reflected off the pickup's windshield, preventing Verlon from recognizing the driver. All the way to Rockmont the truck stayed right on his bumper, then would drop back a couple of hundred feet, then come back close. Verlon sped up until he reached the Rockmont city limit sign, where the truck turned off and disappeared down another dirt road.

The Rockmont Café was on Main Street, facing the Blackrock County Court House. The town was situated on the gentle slope of a mountain, which prevented the customary "town square" found in most Georgia towns. The red brick county courthouse was directly across the street from the café, located on a small ridge which sloped down in the back. County offices were in the two upper stories, the jail and the sheriff's offices were in the "daylight basement" which opened toward the back.

Deputy Sheriff Fred Chilton and Principal Dean Ledford were sitting on the bench outside the café. Both got up as soon as Verlon parked, and walked down to meet him.

"Verlon, I've been bringing Fred up to date on the situation down at the church."

" 'Morning, Preacher," smiled the deputy, holding out his hand for a firm, sincere shake. "Dean's been telling me about on that tragedy down at the church. I just want you to know that the Sheriff's department will do everything we can to help solve that matter."

Verlon shook his head. "Well, Fred, it seems to me like your boss has already washed his hands of that matter."

The deputy nodded. "Ralph is my boss, but he isn't the only person in law enforcement around here."

Dean Ledford studied Verlon's face. Verlon nodded his understanding. "Let's go on in and meet with the gang and talk about it some more after breakfast."

The early risers had already pushed enough tables together to seat a good sized crowd, knowing that everybody would want to get as much first-hand information as they could about the very rare murder right here in their home county. Clyde Edwards, who owned and ran Mountain View Tourist Cabins, and Doc Cantrell, veterinarian, were the first to greet the three men as they came in. Several members had already found chairs and were studying the menu – Billy Jones, who operated a Texaco gas station; Ed Mashburn, also called "Doc," pharmacist at Rockmont Rexall Drugs and Sundries; and Aaron Youngblood, mortician, looked up and waved. Others in attendance were Lloyd Boyd of Boyd Real Estate, Tom Hyatt, shift supervisor at U. S. Fabrics, and Cecil Alverson, the local State Farm Insurance agent.

Out of consideration of the pressure on Verlon, no one jumped right in with eager questions. Menus were studied, lots of eggs were ordered, fried and scrambled, with big helpings of ham, bacon, and sausage, along with hot biscuits and an occasional whole-wheat toast. Pots of strong, black coffee were soon emptied and refilled, except for Realtor Boyd who was nursing an ulcer and stuck with milk.

Waitresses Flo and Minnie hurried back and forth, keeping the table well supplied with more hot biscuits and pots of hot coffee. It was rumored that Minnie was a retired stripper, and there was always some jokes about what it would take to get her to come out of retirement.

Conversation centered around the prospects of Blackrock County High School's football team this Fall, the University of Georgia's Bulldogs, and whether the Atlanta Crackers could get a better shortstop and end up with a good year or not. Then slowly the conversations began to quieten and die down, and Verlon picked up an occasional inquisitive glance.

Finally, Verlon sat up straight and looked around the table, and the conversation came to a complete halt. Then the questions began.

Just what happened down there?

Our janitor was murdered.

How was he killed?

Hit in the head with an ax.

With the blunt end or the blade?

With the blade. Sliced his head half in-two.

Did they hit him from the front or the back?

The front.

Then he must have known the murderer?

Could be.

Where was it?

In the church basement.

Is old Ralph on the case?

That's an issue we are working on right now.

At this point, Deputy Fred Chilton broke into the conversation. "I really think that we ought to leave Verlon alone right now. Verlon has told us the basic facts, and they will probably be in the paper. We are in the process of gathering information, and that's about all we can tell you at this time. I promise you that the Sheriff's office will do everything it can to see that justice is carried out."

Verlon nodded with a smile of thanks to the deputy.

After a few queries about the health of various families, answers to "how's your business?" and a few ribald jokes, one-by-one the men of Blackrock County Men's Breakfast and Discussion Club trickled out to their respective responsibilities.

Verlon started to mention the black pick-up which followed him, but didn't. But he did pull Fred Chilton aside, and asked, "Is Ralph over at the Court House?"

"He was when I left."

"I'm going over and talk to him some more. I just don't understand his attitude."

"OK, but go easy. You know how fast he can over-heat."

Verlon grinned and nodded.

Dean Ledford caught his arm. "Can I help in any way?"

"Don't you need to get on down to the school?"

"I should, but I'll stay and help if I can."

"Go on. There's no need in both of us getting caught in Ralph's wrath."

Verlon walked around to the back of the Courthouse, and was almost run into by Sheriff Ralph Cogburn charging out the back door. Cogburn was red in the face, which seemed to be his usual state, gritting his teeth, and had his flat-brimmed had pulled down tight on his head.

"Sheriff Cogburn," Verlon started, " I need to ask you about…"

"Not now, Preacher. I got a God-damned emergency I've got to take care of."

"Can I just…"

"Preacher, when I say emergency, then it's a damned emergency. You remember that trusty, that son-of-a-bitch Bill Coleman? We let him wander around out of his cell, help with the office work, and sometimes worked the radio as our dispatcher. Well, that SOB has done stole a sheriff's uniform, stole the patrol car keys, drove the damn car over to Valhalla in South Carolina, where he started directing traffic in front of the High School. Well, them stupid-assed Valhallah policemen finally wondered what a Blackrock County deputy was doing directing traffic in Valhalla, South Carolina, so they locked him up and called me to come get him. Now, dammit, preacher, if you can't trust a damned trusty, who can you trust?"

Verlon, deciding that discretion was the better part of valor, stepped back and again watched Sheriff Ralph Cogburn scratch gravel.

* * *

Trixie sighed with relief when she saw Verlon's black Plymouth pull into the shade under a big red-oak tree. She met him half-way between the house and the shade tree, and their greeting hug was a little longer and a little tighter than usual.

"How was breakfast, sweetheart?"

"Had a good crowd. Everybody wanted to know about our murder."

"Did you get to talk to Ralph?"

"No, but I think Fred Chilton might be of some help until we get things straightened out."

Holding hands, they walked back into the house. Trixie went about her household duties of dusting, washing, and straightening, and Verlon sat down at the breakfast table with his Bible and a couple of reference books and started working on his sermon for the coming Sunday. He decided to preach on the sixth commandment, "Thou shalt not kill,"

But then he decided against it. The killer was certainly not in his congregation. No church-going Baptist would be capable of such a heinous crime.

Or would he? The killer knew his way into the church basement, and must have known that the church was operating one of the largest moonshine stills in the mountains. The deacons knew all about it, all except Dean Ledford, and maybe he just had not been there long enough to get involved in the illegal liquor business. No, Dean seemed to be genuinely interested in helping him find the killer. Or was that just a front? Does Dean know more than he lets on? Was Dean the one designated to keep an eye on Verlon, and not let him get too close to finding all the answers?

After an hour of staring at Exodus 20:13 while his mind raced through a myriad of faces and possibilities, the preacher realized that his powers of concentration were not great enough at this time to hold his brain on the task at hand, instead of the murder of a man in the church basement- HIS church basement.

He jumped when the phone rang. It was Deputy Chilton.

"Whatcha doin', Verlon?"

"Uh – preparing Sunday's sermon."

"When can you get away for a while?"

"Why?"

"Well, there's some things I think you ought to know about the illegal liquor business in Blackrock County."

"Yes, I would like to know more."

"Can you get away now?"

Verlon looked at the open Bible on his table. "What did you have in mind, Fred?"

"We need to meet somewhere where we won't be seen together, and where we can talk for a while."

Verlon felt a chill through his shoulders. "OK. Where?"

"Drive out Chadwick Road about two miles and pull off on an old timber trail. There's an abandoned house and barn there. Drive around behind the barn so you can't be seen. I'll be waiting for you there in a County car."

The chill recurred, but he had to trust somebody. "OK. See you there in a few minutes."

He hung up the phone and stared at it for a moment. Trixie walked into the room and stopped when she saw his expression. "Who was that, honey?"

"Fred Chilton. Wants me to meet him out at an abandoned farm to discuss Ole' Milton."

"Want me to go with you?"

"No, no honey. I just want you to know where I'm going, and who I'm going to see."

"Are you worried about Fred?"

"Right nowt I don't know who to worry about."

Trixie walked over to the chair and pulled his head firmly between her bosoms. "I hope we don't have to worry about Fred."

"If you hold me like this much longer ole' Fred will have to worry about me." Verlon stood up, held her tightly to his chest, and kissed her softly several times.

From the church to the abandoned farm was about fifteen minutes. Fred's patrol car was parked behind the old barn, not far off the road, but completely out of sight to traffic. He motioned for Verlon to pull up next to him, also out of sight from the road.

END - FOR NOW

This is a book in progress. I put this aside for a while and have concentrated on magazine and newspaper articles and short stories. MB

NON –
FICTION
SECTION

THE DROWNING BEAR MYSTERIES

Drowning Bear had a nice little farm on Sweetwater Creek, about five miles up from the Chattahoochee River, in what is now a suburb of Atlanta, Georgia. On this farm he had two cabins, a stable, corn crib, 102 peach trees, and 105 apple trees. He also operated a ferry across Sweetwater Creek from which he earned $70 a year.

He was probably a Muscogee native American, or what most white people called "Creek," because their villages tended to be along the banks of creeks, just as Drowning Bear's home and farm were. There were also some Cherokees in the area, and white people had begun to encroach on the Creek's territory, coveting the land, especially land which had already been improved with cabins, orchards, and a ferry. So Drowning Bear was "driven off," but he left many mysteries in his place.

This information is stated in an appraisal dated February, 1837, so Drowning Bear must have fled around 1829. His home and farm were valued at a total of $674.50 for the buildings, orchards, ferry, and his land. The appraisal also states that the land was in Cobb County, but it is in Douglas. That sum of $674.50 may have been a fair price at that time, or it may not, considering that Drowning Bear had been "driven off eight years ago."

A copy of the appraisal, along with a second appraisal of the ferry for Drowning Bear and his cousins, is on display at Atlanta History Center. All Native American lands in north Georgia were appraised in 1837 in order to compensate them before their forced march to Oklahoma, the infamous "Trail of Tears." In essence, the appraisal, hand written and very legible, gives the following details:

No. 21. Feb 11, 1837

Appraisal for Drowning Bear, on Sweet Water, Cobb County, Ga.

1 Hew'd Log Cabin 18 by 20 $40.00

1 do do 16 by 18 30.00

1 Stable 15.00

1 Crib 10.00

102 Peach Trees at $1.00 102.00

105 Apple Trees at $1.50 157.50

40 acres upland at $8.00   320.00

  $674.50

Driven off 8 years ago, worth $3.00 per acre per ann.

South of Coffee's line

No. 22 Feb 11, 1837. Appraisal for Drowning Bear & Cos (Drowning Bear, Stop, C-su-an-ga's heirs, Nickajack's heirs, Sick-cow-a, Crying Snake, Sweet Water's heirs).

A Ferry on Sweet Water 5' miles above the mouth in Cobb County, Ga. Net Income $70.00 per ann.

Driven off 8 years ago.

South of Coffee's line.

"Coffee's Line" was established by General John Coffee, at the command of President Andrew Jackson. Its purpose was to divide the Creek lands from the Cherokees. The line ran from Shallow Ford (Chattahoochee River near the Roswell Road bridge) straight westward to the Alabama line. It passed just north of Marietta and across the foot of Kennesaw Mountain. Lands north of Coffee's Line were considered Cherokee, south of the line were considered Creek.

No specific value was given to the ferry.

These are the few facts we have. They were collected from several visits to the Atlanta History Center, Georgia Department of Archives and History, and Cobb Library's Georgia Room. However, Drowning Bear left many mysteries behind.

WHERE WAS DROWNING BEAR'S FARM AND FERRY?

The appraisal of the ferry says that it was five miles up the creek from the Chattahoochee River. That would put it in the vicinity of Sweetwater Creek State Park. We must assume that the farm and ferry were together, or very close.

The most likely location for the ferry is where old Factory Shoals Road crossed the creek. There was probably a ferry there long before the bridge was built.

The topography along the creek from the river up to the ferry/bridge site is extremely rugged and rocky and would not be desirable for farming. The first good gently-rolling sites are around where the park's visitor center is now, and extending on up to the rich bottom land which is now covered by Sparks Reservoir. Two smaller creeks intersected Sweetwater at that point. Drowning Bear must have lived and farmed in this general area.

WHY DID THE APPRAISER THINK HE WAS IN COBB COUNTY?

"…5 miles above the mouth…," as the appraisal states, is in Douglas County, not Cobb. That area has never been in Cobb. Sweetwater Creek meanders northward through Douglas for six more miles before it enters Cobb.

The appraisal was done in 1837. Cobb had been created out of Cherokee County in 1832. The area was still very sparsely settled, so the local people may have had vague ideas as to where the county line was actually located. The appraiser made his "best guess" as to where he was, and missed.

Actually, in 1837 the Sweetwater area was in neither Cobb nor its present Douglas County. Douglas was created in 1870 from parts of Campbell and Carroll counties. Drowning Bear's farm would have been in Campbell at the time of his disappearance. So the appraiser was in Campbell, thought he was in Cobb, and it's now Douglas.

WHO "DROVE" HIM OFF?

Only one probable answer to that question—greedy white settlers.

SINCE HE HAD TWO CABINS, HE MUST HAVE HAD A FAMILY. WHAT HAPPENED TO THEM?

Another mystery we cannot answer.

WHAT DO WE KNOW ABOUT DROWNING BEAR PERSONALLY?

He was a hard-working, industrious person. He cleared his land, built two houses and other farm buildings, and planted and maintained 207 fruit trees. When needed, he operated his ferry. He would have been considered one of the more prosperous Creeks.

WHERE DID "SWEETWATER CREEK" GET ITS NAME?

There have been many arguments over that question. Today Sweetwater Creek is big enough to be considered a river in most places. As is almost always the case with urban streams, its great natural and rugged beauty is corrupted now by trash and pollution washing down from our densely populated areas. But that has not always been the case. Once the creek ran pure and clean, clean enough to be considered "sweet." Hence, the name, "Sweetwater."

Another theory is that there was a prominent native American named "Sweet Water" who lived on the upper reaches of the creek. The appraisal of the ferry indicates that it was made for "Drowning Bear and Cos," which we take to mean his cousins. The cousins are listed, and among them we find "Sweet Water." Since creeks often pick up the name of early settlers (Nancy, Vickery, Nickajack, Gilberts, Heards) the author must go along with this theory.

The area around Drowning Bear's farm and ferry has had an interesting history. Long after Drowning Bear had fled, and just before the Civil war, a group of Georgians recognized the fast flowing, ample water supply as an excellent site for a water-powered textile mill. The mill they built was one of the largest buildings in Georgia at that time. A "mill village" grew up around it. Then in 1864, the mill was burned by U. S. cavalry because it manufactured cloth used by the Confederate army for tents and uniforms. The mill workers, mostly women and children, were charged with treason, hauled to Marietta, put on trains, and shipped to northern cities to work in mills up there.

Some of the impressive brick walls of the textile mill are still standing.

The author has been hiking the trails at Sweetwater Creek State Park for many years, but had never heard of Drowning Bear until he saw the appraisal at the Atlanta History Center. Was Drowning Bear killed? Were he and his family forcibly removed to Oklahoma or Alabama, along with 60,000 other Creeks and Cherokees who were expelled from the southern states? If so, did he survive the march or did he perish along the way as so many others did?

I hope he ran away and started over somewhere else. His old farm site is a beautiful spot. I'll watch for his spirit as I walk the Sweetwater trails.

END

One of my favorite articles. Published in The Landmarker.

First Train from Atlanta

Atlanta is a railroad town. You don't see the tracks and trains now. They have been covered over by Underground Atlanta and straddled by hi-rise buildings. Our two magnificent passenger stations have been torn down, but beneath all the glitter and traffic still lie the steel rails which connect Atlanta with the world, and which are the city's very reason for existence.

Without the railroads this area might be just a suburb of Marietta or Decatur, which were both well established cities before Atlanta was even dreamed of, and the state capital might still be in Milledgeville. Even the name "Atlanta" is derived from our first railroad, the Western & Atlantic, and was given to us by a railroad engineer. Our first name was Terminus, which was meant to designate the end of the proposed railroad. Between being Terminus and Atlanta we were Marthasville for a short while.

It was in Marthasville on a cold December afternoon in 1842 that citizens assembled to witness a historic event. The Western and Atlantic Railroad, W & A, had been under construction for two years, and so far the only track laid was from Marthasville to Marietta. Many local skeptics doubted that the state-owned railroad would ever carry any freight or passengers, calling it "the railroad from nowhere to nowhere," but the railroad builders and locomotive engineers and railroad managers and Georgia politicians were determined to show what the W & A could do. An excursion train from Marthasville to Marietta would be just the event needed to squelch the scoffing of skeptics and prove the value of rail transportation. It would also be a good test-run on that section of the first 33 miles of iron rails laid by the W & A.

There was one major problem. The Western and Atlantic Railroad did not have a locomotive and had only one car, a passenger car built at the state penitentiary.

Another railroad line, the Georgia Railroad, had been operating for several years from Augusta to Madison, but there was no track yet form Madison to Marthasville. The distance from Madison to Marthasville was 55 miles in a straight line, but much farther following the 1842 dirt roads and trails through Rutledge, Social Circle, Covington, Conyers, Lithonia, Stone Mountain, and Decatur. But while others said "impossible,"

W & A officials were busy solving the problem.

They bought an old locomotive, the Florida, plus one freight car, from the Georgia Railroad, and hauled them from Madison through Rutledge, Social Circle, Covington, Conyers, Lithonia, Stone Mountain, and Decatur on a huge wagon pulled by sixteen mules. At Marthasville it was muscled onto the new tracks, headed north.

The Florida, the passenger car, and the box car were coupled together and the excursion was ready for its run to Marietta.

Dignitaries had been invited from all over DeKalb County (Marthasville was in DeKalb then, Fulton did not yet exist) and Cobb County. Some families the eastern areas of the state had to spend the night in Decatur before making the final buggy ride to Marthasville to board the train.

As the cold morning dawned a huge crowd gathered to witness the historic event. The entire railroad line from Marthasville to Marietta was lined with spectators. Buggies and farm wagons loaded with families crowded every road. Bands played, crowds cheered, horsed bolted, dogs barked, cows ran away, and up in Cobb County a citizen panicked and ran off pulling his farm wagon behind him. The first train from Marthasville was leaving for Marietta!

Finally time came for departure. The Florida's bell clanged (it did not have a whistle nor a cab), guns were fired into the air, and the crowd roared as the Western & Atlantic's first train moved carefully away from the Marthasville station, loaded with dignitaries and families.

The Florida chugged slowly, feeling its way along the new, untested tracks, ringing its bell continually to clear cows and people out of the way. It was a small locomotive by today's standards, a wood-burner, with a large wooden cow-catcher extending out from the front, and a prominent funnel-shaped smoke stack.

Soon the excursion approached the Chattahoochee River, with its new wooden trestle, also untested, stretching high above cold waters. Some passengers were afraid to venture across the tall bridge, so engineer William Adair stopped and allowed them to get off and walk across behind the train.

Safely across and re-loaded, they began a long, gradual climb, moving slowly, with the bell still clanging to clear the tracks. They crossed Paces Ferry Road at Crossroads, later to be called Vining's Station, and then just Vinings. They wound around Vinings Mountain and across another trestle to a place known as Varner's Station, now called Smyrna.

Marietta was also crowded with citizens and visitors from miles around, more people than had ever been in the town at one time, raising a tumult never before heard in north Georgia. Bands welcomed the passengers as they disembarked and were escorted to the Ball Room at the town's finest hotel. Dignitaries made speeches, bands played and citizens and dignitaries alike danced, drank, and feasted through the night. The first train from Marthasville had arrived!

* * *

Author's note: The material for this article was obtained primarily from Atlanta and Environs by Franklin Garrett, and from The First Hundred Years, by Sarah Blackwell Gober Temple.
Ms. Temple states that the excursion was in "early winter," while Mr. Garrett holds that it was on Christmas Eve.

END

HE'S NOT DEAD

It was twilight on a warm summer day in 1943 when the Navy fighter sputtered over my house. Since World War II started, Atlantans had grown accustomed to a steady increase in military air traffic. Atlanta Naval Air Station produced a steady flow of Grumman Wildcats, and then Hellcats. Marietta Army Air Field, with the adjoining Lockheed plant, showed us a variety of army aircraft, including newly manufactured B-29's. Even Candler Field welcomed an occasional military visit.

My home was on the edge of East Atlanta, in a somewhat sparsely populated area, but with enough houses that one or two would have been wiped out if hit by the Hellcat. He was trailing a thin stream of smoke, and was following Bouldercrest Drive to crash-land away from the homes. My buddies and I jumped on our bicycles and lit out down the road to follow him. Fire trucks had been alerted, and passed us on the way.

The fire trucks had turned down an old dirt road which ran along the edge of a ravine, and then wound back through the woods. We turned in to follow them.

We threw down our bikes and started to run down the road when, much to our amazement, we saw the pilot climbing up out of the ravine, dragging his parachute behind him. We saw that he was not hurt, and some adults climbed down to assist him.

Back in the woods, where the plane had crashed, we could see the flames, and flashing lights of the fire trucks, so we ran in that direction as fast as we could. The crash site was a house-sized hole in the ground where the Hellcat had exploded. Airplane parts were scattered everywhere. A fireman was crawling out of the crater, carrying a mud-smeared machine gun, and several other firemen were searching through the dirt and wreckage.

"What are they looking for?" I asked a fireman on the rim of the crater.

"Trying to find the pilot's body," he replied.

"He's not here," I informed him. "He's OK. We saw him back at the ravine."

Much relieved, the rescue team climbed out of the hole. More military personnel arrived to secure the area, and we were asked to leave.

It wasn't much, but it made a twelve-year-old feel like a hero.

Today Atlanta Naval Air Station is Peachtree-DeKalb Airport, Marietta Army Airfield is Dobbins Air Force Base, and Candler Field is Hartsfield International Airport, one of the world's busiest. Also, the area has grown so much that if the crash happened today it would wipe out at least a dozen families.

END

SHARP-BOYLSTON CO.

A Brief History Of Georgia's Oldest Real Estate Company

John J. Woodside & Son, the corporate predecessor of Sharp-Boylston, was established in 1881. To put 1881 in context, Britain was fighting the Boer wars, Barnum & Bailey Circus made its debut, Sitting Bull surrendered, and in Tombstone, Arizona, there was a gun fight at the OK Corral. Woodside was primarily in the transfer and storage business, along with property management.

A few years later, Wister Sharp and Albert Boylston organized Sharp-Boylston Co. to engage in the real estate management business.

The two companies prospered and decided to merge, and to add a sales department under the direction of a Mr. Day. The name of the new company was John J. Woodside, Sharp-Boylston, and Day. Their offices were at 10 Auburn Avenue, about 100 feet off Peachtree. After a few more years Woodside decided to pull out and concentrate on moving and storage, and Mr. Day also left. The remaining company, once again Sharp-Boylston Co., became a full-service real estate company.

However, the main function of the company was property management. This was before the extensive use of checks, so most tenants paid their rent in cash. Sharp-Boylston employed a large team of rent collectors. Armed with a bucket and a hammer, these collectors walked from door to door to collect the rent. The bucket was to carry the cash in, and the hammer was to knock on the door before calling, "rent man."

Many tenants came into the office to pay in person, so the company employed several cashiers to handle the cash. Most landlords were small investors. One of these landlords carried his repair tools on a bicycle and rode from house to house to personally handle all of his maintenance items. He owned 300 houses, so they kept him busy. While he lived a very simple life, his earnings enabled his two sons to become very active real estate developers.

In these early days of Atlanta's real estate business, many "tools of the trade," which we take for granted now, were not available. Some of these valuable new tools are as follows:

Multiple Listing services

Lock boxes

Copy machines

Fax machines

Email

Cell phones

Telephone answering systems

Computers

Data reporting services

Educational opportunities, such as the CCIM

courses

Multiple offices

In the mid 1900's, the company was sold to Cone M. Maddox, Jr. and Willie Cox. The Sharp-Boylston name was retained even after Mr. Sharp and Mr. Boylston left the company. While still a full-service company, emphasis was on residential property management, with over 6,000 units supervised by the management department.

Door to door collections were eventually discontinued.

In 1961 Cone Maddox and Willie Cox decided to put more emphasis on commercial real estate sales and leasing. Marion Blackwell, Jr., formerly with Adams-Cates Co., became Vice-

President and Sales Manager of the commercial department, and the management department was cut back to 3,000 units.

At that time, the oldest real estate company in Georgia was Adair Realty, having been organized in 1865, right after the Civil War. Adair had both residential and commercial sales departments, but had been so successful in residential sales that they gradually phased out of commercial activity, and became one of the residential leaders in Atlanta. They became so successful that they attracted the attention of one of Atlanta's more prominent commercial Realtors and developers, Charlie Ackerman, who hoped that a venture into the residential business would give him a more diversified company. Ackerman bought Adair, but it did not work out as Ackerman had hoped, and Adair was shut down after a few years.

Sharp-Boylston was second only to Adair in longevity. When Adair ceased to exist as an active company, Blackwell requested that Ackerman cede its longevity claim to Sharp-Boylston. Ackerman kindly agreed, and from that point on Sharp-Boylston was "Georgia's Oldest Realtor."

On the death of Cone Maddox in 1970, a 50% interest in the company was acquired by Marion Blackwell and Warren R. Chilton, Jr., with Blackwell becoming President and Chilton becoming Chairman of the Board. Shortly afterwards, several of Sharp-Boylston's leading salesmen acquired the other 50%.

In the mid '70's the residential section of the property management department was sold to the company's employees who ran that department, and Sharp-Boylston became a specialist in sales, leasing, and management of commercial, industrial, and investment properties. A few years later, Blackwell and Chilton bought out all other owners of the company.

In 1986, Blackwell and Chilton sold the company to Richard Felker, who changed the name to The Sharp-Boylston Companies. David Branch became president and Blackwell and Chilton remained with the company as sales associates, until leaving in the 1990's to form their own independent companies. Branch later bought the company from Felker, and in the early 2000's The Sharp-Boylston Companies became inactive.

During its history of over 120 years in the Atlanta real estate market, Sharp-Boylston handled the sale of numerous prominent properties. A few of them follow:

Land sale on Piedmont Ave. and I-75-85 from Central Atlanta Progress to Georgia Power Company for the GPC office building.

Site of Galleria complex on Cobb Parkway and I-285.

Site of Akers Mill Square on Cobb Parkway and Akers Mill Road.

Land sale, construction, leasing, and management of Lakeshore Plaza, a regional shopping center in Gainesville.

Pine Forest apartments, 500 units on Cobb Parkway in Marietta

Re-sale of Pine Forest for demolition and construction of Wal-Mart and Sams.

Pro-bono sale of Island Ford section of Chattahoochee River National Recreation Area from Atlanta Baptist Association to National Park Service.

1,000 acre farm in Morgan County, sold three times

Cone Maddox, Jr. and Marion Blackwell, Jr. both served as presidents of Atlanta Real Estate Board, now Atlanta Board of Realtors.

END

THEY WERE HERE FIRST

Before any white settlers made their appearance in the woodland we now call Cobb County, Georgia, the area was sparsely populated by Native Americans, or Indians as we shall call them. These people belonged to two Indian Nations, the Creeks and the Cherokees.

The Creek Nation was one of the most powerful Indian nations in North America. Its territory covered most of south and west Georgia, as well as most of Alabama and northern Florida. They had completely dominated other tribes such as the Seminoles, Choctaws, and Chickasaws, and had been instrumental in convincing Spain and France that they should abandon North America.

The Cherokee Nation was more progressive, but much less powerful than the Creeks. Cherokees had once thrived in Kentucky and Tennessee, but the northern tribes, primarily Iriquois, had forced a southward migration into southern Tennessee, North Carolina, and Georgia.

The capital of the Creek nation was a town called Coweta, which was on the Chattahoochee River near Columbus, Georgia. The area that is now Cobb county was at the northern extremity of the Creek territory, making it difficult for the Creeks to govern, and enabling the Cherokees to force the Creeks to remain south of the Chattahoochee.

Our image of "Indians" is often warped by Hollywood's version of the western tribes which always show them living in teepees, in temporary villages which could be moved at a moment's notice. Eastern Indians were much more settled than those out west. Cities were permanent, with definite plans featuring council buildings and wooden houses for the people. Specific houses were designated for various officials. Cherokee and Creek farmers cleared and tilled land, lived in log homes, planted orchards, and built barns for their animals.

The system of "tribal" government was abandoned and by 1828 Cherokees had formed a representative form of government, complete with their own legislature and constitution.

The Chattahoochee River was established as the boundary between Cherokee and Creek territories, but it was very loosely enforced. Members of both nations frequently crossed the river to hunt, and sometimes to settle, but they occasionally went to war over territory around the Chattahoochee.

When that upstart country called the United States of America chased the British and Spanish away and bought out the remaining French, it began concentrating on expanding into the Indian territories, including the Cherokee and Creek lands in our area. Since the Creek's center of activity was much further south, they were more willing to sell their northern territory, which included part of Cobb County. The question was, which part?

President Andrew Jackson sent General Coffee, with a surveying party, to establish the line which would divide the Cherokee and Creek lands. This line, called the Coffee Line, started at the Shallow Ford on the Chattahoochee, and extended straight west, passing just north of Marietta and south of Kennesaw Mountain. This meant that Marietta and everything south of the line was Creek territory, and could be bought. This satisfied most Creeks, who then sold out. Cherokees south of the line had to move northward.

All Indian lands, whether Creek or Cherokee, were evaluated by appraisers hired by the Federal government. The appraisals considered the land value, whether cultivated or woodland, plus every cabin, house, barn stable, and fruit tree on the property. Cherokee land owners were people with names like Joseph Chicken, Levi Chincheek, and Bill Downing.

When Creeks sold their Cobb County land, they usually just moved farther southward into Creek territory in Georgia or Alabama. Cherokees were sent northward to await their relocation to new homes in Oklahoma – a procedure which will forever be an embarrassment to the United States.

END

Sources: Detailed map, "Cherokee Lands," by Mike Hitt; My Sojourn in the Creek Nation, by Milfort; Trail of Tears, by John Ehle; The Only Land They Knew, by J. Leitch Wright, Jr.; Georgia Department of Archives and History; The Georgia Room, Cobb County Public Library.

GEORGIA'S GREAT
LAND LOTTERY

James Barnett "Barney" Blackwell was raised on a farm in what is now Hall County, near Gainesville. In 1831, "Barney" was fortunate enough to hold the winning ticket for a 40-acre land lot in Forsyth County. However, he never claimed that land. He instead acquired a 40 acre lot in north Cobb County, in what is now known as the Blackwell Community. It is the author's unsupported opinion that he traded his Forsyth land lot for the Cobb land. He subsequently acquired twelve additional lots of 40 acres each, bringing his Cobb County holdings to 520 acres. Not bad for a Georgia farm boy.

So, what is a "land lot?" Why are they 40 or 160 acres?

For many centuries that part of Georgia north and west of the Chattahoochee River, including all of Cobb County where Barney Blackwell settled, was "owned" by a progressive, powerful group of people we know as the Cherokee Indians. Their even stronger neighbors to the south, the Creeks, would occasionally wander north of the river, but were never able to establish a foothold. Other than these occasional incursions by the Creeks, the Cherokees lived peaceful and productive lives.

Then, starting in the 1500's, a new, more numerous, more powerful neighbor began coveting the Cherokee lands. The Cherokees gladly shared, for there was more than enough land for everyone. But over a period of a few hundred years the white Europeans, primarily the English, soon outnumbered and overwhelmed the Cherokees. Many of the Cherokees moved west, yielding to the pressure, but several thousand made a futile attempt to keep their homes, farms, mills, and towns.

As the majority of the Cherokees fled or were forcefully removed, the nascent United States of America and the State of Georgia faced the task of how to fairly and economically get the vacated land out of the hands of government and into hands of private citizens. The solution was the Great Land Lottery of 1832.

A large part of the state of Georgia northwest of the Chattahoochee River was designated as one huge county, appropriately called Cherokee County. This gigantic county was then divided into smaller, more governable counties, much as they are today. The objective in creating these smaller counties was to enable a person to drive his mule and wagon from his home to the County Seat and back in one day. These new counties included the current Cherokee County, as well as Bartow (originally Cass), Cobb, Floyd, Forsyth, Gilmer, Lumpkin, Murray, Paulding, and Union.

In the spring and summer of 1831, in spite of the fact that many Cherokee farmers were still tilling their farms, government surveyors began dividing the land into squares, called Land Lots. Gold had been discovered in parts of north Georgia, so if a territory was suspected to contain gold, the Land Lots were forty acres each, which is exactly one-fourth mile square. If gold was not suspected, the lots contained 160 acres each, one-half mile square. The land lots were given numbers, and grouped into districts.

One of these district lines runs north-south across the crest of Kennesaw Mountain. East of the line the lots were all so-called "gold lots" of forty acres each, and west of the line, 160 acres each.

The actual lottery was conducted in Milledgeville, which was then the state capital. Those qualified to participate were required to be U. S. citizens over eighteen years old, and a citizen of Georgia. The drawings began in October, 1832. Two "wheels" were used, one containing the land lots by number, the other containing names of eligible citizens. One ticket would be drawn from each wheel, matching a lucky citizen with his new property.

Legally the winners could claim their new land immediately, but actually it was a more gradual process. Some tracts were still occupied by Cherokees, who had to be given time to relocate. Many did move voluntarily during the six year period between the completion of the lottery in 1832 and 1838. Then in 1838, all remaining Cherokees were forcefully herded to new lands in Oklahoma.

If the reader owns a house or land in north Georgia, the "legal description" in your deed will almost always start with these words: "All that tract or parcel of land lying and being in Land Lot ___ of the ___th district of _____ County, Georgia...." The number of the land lot is the original number assigned to your property in 1831 and 1832.

END

(James Barnett "Barney" Blackwell was the great-great uncle of the author)

Sources: Marietta Quadrangle, United States Department of the Interior Geological Survey; The First Hundred Years, by Sarah Blackwell Gober Temple, a direct descendant of Barney Blackwell.

THE BLACKWELLS OF BLACKWELL

A TALE OF GOOD FORTUNE, PROSPERITY, AND TRAGEDY

The Blackwell Community lies astride Blackwell Road, six miles NNE of the Marietta square. It encompasses Blackwell Square Shopping Center, Blackwell Elementary School, two subdivisions named Blackwell, as well as Blackwell Court, Blackwell Run, and Blackwell Valley Drive.

Who was this "Blackwell?" Where did he come from? What did he do that justified having a road and a community and a school named after him?

He was James Barnett Blackwell, one of the pioneer settlers of Cobb County, and the author's great-great uncle.

In 1830 and 1831 the lands which included what is now Cobb County were the subject of much argument, wars, and litigation between the aboriginal Creeks and Cherokees. To complicate the matter, the State of Georgia disagreed with the Creeks, Cherokees, the United States Supreme Court and the United States government concerning how the so-called Indian problem should be handled.

In spite of great pressure from the U. S. courts and government, as well as meddling citizen organizations in the New England states, Georgia took the bit in its mouth and passed a law establishing a territory it called Cherokee County as all lands north of Carroll County and west of the Chattahoochee. This Cherokee County included what is now Cobb County as well as Forsyth, Bartow, Cass, Paulding, Lumpkin, Murray, Union, and the current Cherokee County.

Then began the procedure to get the land out of government ownership and into the hands of private citizens – the great land lottery. Among the lucky winners was a young pioneer citizen, James Barnett Blackwell.

James Barnett Blackwell was the son of Josiah Blackwell and Elizabeth Barnett Blackwell of Hall County. Another son of Josiah and Elizabeth was David Glenn Blackwell, who was the great-great grandfather of the author. Therefore, James Barnett Blackwell, more often known as "Barney," was the great-great uncle of the author. We are all descended from Robert Blackwell of Watford, England, who settled in New Kent, Virginia, in 1645, and prospered. A great deal of his prosperity can be attributed to his marrying Unity (often spelled Ui) Croshaw of a very wealthy pioneer family. Subsequent generations of Blackwells migrated southward through Virginia, North Carolina, South Carolina, and finally into Georgia, settling in Hall County, in and around Gainesville.

Elizabeth Barnett Blackwell, Barney's mother, had once traced her lineage back to the marriage of King Edward I of England and Eleanor of Castile, a Spanish princess. So the Blackwells who are descendants of Elizabeth and Josiah, including Barney and the author, could claim to be descendants of European royalty.

Barney was one of the lucky winners of the land lottery. He won a 40-acre land lot in what is now Forsyth County, but it appears that he never claimed it. Instead, he started buying land in Cobb. He was 31 years old at the time. It is my unsupported opinion that he sold or traded his claim on the Forsyth land for another land lot in Cobb. As his history proves, he was an excellent businessman, a skill which allowed him to acquire thirteen land lots of 40 acres each, totaling 520 acres.

They were scattered, not contiguous. Land lot 362 is located at the intersection of Chastain Road and George Busbee Parkway, in the middle of Town Park. Today it contains banks, hotels, apartments, office buildings, retail outlets, and part of the Kennesaw State campus. LL 161 is part of Lamplighters Cove, including Barrier Rd. LL 376 fronts on Ebenezer Road. Four contiguous land lots, 490, 518, 519, and 520 front on Piedmont

Road, including Harold Dean Drive. His original three land lots, 632, 633 and 665, along with 591 and 592 are now part of Pine Valley, Morgan Farms, and Lansdown subdivisions, including Rex Drive and Newton Road.

LL 605 includes Rocky Springs Drive and Piney Grove Baptist Church, which has been there so long that its cemetery is larger than its parking lot.

None of these land lots actually touch Blackwell Road, so how did the road get its name?

Barney was a director of North Georgia Railroad, which ran from Marietta through Canton to Ellijay. He was appointed manager of a station located at the point where the railroad crossed a road, which then became known as Blackwell Road, and the community became known as Blackwell's, now just Blackwell. The station was abandoned many years ago, and a private home now occupies the site.

In addition to his railroad responsibilities, James Barnett Blackwell proved to be a multi-talented pioneer who held numerous Cobb County offices, and was involved in the organization and management of several businesses in addition to North Georgia Railroad. He served Cobb County as sheriff, postmaster, delegate to the Georgia Democratic Convention, and Representative in the State of Georgia legislature. In business, he was one of the incorporators of Citizens Loan and Trust Company of Marietta, and director of American Marble Company of Tate. Barney also had proved himself to be an astute land speculator and efficient farmer.

He was blessed with twelve children, but suffered the loss of most of them to illnesses and the Civil War. His first wife was Linda Mayes, daughter of another Cobb County pioneer. Linda died in 1863, and Barney re-married Elizabeth L. Bellinger in 1865.

The Civil War cost him dearly. All four of his sons, Thomas, Jasper, Marion, and Andrew, were either killed in action or died of illnesses. Barney himself joined the Confederate army in 1863, but resigned because of the death of his wife, Linda.

James Barnett Blackwell died on May 6, 1894. He was 80 years old. He not only contributed his name to a part of Cobb County, but his leadership and energy helped start our county into becoming the healthy, thriving center of business and industry which it is today. He and most of his family are buried in the Blackwell family burying ground, located on land which was his old home place off Sandy Plains Road.

END

Sources of information:

The First Hundred Years, by Sarah Blackwell Gober Temple, a descendant of Barney Blackwell ; Biography of James Barnett Blackwell, by Robert V. Blackwell, published by Cobb County Genealogical Society; studies and reports by geneologists in England and Hall County, Georgia; Greater Atlanta Georgia map book; Marietta and Kennesaw quadrangles, U. S. Department of the Interior; Ancestry.com; a personal inspection of the area.

Fords and Ferries along the Chattahoochee

Out of the hills of Habersham,
Down the valleys of Hall,
I hurry amain to reach the plain,
Run the rapid and leap the fall,....

So wrote Sidney Lanier in his "Song of the Chattahoochee."

The Chattahoochee River cuts a swath through Georgia from our northeast to our southwest, where it becomes the Alabama boundary. Its rapid waters were once a boundary between the Cherokee and the Creek nations, and now shape the southern boundary of Cobb County.

Early Native Americans and white settlers found the river a significant obstacle. Without bridges or ferries, the only way to cross was to wade, and in most places the water is too deep and the current too swift to safely wade across. During periods of high water, even the fords were too deep to use.

When Roswell was in Cobb County, a state-wide system of trails converged at one of the safest places to cross the river, known as the Shallow Ford, or "Shallowford." There are Shallowford Roads in Cobb, DeKalb, and Fulton counties, all leading in the direction of this crossing. In many locations, the name has become "Hightower Trail," which is believed to be our corruption of the Native American name "Etowah Trail." Those Etowah trails led to the towns along the Etowah River near Cartersville. There is even a "Hightower Trail" in Rockdale County, heading in the direction of Cartersville via the Shallow Ford.

General Andrew Jackson posted a warning to white squatters at Shallow Ford in 1820. The State of Georgia allowed Jacob Brooks to operate a ferry there in 1824. During the Civil War, after Confederates burned the bridge at Roswell, Federal troops waded across the Shallow Ford to attack Confederate forces entrenched along the hillside, where fine homes and a golf course are now.

As the area developed, paths became roads, wagons became common, and fords became much less desirable than ferries. Operating a ferry was profitable, so several were soon in operation along the river, providing access to Cobb County.

As a going business, ferries were often bought and sold, and tended to adopt the name of the founder or a prominent later operator. Some of our more prominent ferry operators were Johnson, Heard, Power, Pace, DeFoor, Mayson & Turner, and Baker. The roads leading to the ferries have all become prominent thoroughfares. Much of Mayson and Turner Ferry Road is still there, but part is now Veterans Memorial Highway. DeFoors Ferry Road now ends at Marietta Boulevard in Fulton County, but originally tied in with Atlanta Road. Bakers Ferry Road probably crossed the river somewhere near the Cobb-Douglas County line, but its actual crossing has been obliterated by Fulton Industrial District.

Artist George L. Parrish, Jr, produced an excellent rendition of how a typical ferry, Pace's Ferry, must have looked. A copy is on display in the library at Teasley Elementary School in Smyrna, and in the author's office in Vinings. In the drawing, a sign on a tree says:

Paces Ferry Rates:

Loaded Wagons   .62
Empty Wagons .50
Cart .37
Gig or one horse
Carriage .25
Man and single horse .12
Footman or lead horse.06 ¼

Cattle .04 per head
Hogs & Sheep .02 per head

The old ferries were replaced by bridges a hundred years ago, but the roads named for Pace, Power, and other ferry operators should always remind us of the important contributions these early citizens made to the growth of the Atlanta area.

END

Sources: Chattahoochee Lands, map by Michael Hitt and Chuck Brown; Poems of Sidney Lanier, edited by Mary Day Lanier; various maps of Cobb County and Atlanta; Atlanta by Jacob D. Cox.

Battlefields on Backroads

Imagine that a Civil War battle was taking place in your back yard, or on your land. Thousands of young men were being killed and maimed. The ground, churned by explosions and fortifications, was being consecrated by their blood, as they fought for a cause in which you may or may not believe.

The battle ends, the defeated retreat, the maimed are removed, and the dead are buried, but the horror, the memory, remains.

President Abraham Lincoln's address at the dedication of the Gettysburg cemetery can apply to all our battlefields, including ours here in Georgia. As he said, "...we can not consecrate, we can not hallow, this ground. The brave men, living and dead, who struggled here, have consecrated it far above our poor power to add or detract."

The dynamic growth which Georgia has enjoyed over the last 150 years has created a severe need to protect our battlefield sites. In the Atlanta area it is already too late. Homes, shopping centers, and expressways now cover the land which saw the Battle of Peachtree Creek, Battle of Atlanta, Battle of Ezra Church, Battle of Jonesboro, and many others. Along with government agencies and other private organizations, the Georgia Battlefields Association (GBA) stands between preservation and obliteration of Georgia's important historic sites.

On a cold, wet winter day, forty members of GBA assembled in Cartersville to begin a two and one-half day tour of significant sites, specifically, the route of The Army of Tennessee and its besieged commander, General John Bell Hood, after the surrender of Atlanta. In addition to internationally renowned National Park Service Chief Historian Ed Bearss and GBA president Charlie Crawford, the tour group included two past presidents of the Atlanta Civil War Round Table, Grady Ireland and Rob Zaworski, and former UGA athletics director Coach

Vince Dooley. Thirty-two participants were from Georgia, three from South Carolina, and others from Tennessee, Alabama, Ohio, Texas, and Virginia.

Our first stop was Palmetto. Atlanta had surrendered to Sherman, and Hood's remnant of a once powerful army licked its wounds and pondered its next move. Federal forces had defeated Hood's Army of Tennessee at Jonesboro and gained control of the railroad from Macon, which had been the last rail line supplying Atlanta. After evacuating the city, Hood initially assembled his army at Lovejoy's Station, closer to Macon, but subsequently moved the army to Palmetto, on the railroad from Hood's designated supply sources in Alabama.

Hood selected a building on Palmetto's main road to use as his headquarters. The building had been constructed in 1831 and was used as a stagecoach inn before the railroad reached the town. Today it is used as law offices by attorney Jim Barfield and his associates.

The second stop in Palmetto was a large colonial home from which Jefferson Davis addressed soldiers of The Army of Tennessee, or at least those who could hear him from the balcony. The Davis visit to Palmetto was on Sept. 25, 26, and 27 of 1864.

This is the house in Palmetto where Jefferson Davis met with Genereal John B. Hood to discuss strategy.

From Palmetto, the tour continued on to the dead town of Campbellton, formerly county seat of now defunct Campbell County, where there were skirmishes between cavalry patrols. In 1932, Campbell County was absorbed into Fulton.

Then on to Lost Mountain, Dallas, van Wert, Cedartown, and Cave Spring, where Hood's commander, General P. G. T. Beauregard, met him to discuss strategy. It was from Lost Mountain that Hood sent a force of 3,276 combatants under Major General Samuel G.French to attack a Federal supply depot at Allatoona Pass.

Rome, Resaca, and Tilton were our next visits, all sites of skirmishes as Hood's army moved on. At Dalton, 800 Federal soldiers were captured. Some of these were the 44th U. S. Colored Troops, which were returned to slavery after being forced to destroy the important Western & Atlantic railroad through Dalton.

The Western & Atlantic Railroad (now CSX) ran from Chattanooga to Atlanta, passing through Civil War related sites such as Ringgold, Tunnel Hill, Dalton, Calhoun, Adairsville, Resaca, Kingston, Cassville, Allatoona Pass, Acworth, Big Shanty (now Kennesaw), Marietta, Smyrna, and Vinings before entering Atlanta. After capturing Atlanta, Federal forces used this railroad to bring in new troops and supplies, and to carry wounded and surplus troops back north. Destruction of this railroad would have greatly impaired the activities of Sherman's armies.

From Dalton, our bus took us through Villanow, then to Ship's Gap, where some of our brave historians hiked through a cold mist to visit Confederate fortifications along a high ridge.

After a brief stop at LaFayette, we were on to Summerville, Gaylesville, and Cedar Bluff, Alabama, where Gen. Nathan Bedford Forrest tricked Union Colonel Straight into surrendering his much superior force to Forrest's cavalry.

While in Alabama, we inspected Cornwall Furnace, a stone structure used by both sides at one time or another to smelt iron ore. It is now on the shores of Lake Weiss, and is still in excellent condition.

After passing through Rome again we stopped at Kingston, a Federal supply depot, where Gen. Sherman had established his headquarters, and where he later received permission from his commander, General U. S. Grant, to begin the March to the Sea. It was also in Kingston that the Federal soldiers who had stolen the locomotive "The General" met their first long delay due to south-bound traffic, which ultimately led to their capture. At the close of the war, Confederate General William T. Wofford formally surrendered over 3,000 Confederate soldiers at Kingston.

The last half day of the tour was spent in the Kennesaw-Acworth area. Kennesaw (then Big Shanty) is where the General was stolen, and where a large Confederate training camp was located. The General is on display there now in the Southern Museum of Civil War and Locomotive History. We passed by the former site of Moon's Station, where Conductor William Fuller obtained a railroad pole-car to chase the General until he could commandeer the locomotive "Yonah" at the Cooper Ironworks spur, just north of the Etowah River. (We had seen The Texas, the other locomotive involved in the chase, at the Cyclorama on a previous tour).

Our final stop was at Allatoona Pass, where Confederate forces under General Samuel G. French had been repulsed after attempting to destroy both the railroad and capture a large Federal supply depot. Hood had sent French's division from Lost Mountain to destroy the railroad bridge over the Etowah River, and tear up as much rail and destroy as much supplies as possible. The deep railroad pass at Allatoona, much of it cut through ninety-five feet of solid rock, was considered extremely vulnerable, even though it was protected by two forts on knolls bestriding the railroad. French's attack failed partly due to the tenacity of the defenders, and to a report that Federal reinforcements were approaching.

The tour carefully explored both forts, including their surrounding trenches and signal stations. Then we walked through the now abandoned railroad gorge to an unknown soldier's grave.

A large home which survived the battle, and was used as a hospital, is now owned by a family that is, fortunately, very sympathetic and understanding of the need to preserve historic structures. The house is not open to the public, but the tour was invited to visit the graves of 21 Confederate soldiers who were wounded in the battle, treated unsuccessfully in the home, and buried in the back yard. The graves were discovered by use of a rod to discern the different textures of earth below the grass.

We were fortunate on this tour to visit many sites which had not been devoured by development, but as Georgia grows, it is just a question of time until the owners of private but hallowed land are tempted to sell, for profit or necessity.

Georgia has almost 400 Civil War sites. Some have no markers, some have only a few. To supplement the State's reduced effort to recognize these sites, GBA has designed and arranged for the installation of ten markers since 2004.

A few of these sites are protected by the National Park Service or the U. S. Forest Service. A few more are operated by Georgia state agencies, a few by county and city governments, and a very few are held by private preservation groups such as the Atlanta Historical Society. The great majority of these 400 significant sites are owned by individuals, and are vulnerable to whatever the owners want to do with them.

Along with government agencies and other private organizations, GBA hopes to preserve these sites. GBA is a private, non-profit organization formed in 1995. It was formed not only to raise money but also to encourage general awareness of our Civil War history by publishing preservation news, giving lectures, conducting tours, and supporting other preservation organizations.

An excellent example of the work of GBA is the Griswoldville Battlefield. This historic site is located about 12 miles northeast of Macon. In November, 1864, during the March to the Sea, citizens of Macon were alarmed by Sherman's "feint" which led them to believe that Macon would be attacked. A poorly trained force of old men, young boys, and wounded veterans home on leave, was quickly assembled. Armed with outmoded weapons and largely ignorant of tactical lessons learned over the last three years of fighting, they bravely marched out to meet the invaders. In this case, the foe was a battle-hardened, well trained infantry unit, armed with the very latest repeating rifles. The result was the slaughter of many Georgians.

Their leader, Brigadier General Pleasant J. Phillips, led his 4,350 "warriors" in a frontal assault – marching through open ground directly at the incredulous Federals. This tactic had long been obsolete due to the improvements in weapons and ammunition. The result was a quick massacre of 51 citizen-soldiers, with another 422 maimed and wounded.

Through the efforts of GBA, this battlefield was protected in 1998 and deeded to the Georgia Department of Natural Resources, which established a state historic site, complete with parking area, flags, and informative plaques.

When 1,200 acres of the Resaca battlefield became available in 1998, GBA staged a rally at the state capitol which convinced state officials that the site should be preserved. The State of Georgia eventually bought over 500 acres. Plans include a visitor center visible from I-75, roads, trails, and signs.

Resaca is the site of one of Georgia's largest reenactments, held in May of each year, the anniversary of the battle.

GBA often pulls several organizations together to accomplish an important acquisition. When a parcel of land opposite the Kolb Farm at Kennesaw Mountain was threatened with having a gas station-convenience store built at a major intersection, GBA coordinated the efforts of a neighborhood association, the Cobb County Board of Commissioners with its Greenspace funds, and the National Park Service, to acquire all four corners of the intersection. The encroachment was defeated, and 4.2 valuable acres were added to the park.

In addition to working with local governments and state officials, GBA aids the preservation activities of Georgia Civil War Commission, Georgia Department of Natural Resources, National Park Service, the Atlanta History Center, Georgia Civil War Heritage Trails, and the Civil War Preservation Trust. GBA does its work without government funding.

GBA publishes a monthly newsletter containing up-dates on preservation activities. With the Civil War Sesquicentennial coming up in 2011, in 2006 the newsletter began featuring important events which led to the war in a section called "150 Years Ago This Month." Newsletters and membership information are available online through the GBA web site, www.georgiabattlefields.org.

GBA's president is Charlie Crawford, a native of Pennsylvania, Georgia Tech graduate, and retired Air Force colonel. Col. Crawford's wealth of historic knowledge, his rapid mind, and boundless energy help make GBA the important factor it is today. Of the five people on GBA's board of trustees, two are originally from New York, two from Louisiana, and one Georgia native, which reflects the national interest in battlefield preservation.

We have the past, the present, and the future. It is essential that we learn from the past in order to deal with the present and protect our future.

This is the Western and Atlantic railroad cut through Allatoona Ridge. The cut is now abandoned.

Bibliography:
Advance and Retreat, by John Bell Hood.
Allatoona Pass, by William R. Scaife
Preserving Georgia's Civil War Sites, by Charlie Crawford

END

BENJAMIN PICKETT AND THE BATTLE OF PICKETT'S MILL

In 1864, Benjamin Pickett's mill was a peaceful, water powered mill used for grinding wheat and corn into flour and meal for local farmers. A long flume channeled water from his dam on picturesque Pickett's Mill Creek, also called Pumpkinvine Creek, and poured it into the slots of the over-shot mill wheel. A drive shaft from the wheel turned large mill stones which ground the wheat and corn into flour and corn meal. It was built by Benjamin's father, Malachi, on land which had been in the Pickett family since 1830.

We do not know the poignant details of how Benjamin Pickett said his good-byes and rode off to the Battle of Chickamauga. The Pickett home was up the hill a short distance from the mill. He must have shook hands with his partner at the mill, J. C. Harris, and then turned to his family. There would have been long embraces and many kisses and tears as he left his 26 year old wife, Martha, and their four young children.

There would have been more tears if they could have known that Lieutenant Benjamin Pickett of the 1st Georgia Cavalry would die at Chickamauga, and that the mill and home would later be destroyed as an intense battle raged through these Paulding County fields and woods.

The site of this battle is now known as Pickett's Mill Battlefield State Historic Site. The Interpretive Center includes a museum, theatre, and maps which enable visitors to understand the complex engagement. Several miles of well-marked trails wind through the rugged terrain and cross Pickett's Mill Creek, offering beautiful hiking opportunities even if one is not interested in the military history of the area.

The Battle of Pickett's Mill was pivotal, literally, in General William T. Sherman's Atlanta Campaign. Federal forces had systematically pushed General Joseph E. Johnston's smaller Confederate army all the way back from Chattanooga to Kennesaw Mountain. This well-fortified mountain effectively blocked Sherman's approach to Marietta, and then Atlanta. In an effort to avoid having to make a frontal assault on Kennesaw, Sherman attempted a flanking movement around Johnston's left. Federal troops moved as rapidly as possible toward Dallas, Georgia, but poor roads, bad weather, and rugged terrain slowed their pace, enabling the Confederates to extend their lines to face them.

If Sherman's armies could get around the Southern lines at this point, it would enable the Federals to attack Marietta from the west without having to attack the extremely heavily fortified Southerners on Kennesaw Mountain.

On May 27, 1864, the armies clashed just north of Dallas. Federal forces under General Joseph Hooker fought Confederate troops at New Hope Church in a major battle. While the battle raged, Federals under General Oliver O. Howard attempted to move around the right flank of the Southerners, but were met by Southern troops under General Patrick Cleburne at Pickett's Mill.

As Howard's Union forces advanced toward Pickett's Mill, they found themselves slowed by extremely thick undergrowth, with briars, bushes, vines, and trees so dense that they could see only a few feet ahead of their lines. Units became separated, lost, and exhausted. The element of surprise was lost.

Waiting for them on strategic high ground, the Confederates soon began pouring rifle and cannon fire into the confused ranks. Federal attempts to gain a better position were only partially successful. A ravine trapped many Yanks, and became famous for its masses of wounded, lost, maimed, and dead boys in blue. Others who were ordered to charge across an open field suffered severe casualties and finally fled back into the woods.

Benjamin Pickett's home and mill were in the center of the Federal attack and were destroyed, but his family fled back toward Dallas, and survived.

The intensity of the fighting can best be described by the official reports of the officers who were there.

Union General Thomas J. Wood reported, "Never have troops marched to a deadly assault, under most adverse circumstances, with more firmness, with more soldierly bearing, and with more distinguished gallantry."

Confederate General Patrick Cleburne praised both his enemy and his own men: "The enemy advanced in numerous and constantly reinforced lines. His men displayed courage worthy of an honorable cause, pressing in steady throngs within a few paces of our men.... Granbury's men... were awaiting them, and throughout awaited them with calm determination, and as they appeared upon the slope, slaughtered them with deliberate aim."

By dark, the battle seemed to be over except for sporadic firing. Confederate General Granbury was ordered to charge into the dark woods and "clear" them of any remaining Yanks, after which Cleburne reported, "The Texans, their bayonets fixed, plunged into the darkness with a terrific yell, and with one bound upon the enemy, but they met with no resistance. Surprised and panic stricken, many (Yankees) fled, escaping in the darkness; others surrendered...."

When the final count was made, Federal killed and wounded totaled about 1,600, while Confederate losses were about 500.

Sherman was so frustrated by the failure of his flanking movement that he declined to include the battle in his official report, or later in his memoirs.

Benjamin Pickett's mill and home were not the only civilian casualties. Another home and mill across Pickett's Mill Creek, owned and operated the Leverett family, fell victim to the fighting. The Zach Brand family had a small farm on a nearby hill which was also destroyed. Most of these buildings were demolished, not by weapons, but were dismantled piece by piece by the soldiers who would use the boards to enforce their fortifications.

In 1984, Georgia State University completed an extensive archeological study of several sites within the park, primarily around the Zach Brand house. This survey produced numerous pottery shards, buttons, nails, and remnants of household goods, as well as bayonets, Minie balls, cannon ball fragments, and rifle parts.

Kennesaw State University is currently conducting a study of additional sites.

Visitors to Pickett's Mill Battlefield State Historic Site will enjoy the modern, informative Visitor Center, beautiful scenery, picnic areas, and group shelters, as well as many well preserved trenches and artillery emplacements. A pioneer log cabin from the 1840's was recently moved to the park from its original location.

As soon as the battle was over, farmers and millers went back to work to feed their families, so farming, erosion, and logging have obliterated some of the battle's field fortifications.

Trails are for walking only. Bicycles, horses, and joggers are not allowed.

The Park entrance is on Mount Tabor Church Road, off Dallas-Acworth Road. It is six miles from Dallas, eight miles from Acworth, 12 miles from Marietta, and 26 miles from downtown Atlanta, as measured in a straight line.

In a recent fact-gathering visit to Pickett's Mill, I was walking along the trench line from which the Confederates poured withering fire into the attacking Yanks when I suddenly felt that I had walked through a time-warp. There in front of me was a dirty, ragged company of Rebel soldiers with muzzle loading rifles, wooden canteens, and a variety of unmatched hats, ragged shirts, dirty trousers, and worn-out boots. They were Company B of the 32nd Alabama Infantry, re-enactors on maneuvers. Every detail of their equipment and accouterments was authentic, as was their attitude and demeanor. One lounging rifleman even told me, "We ain't re-enactors, we're skirmishers."

A hundred yards up the road I found Company A, also on break with their regimental photographer making real ferro-types with his ancient camera on a tripod, then running to his portable developing studio (canvas cover draped on tree limbs) to carefully place the photo plate in a tray of chemicals. I then was privileged to watch the picture of Company A emerge on the metal plate – just as it was done in 1864.

Then a bugle sounded, others answered, and three companies of the 32nd Alabama sprang into formation, loaded their rifles, and marched off in the direction of Benjamin Pickett's Mill.

END

Gunfights in the Old ATL

Atlanta in the mid 1800's was a typical frontier town. People "up north" even considered Georgia a "western" state. Streets were dirt, often mud, and crowded with horses, mules, and wagons. The few sidewalks they had were wooden boards, and the railroads came right through the middle of the town. Railroad crossings were at grade level (no overpasses), and the loud locomotives with thick billows of wood and coal smoke created a constant roar and smog. But no one complained about the railroads. After all, without the railroads, Atlanta would still be just a stage coach stop between Marietta and Decatur.

In spite of the muddy streets, blocked railroad crossings, and clouds of coal and wood smoke, hotels and businesses flocked as close to the train stations as they could get.

The fact that four railroads intersected in downtown Atlanta, combined with the crowds of new citizens immigrating to Atlanta from all over the world, created a great demand for hotels. The Trout House, Terminal Hotel, The Johnson House, Atlanta Hotel, and Washington Hall were all popular social centers as well as temporary homes. Their lobbies and bars were meeting places for Atlantans of all social levels.

Disreputable areas also near the train station were called Snake Nation, Slab Town, and Murrel's Row, which was named to glorify a Tennessee outlaw. Cock fighting, gambling, and brothels operated openly with no fear of what little law there was. Hotel patrons often drifted back and forth between the two areas, as well as the numerous bars and saloons scattered around downtown Atlanta. Occasional brawls were not uncommon among these rugged frontiersmen and farmers, some involving guns and knives. The Civil War raging around them only served to exacerbate their inclination to violence.

Decatur Street passed the train stations and hotels on its way to the center of town, where its name changed to Marietta Road, and where Whitehall Street turned south for White Hall, and Peachtree Road went north to Buckhead, at the intersection now called Five Points.

POOR CHOICE

William A. Choice was a very highly regarded actor. He is described as tall and husky, with blond hair and blue eyes. Like most thespians, Choice relished the admiration and respect of his audiences, and was extremely egotistical.

On the evening of December 30, 1856, Choice was enjoying being the center of attention at the bar in the Atlanta Hotel when, to his dismay and embarrassment, a bailiff, Calvin Webb, suddenly presented him with a court order to pay a $10 fee he owed a local doctor. Choice did not have the $10. A fight was about to break out between Choice and Webb when Atlanta mayor Luther Glenn walked in and calmed the situation.

His tremendous ego crushed, Choice drank himself into a stupor, then retreated to his room to sleep it off.

Choice arose the next morning and armed himself with a pistol and an umbrella. He left the hotel and walked along the railroad to Pryor Street, then walked up the board sidewalk toward Decatur Street. Suddenly he saw bailiff Calvin Webb walking down the other side of Pryor toward the railroad.

Pedestrians scattered as Choice drew his pistol and fired across the street at Calvin Webb. He missed, but the shocked Webb froze in his tracks. Choice then knelt on the boardwalk, carefully braced the pistol on his knee, and fired again. This time his aim was sure, striking Calvin Webb in the breast, and killing him on the spot.

Choice fled the scene, but was soon found and arrested by the town marshal.

While Choice was a famous and popular fellow, Calvin Webb was also well known and highly respected. Fearing a lynch mob, the marshal transferred Choice to the state jail in Milledgeville for his own protection. Milledgeville was at that time still the Georgia State Capitol.

At this point the plot thickens.

The next year Choice was brought back to Fulton County, was convicted of murder, and sentenced to be hanged. His attorney was Benjamin H. Hill, described as a "rising young statesman" who continued to be politically influential in Georgia and in the Confederate States of America for many years to come.

Ben Hill appealed to the State Supreme Court, which confirmed the Fulton court's decision, guilty of murder.

Hill then worked to avoid the hangman's noose by proving that Choice was insane. He succeeded.

The Georgia General Assembly re-tried Choice in the House of Representatives, found him innocent because of insanity, and sentenced him to life in the "Lunatic Asylum" in Milledgeville. The Senate concurred, but Governor Herschel V. Johnson vetoed. Then, both the house and senate over-rode the governor's veto.

At this point there are two conflicting stories concerning the life of gunman-actor William A. Choice. One story is that he died in the Lunatic Asylum in Milledgeville.

The other is that he served in the Confederate army as a sharp-shooter, and was accidentally killed after the war by falling out of the second story window of a livery stable in his home town of Rome, Georgia.

SELF DEFENSE

The Collier family ranks among Atlanta's earliest and most industrious families. Collier Road is named after early Colliers who built a water mill there and operated it until it was destroyed during the Battle of Peachtree Creek in 1864.

As the Federal armies tightened their noose around Atlanta, law and order in the city began to deteriorate. Confederate deserters and stragglers roamed the streets along with local criminals, looking for opportunities to take advantage of citizens who found themselves without protection. Such a lawless band was roaming around the Buckhead area, robbing and stealing at every opportunity.

A special detachment of 100 Confederate soldiers had been stationed near the intersection of Peachtree and 8th Street. Their assignment was to arrest deserters and stragglers and enforce the conscription laws. They were all teenagers, only two being over eighteen. All older, more experienced soldiers were out manning the fortifications around Atlanta.

At the request of Buckhead citizens, twelve of these young men, under the command of Lieutenant J. A. Caldwell, were sent out to Peachtree Road with instructions to inquire at every house after crossing Peachtree Creek, even though the robberies had been committed farther out on Powers Ferry Road, where North Fulton Park is now.

The situation was ripe for accidents and misunderstandings.

The first house they came to after crossing the creek was the home of Wesley Gray Collier, located at what is now 2510 Peachtree Road. They arrived well after dark, just as the Collier family was preparing to retire for the night. The only light in the house was the fireplace. All doors and windows were closed and locked.

Suddenly, Collier heard a call from his front yard, someone demanding water. Then he heard several men on his front porch, and demands all around his house to open the doors and windows. Collier asked them to leave him alone and go away, but they only threatened to chop down his door and break out his windows.

Collier sent his children to a small room for safety, and armed himself with a shotgun and pistol. Still without identifying themselves, the young soldiers began chopping their way into his home.

When one man finally broke into the house, Collier fired, severely wounding a young soldier named Knight. On hearing this the entire troop opened fire on the home, but Collier and his family had escaped out the back and into the woods.

Policemen finally worked their way out from Atlanta, and the soldiers retreated to their camp at 8th Street, carrying their wounded comrade in a buggy they had confiscated from Collier.

Upon investigation and trials, the whole group of teen-aged soldiers was convicted of aggravated riot. Collier, who was only defending his home and family from an unidentified group of assailants, was acquitted. Why the group of young soldiers acted as they did is still a mystery.

2510 Peachtree Road, the site of the attack, is now the site of The Gates condominiums, just south of Lakeview Avenue.

DISSENSION WITHIN THE RANKS

As the Civil War raged around them, Atlanta law enforcement officers were not immune from dissension, grudges, and even violence among themselves.

G. Whitfield Anderson was a veteran of the Mexican War, which had ended in 1848. Since that time he had served as an Atlanta policeman, becoming a police lieutenant before the Civil War. When the war broke out he joined the First Regiment of Georgia Regulars, and was severely wounded at Sharpsburg, Virginia, in 1862. He returned to Atlanta to recover, and became a candidate for the position of deputy marshal.

His opposition was the current deputy marshal, Thomas Shivers, who had been a stage coach driver back in the days when Atlanta was Terminus, then Marthasville.

The Atlanta City Council met to decide between the two. After considering their qualifications, the vote ended in a tie. Mayor James M. Calhoun broke the tie by casting his vote for Anderson.

This led to ill feelings between the candidates. An argument broke out, which soon escalated into a fight. Shivers struck Anderson on the head with his pistol, and then threw a bottle at him. Anderson withdrew from the fight, told Shivers that he was unarmed at that time, but offered to meet him the next day.

The two men met the next day in front of Muhlenbrink's Saloon, which was located on Whitehall Street where Underground is now. Anderson told Shivers, "I am now fixed up. Are you ready?" It was obvious that the time for talk had ended. Both men drew quickly and fired several shots. Shivers was hit twice, collapsed onto the dirt of Whitehall Street, and was dead within an hour. Anderson holstered his pistol and walked away unharmed.

Anderson was indicted for murder by the Fulton County grand jury. He was tried and acquitted on a plea of self-defense.

Whit Anderson enjoyed a long career of public service, holding various positions for the City of Atlanta, Fulton County, and the State of Georgia. In 1881, he returned to his home in Lumpkin County where he died peacefully that same year.

The career of law officer Whit Anderson typifies the dynamic growth of law enforcement in Atlanta during her nascent stages. Before law enforcement was well organized, each man was responsible for the protection and safety of his family and himself. The Mexican War, then the Civil War, combined with native Americans fighting to protect their rights and homes, and the threat of slave uprisings, all created a sense of uncertainty and danger in growing Atlanta. Knives and pistols were as common as our cell phones today. But the profession of law enforcement grew with the town, and citizens learned that it was better to depend upon the professionals for their protection.

Wherever there are people there will always be some who are predators. Today the news media still report on many crimes involving fire arms, but we must remember that when poor Calvin Webb was murdered, the young city had a population of just a few thousand, and now there are millions. We can thank our law enforcement officers that gunfights on the streets have not increased proportionately.

End

Sources of information: Atlanta and Environs, by Franklin M. Garrett, volumes I and II; Pioneer Citizens History of Atlanta, 1833- 1902; the official records of the Georgia General Assembly; The Governors of Georgia, by James E. Cook

CATTLE DRIVE

by Suzanne Blackwell and Marion Blackwell, Jr.

Can you envision a roundup in Roswell? Horses and cattle balking at a wooden, covered bridge across the Chattahoochee River? Cows being herded down Roswell Road and Peachtree Road?

On June 28, 1994, Suzanne Blackwell, my oldest daughter, interviewed her grandfather, Marion Blackwell, Sr., as a project for an English class. This piece is based on that interview. My father was 85 at the time of the interview. My four children all called their grandfather "Paga," which was as close as my first son could come to saying "Grandpa."

Suzanne: "What year were you born in?"

Paga: "I don't remember, ah, nineteen and nine."

"How old were you when you were running cattle?"

"Well, I guess it was just as soon as I was old enough to walk or ride a horse. 'Cause you had to get them down if you had trouble with them, to the stockyard."

"So were you about ten years old?"

"No, I was 13 years old."

This would make his first cattle drive in about 1922.

"There was a boy there named... we called him, ah he was demented. What did we call him? Well, he could throw a rock and hit you as far as from here to that street over there. You had to watch that rascal. Let's see, what was his name... I remember that doggone rock quarry. Let me remember this boy who throwed all the rocks, he could throw a rock across the street and hit you with it and his name... what was it? I'll be darned if I can remember now."

"Where did you live then?"

"We lived out of Roswell. I remember the name of a, what'd they call that, Hangin' Dog Road."

"Why did they call it that?"

" 'Cause it got hung up in a barbed wire fence, and they called it "Hangin' Dog Road."

"Was that out near the farm where you lived?"

"Yeah. There was this barbed wire, they had a rail fence, you put a, they'd use a rail fence to hold it. You had to use barbed wire to keep the cows from pushing the rails in."

"Where did you get these cattle from?"

"Anybody that had one to sell."

"Did you do this with your father?"

"Yea, and some others."

"How many cattle were there?"

"There'd be, uh, everybody'd get together, you know, and they'd, you know when there was a drive, they called it a cattle drive, and they was going to the stockyard so they could butcher the, they had a place to butcher the cattle."

"So you would have about fifty cattle?"

"Yea, I expect we could get anywhere from thirty-five to forty, forty-five maybe. You had to have some good horses."

The cattle were probably assembled at the old square in Lower Roswell. They were then herded down the hill to the covered bridge across the Chattahoochee, which was their first obstacle. Horses and cows did not like to look through the holes in the wooden floor of the old bridge, so they would blindfold the horses, and then force the cattle across.

Paga goes on, "The cattle didn't want to get in that bridge and look down in the water, so you had to drive a horse, and it got kinda dangerous a little bit 'cause you was riding that horse to drive the cattle and the horses were used to making them move the

way they wanted them to, it wasn't too hard. But I knew when they would get down to the river down there you had a time getting them things through there. It was a covered bridge then, they've done away with it now, they put a concrete bridge there."

(According to historian Mike Hitt, the first concrete bridge was built in 1925).

Suzanne: "Why didn't the cattle like to go across it?"

"They just, it was just the way they are, 'cause you could look down and see the water through the cracks. They'd drive herds of cattle, that was the way the farmer then made his living, 'bout half of it."

"So did you ride a horse when you did that?"

"Yes, boy I hada, I hada (good one). Little Man! Little Man, he was dandy, too. He was kinda a red hair, a little bit darker than that thing there," pointing to the brick fireplace in the home which he had built in Cumming.

I suspect that my father's memory played a trick on him there. Little Man was a horse we had in about 1946 when we lived on Bouldercrest Drive in south DeKalb County. I was about 15 at that time. My father had not forgotten his horsemanship – he was the only one who could ride Little Man. But of course, he also could have had a "Little Man" back when he was a boy in Roswell.

After crossing the old covered bridge, the drive continued south through Sandy Springs and Buckhead.

Suzanne: "So did you actually run cows down Peachtree Street in Atlanta?"

Paga: "O, yeah, we run 'em, and did I ever hate it. You'd run them things down and they didn't wanta go there. I rode a horse, and some of 'em drove a wagon with food and it was usually a pretty long thing. But they'd gather these at least once a year up around Crabapple and Roswell and run it into the stockyard here in Atlanta."

"How many days did it take you to do that?"

"It would take about, you had to go on, you just went on, you got started real early in the morning, and you drove 'em until you got to, uh, that man had some, I don't know now it's been so long, but he'd let you drive this cattle, and he got paid something, everybody tried to make something then. Everybody was poor."

"So would you stay the night on his land?"

"Inside his fence."

"So you'd stay the night there and leave the next morning?"

"Yea."

"So it just took two days?"

"Yea."

I don't know anyone today who would know how far a herd of cattle could walk in a day, but ten or twelve miles is probably a good estimate. This would put them somewhere in the vicinity of Sandy Springs for the first night. Evidently there was someone around Sandy Springs who had a fenced pasture in which they would hold the cattle for a night. My father, Paga, once told me about sleeping under the wagon when they would make those drives.

The next big obstacle was around Buckhead, where the cattle encountered strange creatures which roared and rattled and frightened the whole herd – streetcars and model T Fords. Sometimes the cows would "spook" and start running wild through the yards of fine homes along Peachtree Road. Then Paga and the other Roswell cowboys would have to chase them down and bring them back into the herd.

Paga continues, "It was a job getting through there. I was just trying to run it down all the way. This, ah, demented boy is always coming back to my mind, he would sit on that hill out there and he could throw a rock from here to across the street and just about knock your head off with it if you weren't a good dodger."

Suzanne: "Did he hit you one time?"

"Yea, he hit me once or twice with it. T. S. was his name, T. S. His mother was the sweetest thing you ever seen and she had the worst time with that demented child. He could throw a rock though. He didn't need a gun"

"Where was this stockyard, was it in the heart of Atlanta?"

"It was below Atlanta, I mean, it was below where Roswell was on the far side of the river. Oh, it's been so long now, I've forgotten what it was, but you always had a time driving the cattle when you got to that bridge. They'd go through the water, some of 'em would, better than they would, uh, they'd swim across. It was a terrible job."

The stockyard was probably in the vicinity of the old White Provision plant, near the corner of Howell Mill Road and 14th Street.

"Did you have to cross the river more than once?"

"We just, we crossed it one time. If you could get 'em going through there. You'd have to ride a horse well, the horse was almost as hard to get across the river as the cows was. But you had to learn to get in there with 'em and you had a pretty good buggy whip, you didn't beat 'em or anything like that cause they didn't have to, but if one of them started to turn around or something, they'd pop 'em with that long, you know what they'd call a buggy whip, and that'd wake him up and he'd go on."

"Would you have to get off your horse and lead him through?"

"The minute he got across that bridge he'd go down to the river."

"Why did they go down to the river?"

"Trying to get away from that bridge."

"Did you just do that one time?"

"No, I went with them several times. It'd always give me a stomach ache when I knowd I had to go. Well, it did, I was just a young boy and I had a lot of trouble to go through, getting horses, you know, across them bridges."

"What did you do when you were little to get in trouble?"

"Get in trouble? Get up in the morning."

My father died three years after telling Suzanne this story, some of which I had heard previously in bits and pieces. He had a lot of stories to tell about growing up in a poor farm family with two brothers and four sisters, becoming the man of the family at the age of 12, raising his own family through the Great Depression, and a long career as a City of Atlanta policeman and detective. Suzanne's English assignment came at a good time, allowing us to preserve this important part of the Blackwell family's history, which is also an important part of the history of the Atlanta area.

End

This version of "Cattle Drive" was published in The Landmarker. Notice that there are two versions - one is the original interview, which The Landmarker preferred, and the other is my re-write, as requested by Georgia Backroads.

CATTLE DRIVE

The year 1922 in Cobb and Fulton Counties saw women voting for the first time, execution by hanging for the last time, and the openings of the Biltmore Hotel and radio station WSB.

But can you envision a 1922 cattle drive starting in the little town or Roswell? Horses and cattle balking at a rickety, wooden covered bridge across the Chattahoochee River? Cows being herded through Buckhead and down Peachtree Road, complete with a chuckwagon? It happened, and the author's father, thirteen-year old Maron Blackwell, was a reluctant participant.

In the early 1920's, Roswell was a Cobb County farming community. The textile mills provided hundreds of jobs, but the area was still agricultural, with small, family farms covering the gently rolling land north of the river. These highly diversified farms produced a variety of crops, primarily cotton and corn, but several acres would always be set aside for cattle and hogs.

Each year, these Fulton and Cobb County farmers assembled their surplus cattle in preparation for taking them to market in Atlanta. There were usually 30 to 40 cows assembled, probably on the "square" in lower Roswell. Local men and boys, farmers mounted on their best steeds, would then tackle the daunting but most practical and economical method of transporting those cows to market in Atlanta – a cattle drive.

Young Maron participated in several of these drives. He and his father, Jesse, brought their cows over from the family farm on Hanging Dog Road. It was a dangerous, unpleasant chore, but the drives sometimes produced as much as half of a farm family's annual income.

As soon as the herd was fully assembled, the cowboys began pushing and leading the cattle down Atlanta Road to their first hazard, the old wooden covered bridge across the Chattahoochee River. Wear and tear through the years had opened holes in the floor, enabling the cows and horses to see through to the rushing water below. This was a new experience which terrified the animals to the extent that some had to be blindfolded before they would cross. Others tried to escape or swim across and had to be run down and brought back into the herd. Each lost animal was a serious economical blow to these small farmers. The young, inexperienced "cowboys" tackled this frightening chore the best they could.

After crossing the river the cowboys moved the herd on southward, roughly following the course of Roswell Road. Their main responsibility here would be to keep the herd together and keep it moving.

It took one full day to push the herd to their next objective, the little village of Sandy Springs, where a local farmer would rent them a fenced field for the night. A farm wagon, converted into a chuck wagon, provided food and shelter for the young drovers. Sleeping on the ground under the wagon was no problem after a tiring and tension-filled day.

Daylight found them on the road again, along Roswell Road, which did not follow the exact route that it takes today. Mules and horses could not pull a wagon up a hill as easily as a T-Model Ford could make the ascent, so old roads tended to wind around hills rather than go straight up as they do now. Once again, their main responsibility was to keep the herd moving and bunched together. But even their best efforts would not deter some cows from occasionally galloping off through the woods to a patch of grass or a cool stream. Then it was the cowboy's job to run them down and bring them back to the herd, a difficult and often dangerous task for a 12-year-old boy.

One of many hazards they met along the route was a somewhat handicapped boy named T. S., who would pelt them with rocks. T. S. could throw a rock a great distance with perfect accuracy. "He didn't need a gun," said one of the young drovers.

The farther south they moved, the more development they encountered. Then came Buckhead and Peachtree Road, with paved roads, automobile horns and engines and rattles, and the roar of streetcars to terrify the poor farm animals – and the farm boys. There were several fine homes along Peachtree Road with expansive lawns and immaculate landscaping, which looked just like a pasture to a hungry cow. They could not resist the temptation to stop and feast. Irate home owners joined in the din as cows and cowboys galloped across their lawns and gardens.

In spite of all these obstacles and confusions, the cowboys would finally deliver their animals to "the stock yards," in the vicinity of the old White Provision Company, near the intersection of Howell Mill Road and 14th Street. The old building is still there, but the slaughter-house operation was discontinued many years ago.

This was the end of the line for the cows. With relief, young drover Maron, with his father and friends, could now begin their more relaxed journey back to Roswell and home.

The slaughter houses are closed now, but the collection of small businesses and stately homes known as "Lower Roswell" has changed little since 1922. However, Hanging Dog Road has vanished into oblivion and the family farms are now sprawling subdivisions. That part of Cobb County, the Roswell area, was transferred to Milton County during the Great Depression, and was later absorbed by Fulton.

The wooden covered bridge was torn down just a few years after this cattle crossing and replaced by a steel bridge, which was itself replaced by a series of concrete bridges as traffic increased. Sandy Springs has grown from a "village" to a major commercial center. The commercial district in Buckhead, and the fine old homes on Peachtree Road, have been replaced by office buildings and high-rise apartments. White Provision Company killed its last cow 60 years ago. Its old building is a part of an office, retail, and residential complex, which includes a restaurant appropriately named "Abattoir."

Author's note: My father's name was originally "Maron," as was mine. At one point in my early youth, Dad changed our names to

·

"Marion." Information for this article was obtained from a 1994 interview in which my daughter, Suzanne Blackwell, interviewed my father for an English project. My father was born in 1909, and was 85 at the time of the interview. Other sources were Atlanta and Environs by Franklin Garrett, and the History Centers in Roswell and Sandy Springs.

END

This article has been published twice. This version was in Georgia Backroads, and the original interview version was published in The Landmarker.

TRUE ADVENTURES OF JOHN ROBB, UNITED STATES ARMY AIR CORPS

By the time he reached 22 years of age, John Robb had earned his wings in the United States Army Air Corps, learned to fly the most challenging B-26 Martin Marauder bomber, was shot at and shot up by hordes of German fighters, dodged flack, overcame every conceivable equipment failure, and completed forty raids on factories, rail heads, airfields, and bridges in Italy and France.

The B-26 Marauder was a formidable and intimidating aircraft, some say designed ahead of its time. Many pilots could not fly it, many refused to fly it, and some died trying to fly it. It was described as a ship, which would glide like a rock. None of this bothered John Robb, who delivered bomb loads of 5,000 pounds on targets 500 miles away from his base in Tunisia.

A certain amount of luck is involved to enable a pilot to complete forty missions, and John Robb was happy to receive his share. On two occasions when he was not flying, when John was ill and again for disciplinary reasons, his B-26 was lost. In one of these disasters his entire crew went down with it.

Many of his bombing missions required visits to such places as Mt. Etna, Rome, Naples, Salerno, Nice, Cannes, Genoa, and Pisa. John vehemently denies that his Pisa raid had anything to do with the way the tower leans.

There is always one experience in the hazardous life of every pilot which becomes so harrowing that he recognizes it as a "near death" experience. That harrowing experience was John Robb's fifth raid. Here is the story in John's own words.

"Whew, my 5th raid was a lulu. The 'big show' or invasion of Sicily started at 0300 on July 10th. Everything was going according to plan. While standing by for a target of opportunity, we were sent to a target at the base of Mt. Etna in northeastern Sicily. We had no fighter escort and I was Tail-end Charlie, the last bomber in the formation. We were attacked by about thirty German ME-109's. My crew shot down two fighters, but they shot out my hydraulic system, punctured my wing tanks and hit my bomb bay air bottle, making it impossible to close my bomb bay doors.

"We had to use full power to keep up with the rest of the formation. I realized that we could not get back to our base as we were losing too much gasoline out of our wing tanks. I decided to go to Malta to land at a fighter base there. When we arrived, I decided to use a dirt runway. With our hydraulic system shot out, we were unable to lower our landing gear. A belly landing was our only option.

"We set up final approach to land and I feathered both engines in close because the prop tips would break off on contact with the ground and the tips sometimes came through the cockpit. As we touched down, the plane started skidding and turning around until we were facing the way we had come in. Before we started the backward skid, I saw a concrete wall at the end of the runway, built to discourage German glider attacks. We stopped skidding about ten feet from that concrete wall. No one was hurt on landing but the airplane was totaled. We got out and counted 350 bullet holes. Our tail gunner had a shell fragment in his ribs, but he recovered and joined us on later raids."

That's just one of forty missions. Many of the other 39 were almost as exciting.

"…the flak was moderate. We had five holes in our airplane from flak. We lost one plane out of the 437th Squadron.,…."

"My 7th raid was made on the Ciampo Airdrome at Rome. This raid occurred on July 19th. Our show tonight is 'Tarzan Triumphs'."

"On my 9th raid we bombed the town of Adrano…. English Spitfires and P-38's were our escort."

"I had my 11th raid on August 16th. The target was a bridge over the Angitola River in southern Italy. We destroyed the bridge. Heavy flak, but no fighters."

The thing that scared John the most was flak. "You can't fight back against flak," he said.

"We hit some railroad yards and really damaged the tracks. The yards were located about 50 miles south of Naples...."

"Well, this was a hot one. My 13th raid, on Salerno. The flak was very intense.... We were out over the Mediterranean and were jumped by a large number of German fighters. I saw a whole bunch of tracers go by the window.... The formation descended from 11,000 feet to 1,500 feet at a speed of 325 mph. On the way down, two B-26's collided and exploded in mid-air. Part of an engine fell just in front of us, barely missing us. Then another B-26 plunged into the sea with his right engine on fire. I didn't see anyone bail out and he went into the sea like a submarine. Another B-26 with his left wing burned off went in. Bradford damn near had his rudder shot off and with one engine on fire he made a successful water landing. Four of the crew got out but two gunners were missing. During the fight, 35 German fighters were shot down. The Germans shot down 19 B-26's out of 36 in our formation. I was lucky that I made it back." Nineteen out of 26 bombers is more than a 50% loss in one raid.

John's luck continues.

"We hit the target okay but the P-38's had one hell of a fight with the German fighters."

"We had flak three minutes before our bomb run, on the bomb run, and three minutes after. It was very intense. We caught about 100 JU-52's on the ground and destroyed about 80 per cent of them."

"I lost my airplane yesterday. Callahan was flying it and he had his left oil tank shot out. He made a crash landing in Sicily and his whole crew got out okay. It was a good ship."

"…Parry Thomas was hit twice. His tail gunner was wounded in the hip and is in bad shape. Kaminski, his bombardier, had part of his nose glass shot away. He was cut in the face."

"German Headquarters is reported to be in Alife along with a large troop concentration. We hit the town and literally blew it off the map. The flak was moderate and accurate. We were hit by a piece of flak in our left engine. Another fragment severed a hydraulic line in our right engine. When we came in to land, we could only get our main gear down. Using a hand crank, we finally were able to get our nose gear down also. We cranked half flaps down by hand on the approach leg. We made a nice landing and slowed the airplane up as much as possible and then used the air bottle for braking. The only damage was two tires burned out and no one was hurt."

"…no one was hurt' only because of John's courage and exceptional skills.

Good fortune and skillful flying kept John Robb alive, but his fellow pilots were not always so lucky.

"I picked up a cold and was grounded on October 15. George Hanchin took my crew on a raid on October 22. They got back to within 30 miles of Bizerte when they ran out of gas and had to make a water landing. Air-sea rescue was sent out but they could not find a trace of the plane or crew." John then went on to name each member of his lost crew and tell something personal about each one.

"…The boys ran into bad weather and two of them collided in mid-air and another B-26 iced up and crashed. That is the worst day in our squadron history."

"…Ed Brent made a beautiful water landing off the coast of Sardinia. The whole crew got out all right and paddled ashore in their life raft."

"…Lt. Stewart's left engine was hit and set on fire. We saw three men bail out and pinpointed where the airplane crashed. I hope the rest of the crew got out all right."

Near Cannes, mission number 32: "We received four flak holes and were jumped by five aggressive German fighters. My plane was damaged but we all got back. We destroyed the bridge…."

"We made a left break off the target and really got a good view of Rome. The city looked nice…."

On January 7, 1944, John Robb completed his 40th and final mission, a traditional low-risk "weather mission," this time to Leghorn, Italy. Three weeks later he received orders to go to Casablanca, where he boarded a troop ship for home.

A native of Danville, Illinois, John lived in Georgia for 52 years. After World War II, his love of adventure and flying led him to a long and successful career as a pilot with Delta Air Lines. John admits that it is quite a change from dropping 5,000 pounds of bombs on an enemy who is shooting back, to cruising at 30,000 feet in a smooth Delta L-1011.

End

John Robb was a personal friend and neighbor of the author. He told the story about crash-landing on Malta at a breakfast meeting of Vinings residents. I asked him if any of his adventures had ever been published, and they had not. So I interviewed him for the above details. The article appeared in the spring 2009 edition of Friends Journal, which is published at Wright-Patterson Air Force Base. Friends Journal has a "pipeline" of articles which takes over two years to publish a submission. Unfortunately, John died during that two-year period, and never got to see his adventures in print. Copies were provided to his family.

11,000 Killed or Wounded in My Old Neighborhoods

When I was five years old, in 1936, we moved from Buckhead to East Atlanta. Our new home was a brick duplex at the corner of Gresham Ave. and Pendleton St., adjoining Brownwood Park. Some of my friends lived on Hardee Street and McPherson Avenue, but I never stopped playing to wonder who Gresham, Pendleton, Brown, Hardee, or McPherson were, nor what they did to merit having a street named after them.

For six years I attended John B. Gordon elementary school, and never once asked, or even wondered, who John B. Gordon was.

We rode our bicycles to Grant Park, named after Colonel L. P. Grant, an engineer in the Confederate army who designed the fortifications around Atlanta. There we played on Fort Walker, a remnant of Colonel Grant's fortifications. Fort Walker is named after Confederate General William H. T. Walker, who was one of the first casualties of the Battle of Atlanta, shot by a Federal picket near Glenwood Road.

When I was ten we moved to a newer house on Bouldercrest Dr., very near Fayetteville Road. There were thousands of acres of undeveloped land around us then. It was a safe and exciting place for a boy who liked to wander and explore the woods. My friends and I often found Minie balls in the fields and woods along Fayetteville Road, which we knew only as old lead bullets, having no idea why so many were scattered around our playing areas.

As all of us have often said, "I wish I knew then what I know now," particularly about the history of Atlanta, and about history in general.

In July 1864, a tremendous battle, which we now call The Battle of Atlanta, raged all the way from East Atlanta to Little Five Points. Estimates indicate that approximately 11,000 soldiers were killed or wounded. But Atlanta's phenomenal growth could not be held back, so the trenches of the dead and the blood-stained fields of conflict slowly became neighborhoods, parks, streets, schools, and shopping areas, with present day Moreland Avenue and Memorial Drive running right through the center of the battlefields.

Hardee Street was named after General William Hardee, who commanded the Confederate forces making the attack. Just three short days earlier, his exhausted soldiers had faced U. S. General George Thomas at the Battle of Peachtree Creek along Collier Road and Northside Drive, where the Southern forces lost 5,000 men. With almost no rest at all, Hardee's tired soldiers marched fifteen miles from the Collier Road area southward through downtown Atlanta, then further south to the area of the Federal Penitentiary, then eastward across to Bouldercrest (then McDonough Road), and then north on Bouldercrest to Fayetteville Road. There Hardee split his troops, sending some up Fayetteville and some up Bouldercrest.

That's where we found the old bullets. They had never been fired, and are called "dropped shot." Worn-out from fighting at Peachtree Creek, barefooted, and carrying heavy arms and equipment in a hot July sun, it's not surprising that they "dropped" a lot of Minie balls to lighten the load during their fifteen-mile march.

I lived on Bouldercrest for twelve years and never realized that it was the route of a famous troop movement, Hardee's "end around" attempt to attack the Federals on their flank. Again, I wish I knew then what I know now.

Many Confederate officers were honored by having streets and schools named after them. Hardee, Pendleton, Walker, Cleburne, and Gordon, were, of course, Confederate generals. John B. Gordon was an outstanding General, a citizen-soldier fighting in Virginia, and was later governor of Georgia. Another Georgian, William Hardee, who "wrote the book" on infantry tactics, was highly regarded by BOTH armies. There were several Pendletons fighting for the Confederacy, but the one most likely to have lent his name to the street was William Nelson Pendleton, an artillery commander with Robert E. Lee. Patrick Cleburne was an outstanding commander who later lost his life with Hood in Franklin, Tennessee. There is a Cleburne Avenue, Court, Ridge, Terrace and Parkway.

One of historian Bill Scaife's excellent maps shows Cleburne's division formed for battle on what is now Gresham Avenue and Pendleton Street, exactly where my home was 62 years after the battle, and where our old red-brick duplex still stands today.

General W. H. T. Walker led the force which marched out Fayetteville Road and then moved up Sugar Creek, through dense swamps and thickets, to hit the Union flank. He was shot and killed by a picket when he emerged from the woods. Walker was a West Point graduate and had served in the United States Army in the Mexican War. He was 48 when killed. An upright cannon monument to General Walker is just off Glenwood Avenue near Sugar Creek and I-20. My pals and I would often spend all day trying to dam-up Sugar Creek. We never succeeded.

The early developers of East Atlanta must have been very forgiving. James B. McPherson was a bright, 35-year-old U. S. General who was killed at the site where his monument, also an upright cannon, is now placed. I passed it many times walking down McPherson Avenue to Murphy High School, and did not have the slightest idea of its significance.

Walter Gresham also was a U. S. general who had his knee shattered by a sniper on Leggett's hill, which was where Moreland Avenue crosses I-20 now. The hill, also called "Bald Hill," disappeared when I-20 was constructed. There had been a large old "haunted house" on the hill which my pals and I tried to muster up the courage to run through at night.

Brownwood Park and Brownwood Avenue are named after Joseph E. Brown, governor of Georgia during the Civil War. We also tried to dam up the creek in Brownwood Park. Creeks just don't like to be dammed up.

Now I live in Vinings, where both armies camped, fortified, and used it as a supply depot. The railroad which runs through Vinings was like an umbilical cord for both armies. U. S. supplies and troops came down from Chattanooga to Sherman's forces, and CSA supplies came up from Atlanta for Confederate forces.

I cross the Chattahoochee River every day, fifty feet from the place where parts of both armies crossed on pontoon bridges and ferries, very near where Hardy Pace had his ferry. I'm glad that now I know about and understand what happened here 150 years ago, particularly since I have discovered that I had a great-great grandfather who was killed in action in Vicksburg, another great-great grandfather from Alpharetta who served briefly in Savannah at the end of the war, and three distant cousins, all Blackwells from Cobb County, who died shortly after the war as a result of wounds and illnesses. One of them was also Marion Blackwell.

U. S. General James B. McPherson, killed in East Atlanta as mentioned above, graduated first in his class at West Point in 1853. Early in his career, while serving as officer in charge of harbor defense in San Francisco, he met and fell in love with a pretty young socialite named Emily Hoffman. However, the prominent Hoffman family, from Baltimore, were vehement Confederate sympathizers, and did not approve of their daughter loving and later becoming engaged to a Yankee officer.

When Emily's mother received the telegram that General McPherson had been killed, she handed it to Emily with the comment, "some good news."

Emily fled to her room where she stayed in recluse for one year. She never married.

We have the past, the present, and the future. We cannot change the past nor control the future, but a better understanding of our history will help us enrich our lives, accept our present, and deal with our future.

END

VININGS' LITTLE-KNOWN CHATTAHOOCHEE RIVER LINE OF THE AMERICAN CIVIL WAR

Long before the French even dreamed of the Maginot Line along their border with Germany in World War I, an equally impregnable version of that famous defensive fortification was built in Cobb County, Georgia, in 1864.

Both met the same fate – outflanked by the enemy.

General William T. Sherman's flanking maneuver was used extensively in the spring and summer of 1864 as he pressed the Confederate Army of Tennessee from Dalton back to Atlanta.

The maneuver consisted of attacking the enemy's front with a large force and then sending another large body of troops around to attack the side, or flank, of the enemy. Sherman could use this tactic easily since his force consisted of 120,000 Union soldiers, while Confederate General Joseph E. Johnston was opposing him with 65,000 Confederates. Johnston would withdraw and re-entrench rather than allow an attack on his vulnerable flanks.

This pattern of flanking and withdrawing, which historian Bill Scaife referred to as a "red-clay minuet," continued until the Confederate forces were backed up to the Chattahoochee River. At this point Johnston built a fortification the likes of which even Sherman had never seen – the River Line. Built almost entirely with a labor force of over 1,000 slaves in July, 1864, the Chattahoochee River Line was a series of connected fortifications intended to stop Sherman's attack on Atlanta.

This masterpiece of military engineering was six miles long, extending from Vinings to just south of Veterans Memorial Highway. The northern terminus of the fortification was located at a point off Polo Lane on a hill overlooking the Chattahoochee River where a large artillery fort was constructed. The line of forts crossed Atlanta Road south of I-285. Then turning in a more southerly direction, running parallel with the river, the line extended through Oakdale, and followed the ridge on which Oakdale Road is now located. Then it extended to the southernmost fort south of Veterans Memorial Highway, overlooking Nickajack Creek.

In June and July of 1864, after failing in an attempt to outflank Johnston at Dallas and Pickett's Mill, Federal armies attacked Confederate forces on Kennesaw Mountain. The Confederate forces repulsed them in some of the bloodiest battles of the war. Seeing the futility of continuing to attack such a strongly fortified hill, the Federals once again resorted to flanking movements.

General Johnston did not want to allow Sherman to get between the Confederates and Atlanta, so Johnston withdrew, abandoning Kennesaw Mountain and its line of fortifications. At this point the Confederate army was in the perilous position of being caught between the Yankees and the Chattahoochee River.

On Johnston's staff was a brilliant officer with a variety of experience, Brigadier General Francis Asbury Shoup. In an effort to stop the pattern of retreating, and to stop the Federals short of Atlanta, Shoup conceived the plan for a string of strong fortifications backing up to the Chattahoochee River. He presented his plan to Johnston, and the plan was approved in time to complete the fortifications before the rebel forces fell back from Kennesaw through Marietta and Smyrna.

Shoup had spent a part of his life prior to the war in St. Augustine, Florida, where he was doubtlessly inspired by the imposing Castillo de San Marcus. This old Spanish fort is a classic example of the use of bastions, small arrowhead-shaped forts which protrude out from the main fort. Gunners in the bastions could fire into the sides and backs of enemies who may be attacking another part of the walls. Likewise, fire from the walls could protect the bastions. This pattern enabled a crossfire which few attacking forces could penetrate. A graduate of West

Point, Shoup was also well educated in the design and use of military fortifications.

The Chattahoochee River Line, sometimes called Johnston's River Line, consisted of 36 of these arrowhead shaped forts, connected by a strong wall of log palisades and trenches. The forts are commonly called "Shoupades" after their designer, General Shoup. Most of them were graded away as Vinings and Oakdale developed. Very little evidence of the connecting palisades can be found.

The section most likely to be preserved is near the southern end of the line at Veterans Memorial Highway. Fortunately, this land is now owned and protected by Cobb County, and will hopefully be developed as a park. There are no trails leading to this part of the fortifications at this point, and no parking areas.

A remnant of a Shoupade is on Oakdale Road, squeezed in between an apartment complex and a residential development.*

Part of another is off Atlanta Road in "Olde Ivy" development, but it is difficult to get to and hardly recognizable. On Fort Drive, off Oakdale Road, parts of a Shoupade and an artillery fort were recently saved from destruction by the hard and persistent work of local preservation groups and activists. A few scattered Shoupades and artillery forts are in the yards of homeowners and on church grounds. Many home owners live on or near the ancient fort and have never heard of it.

Did the Chattahoochee River Line perform the task for which it was designed and laboriously constructed? This question is often discussed among students of the Civil War. Some feel that Johnston had hoped to stop Sherman at that point, and others feel that it was only meant to divert and delay the Federal armies until the Confederates could safely withdraw across the river. Being caught with half his army on one side of the river and half on the other would have been disastrous to Johnston.

The designer, General Shoup, felt that it should serve as a permanent fortification, but Johnston disagreed, much to Shoup's disappointment, and to the disappointment of other generals of the Confederate army. Confederate forces briefly occupied the River Line after their withdrawal from Smyrna and Marietta. When Federal forces, in hot pursuit, encountered the line, bristling with cannons and Shoupades, they wisely decided not to waste lives by throwing men against such an imposing obstacle. Sherman himself stated that it was the best field fortification he had ever seen. He then resorted to the tried-and-true tactic which had brought him from Dalton to the edge of Atlanta, the flanking movement.

As soon as General Johnston was informed that he had been out-flanked again and that Sherman's troops had crossed the Chattahoochee above and below his fortress, Confederate troops abandoned the River Line, crossed the river on pontoon bridges, and withdrew into the fortifications around Atlanta.

Just as German forces negated the strength of the Maginot line by going around it, so did United States forces negate the long-term effectiveness of the Chattahoochee River Line.

Historians William R. Scaife and William E. Erquitt wrote a book on the line in 1992, entitled *The Chattahoochee River Line*. This book contains much more information, including photographs of model Shoupades, details of construction, maps of the line and of troop movements, and more details about the Civil War in Georgia, and has been extremely helpful in writing this article.

POSTSCRIPT

This article has been published in three periodicals and one pamphlet. The most prominent periodical was Georgia Backroads magazine. The pamphlet is widely used by Mableton Improvement Coalition in their efforts to preserve historical structures in the Mableton-Oakdale area.

They were partly successful, but development of the area had already become so active that many fortifications were lost. The tale is told of one land owner who, on learning that he had several

Shoupades on land he hoped to develop, immediately had some of them graded away by bulldozers. One Shoupade mentioned in the story above (see the *) has completely disappeared, swallowed up by an apartment complex and a residential development.

Since 1864, most of the River Line has been leveled a little at a time by home owners and developers, and by Cobb County and The State of Georgia in the construction, widening, and paving of Woodland Brook Road, Polo Lane, I-285, South Cobb Drive, and Oakdale Road. The Line followed Oakdale Road for over half its length.

However, we can thank the Mableton and Smyrna activists for preserving one Shoupade in the creation of River Line Park on Oakdale Road. And in a way, we can thank General Joseph E. Johnston, also.

Mayson & Turner's Ferry was located where Veteran's Memorial Highway crosses the river today. General Shoup's plan called for the line to end by leaving the Oakdale ridge and curving down to the Chattahoochee, just up-stream from Mayson & Turner's Ferry. The line was quickly built to that point above the ferry. Immediately after construction, General Johnston inspected the line and decided that Mayson & Turner's Ferry was an important river crossing, so he had the line extended southward to protect the ferry.

While most of the forts along Oakdale Road were destroyed by development, some of the forts on Shoup's original line, which curved down off the ridge, were not destroyed because they were back away from Oakdale Road. Fortunately, an untouched Shoupade in excellent condition is now within the park's boundary, and was saved from destruction. This old fort is easily accessible by a paved path, and its importance is very well explained by a historical plaque. Of course, its log outer walls and its log palisades have long ago rotted away.

Another Shoupade is preserved on Fort Drive, off Oakdale Road.

Of the original 36 Shoupades, only eight remain, and most of them are damaged to the point that they are hard to recognize as a fort.

At this point the author speaks for those of us who realize the importance of preserving our history by thanking a few of the individuals and organizations which worked to preserve this part of The River Line:

Roberta Cook, River Line Historic Area Coordinator
Brian Smith, The Columns Group
Wade Lnenicka and the City of Smyrna
Barry Brown, Georgia Civil War Commission
Charlie Crawford, Georgia Battlefields Association
John Wieland, John Wieland Homes
Mableton Improvement Coalition
Mary Rose Barnes, preservation advocate

A model "Shoupade," made by historian Bill Scaife

END

TAKING DAD'S KEYS

The phone call came at about 8:30 one summer evening. The Forsyth County police had corralled my father for reckless driving.

They had been "chasing" him all over Cumming at twenty miles per hour.

Dad was 85 at the time. He had been declining mentally and physically for a few years, but had still been able to drive without problems. He and Mother took their big Chevrolet Suburban to run errands, go out to eat, and more and more frequent trips to their doctor and the hospital.

When I arrived at their home in Cumming about an hour later, Dad's Suburban was in the driveway, blocked in by three police cars with red lights flashing. But the scene was peaceful. Dad and four policemen were standing in the driveway, leaning on the cars, and chatting calmly.

A policeman walked out to meet me. "Mr. Blackwell," he explained, "we have been chasing your father all over Forsyth County for over an hour. I think he hit every curb in town. I believe you need to stop him from driving."

My relationship with Dad was still very much father-son. He was unquestionably the head of the family, in spite of his mental and physical failings. There was no way that I could ever get him to turn over his car keys to me, and I explained that to the policeman.

Most of my father's working life had been spent as a City of Atlanta policeman. He was a lieutenant when he retired in 1968. As long as he was able, he spent his retirement years fishing on Lake Lanier, playing golf, and traveling with their Airstream trailer pulled by the Suburban. He was the oldest son in a family of seven children and was always the leader of family affairs.

I explained that to the policeman, and asked him to try to get the keys, feeling that Dad would respect a fellow law officer.

He agreed, and simply asked, "Mr. Blackwell, could I have your keys?" Dad fished the keys from his pocket, held them up and studied them for as moment as if he realized that he would never drive again, and then placed them in the policeman's hand.

The policemen shook Dad's hand, and mine, and quietly left. I still greatly appreciate the calm and professional manner in which they handled a very sensitive situation.

Of course, Dad never drove again. The big Suburban sat in their driveway, unused. Three years later he and Mother died within a few months of each other, and we sold the Suburban. But Dad got his revenge – while cleaning up their home to sell it, we found a note which said, "Money hidden in spare tire of Suburban."

END

Published in Atlanta Journal-Constitution

STREETCARS

A slightly different version of this was published in the AJC.

Iron wheels on iron rails and a loud clanging bell- you could hear them coming from two blocks away. Powered by electricity, streetcars were economical to operate and did not pollute the city's air.

Streetcar lines converged at Five Points, in the heart of downtown Atlanta. This virtually guaranteed a prosperous downtown business district – wherever you wanted to go, you had to go through downtown, and usually you would have to get off and transfer to another line.

When I was twelve years old, in 1943, I lived in East Atlanta. My home was an easy walk to the streetcar line on Moreland Avenue, and about five miles from downtown. I could walk to the line, catch a streetcar, and for fifteen cents be downtown in twenty minutes. We could shop at Woolworth and Rich's, get a Krystal or a Frosted Malted, and maybe see a movie at the Paramount or Lowe's Grand. Later when I was dating but still too young to drive, I tried to pick girl friends who lived on streetcar lines.

There were two long streetcar lines which carried larger and faster streetcars. One line stretched 18 miles from Marietta to Atlanta, and the other from Atlanta to Stone Mountain, 14 miles east. Both met at Five Points. As soon as these high-speed streetcars cleared the downtown Atlanta area they would leave the usual network of trolley tracks and speed away on their private lines. No clanging trolley bells for them, their warning blast sounded more like today's diesel locomotives. It was a real adventure for my pals and me to ride all the way to Marietta or Stone Mountain, and a thrill crossing the Chattahoochee on a high trestle.

At one time, the Atlanta school system tried an ill-conceived plan which required us to go to a high school on the far side of downtown. Our mode of transportation was, of course, streetcars. So from East Atlanta students had to ride through downtown Atlanta, and through several residential neighborhoods to get to Boys' High School, which was where Grady High School is today.

That year the ROTC students at Boys High had to march in a parade downtown. Riding in front of us were the Shriners with their "Mounted Patrol," which was about forty fat men mounted on fine horses. After the Mounted Patrol came our Boys' High band, our ROTC platoon marching with their 1903 Springfield rifles, then behind us the Tech High band. We were trying to march in step while we heard the Tech High band behind us and our band in front as we dodged horse manure and tried not to turn an ankle on streetcar tracks. We looked more like a mob than a military unit.

When the parade ended downtown we went straight home, with our rifles. The next morning our ride to school on a streetcar looked like an invasion, with Springfields pointed out of every window. People scattered and ran behind houses as some neighborhoods were terrified when we roared through, bristling with armament.

That experiment ended after one year – my 10th grade. I guess they decided that Springfields and streetcars don't mix.

In spite of streetcars being a nearly perfect mode of transportation, flaws began to be noticed as the metropolitan area grew.

The tracks usually ran down the middle of the street, which meant that you had to step off the curb and cross a lane of traffic to get to the trolley car. Noise from the wheels and bells became a nuisance to some quiet neighborhoods.

Automobiles were increasing in number, and drivers complained about streetcars always being in the way. When steel tracks got wet they were slick and dangerous to drive over. All of these problems were exacerbated by the exponential increase in automobiles.

The greatest flaw was seen to be the over-all inflexibility of the network of streetcar tracks. Steel tracks were expensive to relocate or extend. As some neighborhoods grew, others declined, and new areas were developed. Metropolitan Atlanta's dynamic growth pushed the population from 500,000 in the 1950's to over 4,000,000 now. Our streetcar system could not be economically changed to meet the new demands.

So streetcars were gradually replaced by quieter, more flexible "trackless trolleys" and busses, and eventually the steel tracks were removed or paved over.

But now we may have come full circle, as most things do. Streetcars are being re-considered as a practical and inexpensive mode of transportation, particularly along major thoroughfares such as Peachtree or Cobb Parkway. I wonder if I will still be able to get a token for fifteen cents. Probably not.

In these days of dependency on the federal government for almost everything, Georgia and the Atlanta area are lagging behind the rest of the nation in our funding applications. Out of 27 recent applications, Georgia made none. While we have not even applied, huge grants have gone to Charlotte, Tucson, New Orleans, Dallas (TX), and Portland, among many others. I rode Portland's streetcars several years ago. They are quiet, smooth, practical, economical, and widely used.

While our sister/competitor cities around the nation move quickly and take advantage of the tax money we paid the Feds, Atlanta area governments prefer to consume our funds and time by making studies and employing exorbitantly expensive consultants.

END

Published Twice

A different version of "Streetcars" was published in the Atlanta Journal-Constitution in 2010. A recent visit to several European cities showed "streetcars," often coupled together in trains of three or four cars, to be an important and efficient means of urban transportation. A shorter version of this article was published in the magazine "Loftlife" in 2008.

SCREAMS UNDER WATER

Off the coast of Bon Aire, in thirty feet of crystal clear water swarming with sea life, one of our diving instructors encountered a Moray Eel about five feet long. A Moray Eel looks like a fat, green snake, except where a snake has two fangs, an eel has a mouth full of long, sharp teeth. He is the nearest thing to a sea-monster which we have around today.

As the instructor related the story to his group of divers, he and the eel had studied each other at close range for a while. Then the instructor decided to swim away, so he extended his right arm to wave by-by to the eel. Like a lightning bolt the eel's long sharp teeth ripped the arm open from elbow to wrist, and was gone in a flash.

The instructor was severely injured, but he was a professional, so with his one good arm and strong legs he surfaced and got immediate medical attention. When we saw him, his arm was in a sling and bandaged from wrist to elbow. We were swimming at the same depth and not fifty yards from him and did not see it happen.

A few months later, my wife and I were diving off the British Virgin Islands. We were spending a week there, diving almost every day. When not under twenty to fifty feet of water, we would explore the islands in a rented car.

Motels which cater to divers always have dive shops, where scuba divers can purchase souvenirs and equipment. The lady who operated the dive shop at our motel was also an under-water photographer. A television in her shop was always running some of her under-water movies, with beautiful shots of marine life you never see while swimming on the surface. Between dives, we would hang out there and admire her talent.

One day she offered to dive with us and film our adventures, and suggested the site of the wreck of the Rhone.

The H.M.S Rhone was a steam powered, two-masted ship which carried mail, a few passengers, and cargo around the islands in the 1860's. It was the first steam-powered ship to cross the Atlantic, and was reputed to be the fastest ship in the area.

With its cargo of mail and merchandise and 147 people, the Rhone was making a long crossing from one island to another when a bad storm blew. The Captain felt that it would be safer take shelter in a cove until the waters became more calm, which he did. As the winds began to die down, he decided to make a run for a better shelter in a well-protected harbor. The passengers were tied into their beds to prevent them from being thrown around and possibly injured. However, halfway across the bay, the storm turned into a full-fledged hurricane.

The first disaster happened when the Captain was blown overboard and never seen again. They had gone too far to turn back, and were caught in the middle of the hurricane. Finally the mighty ship endured all it could, and broke into two sections, one section sinking into eighty feet of water, the other section sinking thirty feet. 124 people drowned, 23 survived. Many, still tied into their beds, did not have a chance.

We decided to let her photograph our dive to the more shallow of the two sections. Shallow dives are safer, and the light is much better, making colors more vivid.

As we swam down to the wreck, I first saw that it was almost un-recognizable as a ship. Huge slabs of twisted metal were piled and strewn around the area. We started exploring, and the photographer started filming.

I was standing with one foot on a large section of the hull and the other foot on what looked like the rudder, holding a twisted rusty beam for stability, when I heard a strange noise. Underwater, you usually don't hear anything but your bubbles, but this sounded like a scream. Then, two screams. Two women screaming. I looked around until I found my wife and the photographer, both showing hysterical expressions and pointing at something which I could not see. I gave them a "thumbs-up" signal to surface.

We met at the surface and removed our masks so we could talk.

"Did you see it? Did you see it?" they both asked with bug-eyed expressions.

"See what?" I asked.

"The eel! The Moray Eel! He was huge – fifteen feet long and swam right between your legs!" That's three times as large as the eel which attacked the instructor.

I had not seen it, and the photographer was too terrified to shoot a movie of one of my more harrowing experiences, or so they tell me.

END

To Shoot the Chattooga

In 1970, Atlanta poet-writer James Dickey wrote his best-selling novel *Deliverance*. By 1972, Hollywood had realized the importance of the story and made it into an action-packed movie starring Burt Reynolds, Jon Voight, Ned Beatty, and Ronny Cox.

The story was about four men who were determined to canoe a white-water river in north Georgia which was scheduled to be inundated as the waters of a lake backed up. The lake was the product of a new hydro-electric dam. The four amateur canoers, with two canoes, did not know what they were getting into, and had very limited white-water experience. The result was a series of disasters, causing the death of the fourth canoer, played by Cox.

It was a fascinating book and a great movie.

Shortly after the movie came out, boaters all over Georgia were lured to the beautiful, exciting white water rivers, primarily the Chattooga. Few of them had any idea what they were getting into.

At that time I was president of a commercial real estate company in downtown Atlanta, Sharp-Boylston Company. I had a canoe, but only used it to paddle my four kids around on lakes and the calm sections of the Chattahoochee River as it meandered its way through Atlanta. At that time, a gentleman named Hal was associated with us at Sharp-Boylston. Hal knew I had a canoe.

One day at the office, Hal approached me with an idea. He knew four other guys, lawyers and realtors, who were planning to challenge the white rapids of the Chattooga. If I would furnish the canoe, he would rig it to run the rapids, and supply some food and drink, which turned out to be pina-coladas.

It sounded like great fun to me. Hal somewhere found a truck inner-tube which he placed in the center of the canoe, then inflated it tight against the sides. It was a brilliant idea. It kept the middle section of the canoe from filling up with water, and its pressure on the sides kept the canoe from suffering too many dents from crashing sideways into rocks.

On the appointed day, we roped the canoe to the top of my Buick Electra 225 and headed for Rabun County. The other four men, with their canoes, were to meet us at Earl's Ford, which was accessible only by a rugged dirt road. Our launching point was three miles from the nearest paved road, War Woman Road. A Buick Electra 225 was not designed for dirt roads, but somehow we made it without any problems. We even forded a couple of small creeks. I recall thinking that, if it rained and that dirt road got slick, we might as well just abandon the Buick at Earl's Ford.

There was a scene in Deliverance in which Ned Beaty had a very unfortunate sexual experience with some mountain boys, sometimes referred to as "the love scene." We had joked about which of us would be the volunteer sex object if we encountered any such people.

Hal and I were the first to arrive at the ford. We were immediately concerned about the smell of meat cooking and smoke from a camp fire a short distance downstream from us. We had no idea how long it would be before our four other boaters would arrive. This was before cell phones.

I volunteered to check it out while Hal guarded the Buick and canoe.

Climbing over rocks and washed-up trees, I made my way down the riverside. Finally, I came upon four young mountain boys with a cook-pot smoking over a campfire, and four rifles propped against trees. They were just as friendly as they could be.

"That sure smells good," I complimented them. "What is it?"

"Squirrel stew. Want some?"

I told them that I appreciated the offer but we had brought food with us. With that I returned to Hal, who was relieved to know that we did not have to worry about requests for a date.

Soon the rest of our party arrived in one car – two canoes and four people. They had left the other car at the take-out point, Highway 76, to give us a ride back to our launch site.

It was getting late and we were ready to set up camp, have dinner, get a good night's rest, and be ready for an early start down the rocky, rapid Chattooga River. But then some of our crowd got concerned about the well-armed mountain boys and their squirrel stew, camping within smelling range, so we decided to load the three canoes and paddle across the river to a camp site on the other side. This we did, and that was our first little mishap.

A canoe handles better if the heavier person is at the back. I was the heavier of the two, so Hal was at the front. We ran the bow of our canoe into the opposite bank, Hal stepped out of the bow and pulled it up securely, then I stood up to walk to the front, at which time Hal decided to reach back and make the canoe a little more secure by giving it another tug, causing me to flip over backwards into the river.

Thankfully, this was not a problem. We built a big fire and I dried out quickly. Hal had brought delicious food and drink, so we all enjoyed a gourmet feast by campfire before turning in for a good night's rest.

The following morning we built another fire and cooked a big breakfast. While standing around the fire, eating and warming up, two men in a canoe came floating by. At Earl's Ford we were between the rapids, and the Chattooga looked like a placid stream. The two men held up life jackets and yelled at us, "Do you think we will need these?" The experienced canoers among us called back that, yes, they should definitely wear their life jackets.

Breakfast over and all our camping gear ferried across the river and stowed in the cars, we were ready to challenge the mighty Chattooga, so off we went.

We drifted quietly through the calm waters, giving us an opportunity to enjoy the beautiful mountain scenery around us, and to get accustomed to handling the canoe as a team. Soon we heard what we came for – the roar of rapids ahead, growing louder as we approached white water. We paddled harder to get better control of the canoe as we sped to the rapids.

Water rushing between two boulders makes a "V" pointing downstream, and we knew to aim the canoe directly through the point of the V. The sudden surge of speed was thrilling, and we "shot" the first few rapids with no problems at all. This was not only thrilling, it was easy boating. The water provided most of the speed, all we had to do was steer.

Then the boulders grew larger and more numerous, and the river picked up speed. We took careful aim at one V only to see another boulder awaiting us at the point of the V. There was no way to miss it. The collision flipped the canoe onto its side and pitched Hal and me right out into the foamy waters. Hal's inner tube kept the canoe afloat, so all we could do was go with the flow and wait for the canoe to get stopped by rocks or a beach. Another good idea Hal had was to tie the paddles to the canoe with a light rope to keep them from getting washed away. Without his keen foresight, we, literally, would have been left up the creek without a paddle.

Here we learned our first white-water lesson. Floating downstream, watching for the canoe to get stopped, was fun – that is, until we hit submerged rocks with our knees and bare legs. In self-defense we learned to float in a sitting position with our feet extended out in front. Our tennis shoes would hit the rocks and we could push away without any harm.

We were surprised to find many white, sandy beaches along the river. As soon as the canoe would get stopped by rocks or one of these beaches, we would drift to it, pour the water out, climb in, and be gone downstream.

This procedure happened over and over again, but we never got tired or dreaded it – it was fun!

Occasionally, the rapids ahead would make such a loud roar that we would beach all three canoes and walk down the river bank to reconnoiter and decide the best way to handle that particular challenge. At one point, almost the whole river was funneled between two huge boulders, then dropped straight down about six feet into a cauldron of foam boxed in by other boulders, which then spit the foam out to the right at a 90 degree angle. Five out of six of us were in favor of a portage, but Hal wanted to give it a try.

We watched on the edge of the cauldron as Hal walked over to our canoe, positioned himself to have maximum control, and shoved off.

The speed of the water quickly brought him to the edge and over the rocks. He was immediately pitched out of the canoe into the swirling white foam. We watched helplessly as Hal and the canoe spun around several times between the rocks, waiting for them to be flushed out into the main stream. As the canoe bounced around, I was afraid that it would hit Hal and maybe knock him unconscious. I was about ready to jump in with him, but the river decided that he had had enough and spit Hal and the canoe out into the main channel. We applauded as he grabbed the canoe and drifted to a beach where we could dump the water out and start again.

The all-day trip was one adventure after another. I couldn't count the number of times we turned over. When we would angle for the shore to avoid some rocks, the current would push against the side of the canoe and we would lose control. We often found ourselves floating sideways – or even backwards – down the river. Then it was a race with time to either get better control or have an underwater boulder catch us and tip us over.

During peaceful stretches when we did not have to concentrate on the rapids, we just drifted and enjoyed the scenery. Vertical rock cliffs were often as tall as a five or six story building. Huge trees and deep woods hugged the river on both sides. Any sign of civilization was almost non-existent.

At one sandy beach we were amazed to find a canoe which had been ripped in half by the power of the river.

We had heard about Bull Sluice before we arrived at the Chattooga. Boaters hear about Bull Sluice as the knights of old heard about dragons. The odds of successfully shooting Bull Sluice were slim, but some had to try it. By the time we arrived at Bull Sluice, a crowd had gathered along the river banks to watch the few brave souls who had the skill and courage to try. We joined the crowd to evaluate our chances.

Canoes, kayaks, and rubber rafts with five or six people tried their luck, and nearly all failed. Boaters would get tossed out into the roaring foam and flipped into every conceivable position as they banged against the boulders before being spewed out into the river below. Occasionally, a kayak would get through, but nothing else.

We decided to portage. After all, discretion is the better part of valor.

A very short float below Bull Sluice was Highway 76, our take-out point. We were surprised at the number of people gathered there, possibly fifty or a hundred boaters who had gone before us, and a few spectators who had arrived by car. Several huge bonfires had been built to dry out the wet, and by this time chilly, boaters. We joined the crowd and swapped a few stories.

A somewhat familiar face came up and shook our hands all around. I recognized him as one of the boaters who had floated by our camp that morning, and had asked us about wearing their life jackets. "You saved our lives," he said. Thinking back over what we had been through and all the adventures of the day, I guess we did.

END

ESSAYS

SIGNIFICANT TRANSACTIONS

180 DECATUR STREET – MY FIRST SALE

In March 1955, I was released from the Army after serving 21 months during the Korean conflict. The first sale of my career was in April, one month after being discharged. I do not recall the exact details of how this transaction happened so fast, but, since I was stationed at Fort McPherson and was working real estate on weekends, I had probably been working on it before my discharge. My civilian employer, Adams-Cates Co., had been very understanding for the entire 21 months of my military service, and had reserved my desk for me. Occasionally, on my way home from Fort McPherson, and on weekends, I would come in to the Hurt Building office and answer mail, return calls, and handle anything which might have come up.

This first sale, 180 Decatur Street, was a vacant lot located next to Garner Bonding Company, a company which was owned by my grandmother and operated by my uncle, Gene Garner. Gene had probably asked me to look into it for him. Walking from Adams-Cates' office in the Hurt Building to the Fulton County Courthouse, I followed the standard procedure of finding the information. This was before the advent of computers and plat books. To find information at the courthouse, you had to ask a clerk in the tax assessor's office for a certain plat book, and then trace the plat of the property with a ruler and paper which you had brought with you. Then, using an index in the plat book, look up the owner's name and address in the tax assessors directory. It took two hours to get information you can get in two minutes today.

The lot was owned by a gentleman named Taft Mansour, who ran a dry-goods store in Newnan. A couple of trips down there (on Roosevelt Highway, there was no I-85 then) and a few phone calls and we worked out a sale at a price of $8,450.

My commission was $211.25, which was a lot considering that I had been making $85 a month in the Army. 180 Decatur Street was directly across the street from the Atlanta police station, and is now a part of the Georgia State University campus.

From this transaction I learned a very important lesson: your most likely buyer is always the next door neighbor or someone very near the property. This eventually developed into what I thought of as 'The Spiral System' of offering listings first to the tenant, if there is one, and then to all adjoining owners and then gradually spiraling out farther and farther from the property. Later, I would teach 'The Spiral System' to salesmen at Sharp-Boylston Company. They used it profitably and to this day often comment on how practical and productive it was for them.

SPECIALIZATION? WHAT'S THAT?

The population of metro Atlanta was only about 500,000 then, compared to about 4,500,000 now. There were no Interstate highways and very few four-lane roads.

There was not enough of any one type of property to specialize. Adams-Cates was beginning to evolve into a commercial company, but in 1955, they handled whatever came along, including houses. My other transactions in that first year were as follows:

Leased 180 Decatur St. (the lot I sold to Gene Garner).
225 acres on Lum Crow Road, in north Fulton, for $28 per acre
House at 888 Emerson Avenue, SE, for $9,300.
Residential lot on Lake Talmadge, Clayton County, for $3,000
113 acres in Cherokee County for $7,500 (That is $66.40 per acre)

House at 1821 Buckeye Street, SW, for $10,800

New house in Meadowbrook Heights (in Buckhead) for $19,000

Small acreage on Union Road, S. Fulton, for $19,500

Another new house in Meadowbrook for $18,500

House at 2298 Burroughs Avenue, SE, for $9,900

Lot on West Garmon Road for $7,650

588 14th Street for $11,000 (near where Atlantic Station is now).

In my first year out of the army I made $3,884.38. On this I supported my wife and first child, Danny.

Then, in 1956, I sold 14 houses, six tracts of acreage, three residential lots, and two commercial buildings. On seven of these transactions, I worked with another Adams-Cates salesman, and on one I worked with another company – Sharp-Boylston Company. My 1956 earnings were $12,162.40 – more than I ever dreamed I could make at age 25.

NORTHSIDE DRIVE INDUSTRIAL LOT

The Spiral System lesson was reinforced with this sale.

Northside Drive was (and is) a major thoroughfare in downtown Atlanta, one of our first four-lane roads. Grinnell Company had a large industrial plant on Northside, just south of Marietta Street. Since I drove this route frequently, I often noticed that another broker, Sam, had a large For Sale sign on a very nice looking two or three acre lot adjoining Grinnell. I coveted the listing, but ethics prevented me from "going around" Sam. The sign stayed there a long, long time and eventually the posts rotted and it fell. This is usually a pretty good indication that the broker has lost interest or lost the listing, so I felt free to investigate.

The owner said that he had not heard from Sam for a year and gave me an open listing. I walked into Grinnell's office, asked for the boss, got in to see him, and asked him if he had ever considered buying the lot next door. He asked, "Is that lot for sale?"

I could not believe that Sam had never offered it to him, and that he had never noticed the sign, which had been there for a couple of years. He quickly bought the lot at the asking price.

The significance of this sale is that I learned not to assume that all of my competitors were competent.

The lot is still vacant after 44 years, and I regret to say that the former Grinnell building is now abandoned, with broken windows. A sign indicates that the last occupant was "Creative Fine Arts." That section of Northside Drive has really gone down, but shows signs of coming back.

GRESHAM PARK

The two people who were most influential in my real estate career were my uncle, Gene Garner, who patiently walked me through several early transactions, and Henry Robinson. Mr. Rob was my sales manager at Adams-Cates. He taught me 99 percent of everything I know about real estate, and was the best role model any young person could hope for.

One day, Mr. Rob approached me and asked if I would be interested in an unusual project. The U. S. Prison Service had asked us to appraise all of what they called their "non-custodial" properties in Atlanta, that is, everything outside of the tall, gray concrete walls on McDonough Boulevard, known as the Federal Prison. These non-custodial properties consisted of the homes occupied by the warden, chaplain, and other prison officials, all located around the main prison, as well as what they called "the farm," which was 1,200 acres on Panthersville Road in south DeKalb county. A fee was involved, so I was interested.

The assignment was fascinating, and included an extensive tour, conducted by the warden himself, of everything inside the walls, as well as outside. Once inside the bars, we walked freely among racketeers and murderers while we toured the city behind the walls. And a complete city it is, with factories, athletic fields, offices, stores, eating facilities, chapel, hospital, and a communal shower where the inmates were herded once a week, whether they needed it or not.

Then we toured the farm, which was an immaculate operation, with all labor supplied by trustees. They raised prize-winning hogs, and grew enough crops and beef to feed the 1,000 inmates at the main prison.

This assignment was repeated the next year. By this time, I had gotten to know the warden very well. In one of our conversations, he mentioned that part of the farm had been declared surplus by the government. This surplus tract was 35 acres at the intersection of Clifton Church Road and Gresham Road which they had never used, and was just a few blocks from where I lived at that time.

This part of DeKalb County was growing very rapidly, and we needed a park for playgrounds and ball fields. This 35 acres would be ideal if there were some way I could get the U. S. government to give it to the County.

When the U. S. Government declares something to be surplus, a specific procedure must be followed:

1. The property must be offered to all other U. S. government agencies.

2. If no U. S. agency wants it, it is then offered to state agencies.

3. If no state agency wants it, it is then offered to the local county.

4. If the county has no use for it, it is offered to the public at auction.

This was truly a case of being at the right place at the right time. I was the only non-government person who knew in advance that the tract was available, and I was close enough to it to recognize that its highest and best use would be as a park. At that time we were beginning the organization of Gresham Park Little League, and had no place to play. Gresham Park was also the name of the area in which we lived.

First, I approached the county to be sure that they would develop it as a park if it became available. The answer was yes, if it did not cost them anything.

Then a hitch developed. A National Guard unit had requested it for use as an armory. I met with the commanding officer, a colonel, at their old armory on Ponce de Leon. I was a little bit intimidated, a recent ex-corporal talking to a colonel, but somehow I convinced him that it was not a good site for an armory, and that he really did not want it after all, and that the property would be much better for the people of America if he passed on it and let the county develop it as a park, with Little League fields. Letters to Senators and Congressmen may have helped. Danny, my first son, was not big enough to play baseball then, but I could picture him there in a few years.

We Gresham Park citizens opposed the armory every way we could, primarily by contacting every elected official we could think of. The colonel must have felt the pressure, because at one time he offered me a direct commission as a captain if I would stop working against it. I briefly pictured myself in an officer's uniform with two silver bars on my shoulder, but I quickly realized that army life with its regimentation could not compete with real estate, with its freedom and unlimited earnings opportunities.

Forty years later, Gresham Park is a well-developed DeKalb County park, containing nine baseball fields, some of which are lighted, a football/soccer field, pool, gymnasium/activities building, and several picnic shelters. It looks bigger than I remember – the county may have added some more land.

I did not make a penny on this transaction, but I consider it one of the most significant I ever helped put together. We moved to Dunwoody before the park was developed and Danny never got to play there.

My First – and Last – Assemblage

Adams-Cates had a client who needed several acres near downtown, and had selected a block located on Northside Drive in the vicinity of Spelman and Morehouse Colleges. The block was cut up into 30 or 40 small lots, each about 50 X 150, each with a small house about fifty years old. I had absolutely no experience with assemblages, so I thought I would give it a try.

All of the homes were occupied by the owners. Several months were consumed in talking to the owners, getting them to agree to sell, and then getting a contract or option signed. In most cases, I had to make several visits to earn the owner's trust and to help decide on a price which not only included the value of the property but also included a "bonus" for selling and moving.

Finally, all properties were under contract, except one. The owner was an elderly African-American lady who was always friendly and was always glad to see me come by, but just would not agree to sell. The buyer, still unknown to me, would not buy just part of the block – he had to have the whole thing or nothing at all.

It was like juggling plates on sticks. While I was trying to get her to sell, some of the other contracts were expiring, so I had to run back to the owners and get them extended, sometimes at increased prices. Then, one day, while standing on her front porch, she told me, "Mr. Blackwell, when I bought this house I promised The Lord that if I ever got it paid for, I would never sell it. Now, Mr. Blackwell, do you want me to break my promise to The Lord?"

Of course I had to say no.

When I thought about how much time I had consumed on this project, and how much I could have earned if I had been working on other properties, I decided that assemblages involved entirely too much risk. So I made a rule for myself: no more assemblages. I obeyed that rule for the rest of my career.

However, assemblages do not always turn out badly. An old friend and boyhood buddy, Jimmy Hackney, mastered the art of assemblages and made them an important and profitable part of his successful career.

FULTON INDUSTRIAL DISTRICT

Fulton County owned over 1,000 acres on the Chattahoochee River at Gordon Road, now M. L. King Jr. Drive, which they called the County Farm. It was worked by trustees convicted of minor, short-term offenses. Most of it was woods and cultivated fields, tended by the prisoners, who plowed it with mules. It was bounded on the north by Fulton County Airport, now called Charlie Brown Field after one of the county's more dedicated commissioners.

Access from the tract into Atlanta, or anywhere else, was very poor. However, when it was determined that Interstate Highway 20 would pass somewhere in the vicinity of the farm, the county decided to close the farm and develop the land as an industrial district.

Fulton Industrial Boulevard, a four-lane divided thoroughfare, was constructed for several miles through the site. A few side roads were also built. A site plan was prepared showing industrial lots of a wide variety of sizes and shapes, many with rail. Heavy-duty water, gas, electrical service, and sewer lines were installed. Very colorful, expensive marketing materials were prepared. A retired corporate executive, Bill, was hired to market the sites, which were very reasonably priced.

Bill presented Fulton Industrial District to Adams-Cates, Draper-Owens, Haas and Dodd, Sharp-Boylston, Adair, and other companies which had commercial departments, encouraging their assistance. Then he waited for the industries to line up for sites. And waited. And waited. And after much effort and expense, he finally sold a five acre site to a good local firm, Walker Die Tool and Engineering Co., and another site to a company which manufactured batteries. Then there was another long period in which nothing happened.

About this time, I had completely made the switch from a multi-purpose agent to a commercial-investment specialist, and I was looking for something to work on. Fulton Industrial District looked like a good opportunity because of its size, competitive pricing, huge investment by the county, and lack of activity because of its current marketing program.

I met with Bill and told him that I would like to be the County's exclusive agent for FID. Bill said no, that was his job. But he was an intelligent person, and realized that he was not producing results. With the blessings of the Adams-Cates officials, I outlined a comprehensive marketing program to him, and emphasized the importance of having a sales team which was motivated by commissions.

Bill agreed. Then he resigned his job and recommended to the county commissioners that Fulton County turn FID over to Adams-Cates. Adams-Cates then appointed me the agent in charge of marketing this huge project, which at that time was exceeded in scope only by Peachtree Industrial Boulevard (now known as just Peachtree Boulevard).

Dallas, Texas, was way ahead of Atlanta in the development of industrial parks. In order to advise our client, Fulton County, on future development, I spent a week in Dallas studying their parks and talking to the developers.

(I had never traveled by air, so I rode a train all the way to Dallas, but Mr. Rob convinced me that I should fly back. The flight on a Delta DC-6 four engine prop plane was fascinating and showed me that flying was here to stay).

But I-20 was yet to be constructed, and prospects were very cool to a site with poor accessibility.

Finally, the state settled on the exact location of I-20, and agreed to build an interchange at Fulton Industrial Boulevard. As luck would have it, the one site already sold, to Walker Die Tool and Engineering Co., was exactly in the middle of the proposed interchange. My first transaction in FID was to exchange the Walker site for another tract outside the proposed I-20 right-of-way, which was also my first exchange.

For several years, Fulton Industrial District was my primary concern, and I was successful in bringing many industries and businesses to the park. My largest sale there was 57 acres to Amarlite, an aluminum extruding firm which was later acquired by Anaconda. Now the property, 340,000 square feet, has a "for lease" sign on it, and is partly being used as a recycling plant.

Industrial transactions were very interesting. I always enjoyed getting to see how different industries operated, how various products were made. I was very pleased when Walter Clifton, the owner of Amarlite, completed his new building on his 57 acres and proudly showed me through the plant in his golf cart – the plant was too huge to walk through. It's sad to see that this once fine building is now not fully utilized, but it has been 50 years since Walter Clifton rode me around in his golf cart.

One significant feature of the FID listing and subsequent sales is that I had to talk Bill into quitting his job in order for me to get the listing, and it showed me the importance of working hard to control a good listing.

Everything relating to FID had to be approved by the Fulton Industrial Authority, which was a group of prominent business advisers, and finally by the Fulton County Board of Commissioners. At that time, Fulton County had a three-man commission. Carlyle Frasier was founder and president of Genuine Parts, Jim Aldredge had a hardware store on Bankhead Highway, and Archie Lindsey was a real estate broker from Alpharetta. All three were impeccably honest, intelligent, and wonderful to work with. I doubt that I would want that job today.

SINGER

Singer & Co. was a dry goods wholesaler operating out of an ancient multi-story warehouse on Mitchell Street in downtown Atlanta. They needed a more modern building and asked me to find a site for them.

I had been showing the owners, Sol and Marvin Singer, sites for several months before the FID listing. I picked out a good site for them in FID and took them out there, but they didn't like it.

They were hard to please, but I kept showing them other sites. Each time they would turn one down, I would bring up FID. To me, it seemed like a perfect match.

Finally, they agreed and bought a site with frontage on I-20. Their new, efficient, one-story warehouse was their pride and joy. I kept in touch with them for many years after that, and they never stopped thanking me for being persistent. Their building is still there, but no longer used by Singer.

This transaction showed me that sometimes I understand a prospect's needs better than the prospect does himself.

THE JAIL SALE

Fulton County also owned an old, closed prison located on 154 acres on Fairburn Road in Ben Hill. When it was declared surplus, they asked me to sell it for them.

It was a granite building, built like a fortress. Rows of tiny, dark cells still had their rusty iron bars. An alternative use was hard to imagine.

After several months work, I had reached an impasse at finding someone who wanted to go into the jail business.

Directly across Fairburn Road from the prison was the office of a real estate developer, Ralph Eskew, who also happened to be one of Gene Garner's fishing buddies. Ralph contacted me – I had neglected the Spiral System and had not contacted him – and asked about the property. He wanted to open a private school. The county liked the idea and sold it to him for a good price, thereby making me the only real estate agent I have ever heard of who sold a jail. In addition to the Gresham Park transaction I handled for the Federal Prison System, and the former prison-farm land in Fulton Industrial District, the jail sale made three transactions involving "custodial properties."

Maybe I missed a good bet by not specializing in "custodial properties."

The fortress-like building is gone, and the exact location is hard to determine, but it looks like the site is now being used by Mount Calvary Baptist Church.

Coincidentally, Arlington School was built around the old jail on Fairburn Road, and was briefly attended by my children during the integration turmoil of the 1960's.

THE SOUTHERN RAILWAY ACQUISITIONS

Southern was the most progressive railroad serving Atlanta in the late 1950's. They had been working on a large assemblage in Gwinnett County, consisting of most of the land between Buford Highway and the then newly announced right-of-way for I-85, from Oakcliff Road up to Norcross-Tucker Road, now Jimmy Carter Boulevard. They became unhappy with the broker who started the assemblage for them, and called Adams-Cates to take over. Adams-Cates then turned the project over to me. It was like a jig-saw puzzle with several important pieces missing, and my job was to acquire the missing pieces.

The targeted area consisted of a multitude of small farms and small acreage tracts, five to 100 acres, owned by people who worked around Atlanta and enjoyed their homes in a rural atmosphere, with a sprinkling of old-timers who had farmed the land for several generations. This meant that I could only talk to them in the afternoons after they had come home from work, or in from the fields. Since this was before I-85 existed, the only way to get to the area from my office downtown was to go out Piedmont to Cheshire Bridge, then out Buford Highway to the Norcross area. Fighting afternoon traffic out from Atlanta and dealing with unwilling owners and their watch dogs when I got out there, made this one of my more difficult projects.

A fringe benefit was getting to meet and dine with Southern Railway officials in their luxurious private cars, with gourmet meals prepared by their own chefs.

I was able to acquire several of the puzzle's missing pieces and help Southern begin development of the district, which is now one of the largest industrial districts in Atlanta.

BUYERS IN THE SKY

Madras is a small community off U. S. 29 between Palmetto and Newnan. I had a listing there, an antebellum home with some acreage. This was a real antebellum home, not just a big white house with columns. A Delta pilot contacted me and bought it. He explained that as he would take off from Atlanta International Airport, he would bank to turn into his route, and as he banked he would be looking down on this property. He often thought about how wonderful it would be to own it, so when he saw my "For Sale" sign, he acted immediately.

ON THE MOVE

In the late 1950's, I began getting interested in sales management. I had learned that most sales managers were compensated by a 10% fee off the top of all commissions produced by their salesmen. It seemed to me that if I could manage ten salespeople who averaged earning as much as I did, then I could earn as much as I earn selling, and without the many ups and downs. Also, with more than 10 salesmen, I could be earning more than I earned selling.

Mr. Rob encouraged this interest, subscribing to a sales management magazine for me, and introducing me to the organization Sales and Marketing Executives of Atlanta. I suspect that he felt that someday I would succeed him as the sales manager at Adams-Cates. However, I grew impatient, and along came Hue Lee.

Hue Lee was a member of a very prominent, very wealthy Atlanta family, which owned a lot of real estate, and had roots in the Texas oil business. Several of the socially prominent salesmen at Adams-Cates knew him, and I had met him through them.

Hue had acquired a couple of small tracts of land in Cobb County, across the river from Fulton Industrial District. He had visions of another industrial park similar to FID, and asked me to help him acquire more land. I negotiated a few purchases for him along River Road, and we got to know each other fairly well. This assemblage formed the nucleus for Six Flags, which Hue subsequently sold to them without my help.

When Hue decided that he would like to open his own real estate company, he approached me to run it for him. I would be President and Sales Manager. In addition to his and his family's many land holdings, Hue also owned a building on Luckie Street downtown which he wanted to renovate for his new company's offices. The temptation was timely, and the opportunity was too great for me to resist, even though I was still very happy at Adams-Cates.

One of the most difficult tasks with which I have ever been confronted was telling Henry Robinson that I was leaving Adams-Cates. But I did, and Hue and I proceeded to open Tye Realty Company, a name chosen to honor his maternal grandmother.

Right away, my first job was to hire some salesmen. Since I was new at interviewing and hiring, I hired several good salesmen and several not-so-good salesmen. The best of the bunch, by far, was Warren Chilton. Warren and I worked together on numerous significant transactions, and through many difficult times, for 29 years.

I had very little time for personal production while getting Tye Realty Company up and running. However, one sale I did make was 64 acres on Woodland Brook Drive in Cobb County, owned by Hue's grandmother, Frania Tye Lee. The buyer was Dean Spratlin, a very active and prominent developer. The property was listed at $1,400 per acre. Dean offered $1,200, and Mrs. Lee countered at the asking price. Dean agreed to pay it, but then Mrs. Lee refused to take the listing price, instead demanding $1,600 per acre, $200 more than the asking price. After much negotiating, Dean finally agreed to buy the property for $1,600 per acre. This is the only property I recall selling for more than the listing price, although I have heard of other instances in which this happened. Dean Spratlin went on to develop Farmington on the property, still a beautiful riverside community.

Little did I suspect then that, 18 years later, I would buy a home in Farmington and live there happily for 20 years.

Hue Lee was a dreamer and a visionary. After about a year, I found that his dreams and visions were consuming too much of my time, and I did not necessarily share his enthusiasm for all of them. I had begun to suspect that I had not made a very good move in helping organize Tye Realty.

Sharp-Boylston Company, organized in 1881, was Georgia's second oldest Realtor, second only to Adair Realty Co. Sharp-Boylston had a property management department which managed over 3,500 residential units, and a large sales department. The company was owned by Cone Maddox, Jr., and Willie Cox. Their sales manager was Lamar Pierson.

Problems which I never understood weighed too heavily on Lamar, so he took his own life.

This left the commercial sales department without a leader, so Cone Maddox, Jr. and Willie Cox began searching for a replacement for Lamar Pierson. In those days, there were very strict rules and customs which prohibited proselytizing from a fellow Realtor company.

A gentleman named Harry Goodman, the owner of Goodman Decorating Co., was well known to all of us. I first met him and did business with him at Adams-Cates, and Cone and Willie had known him for many years. When Cone and Willie decided that they wanted to approach me about becoming Sharp-Boylston's sales manager, they circumvented the rules and got Harry Goodman to do it for them. Harry took me to lunch one day and asked me if I would consider switching to Sharp-Boylston and becoming their sales manager.

I liked the idea, and in 1962, I became Vice President and Sales Manager of Sharp-Boylston Company.

At that time, the only company in Georgia older that Sharp-Boylston was Adair Realty, which had been around since the Civil War. They had a commercial department, but their primary business was residential. Charlie Ackerman, a well-known commercial developer, wanted to get into the residential business, so he bought Adair as a diversification. But the residential business did not work out for Charlie, and he eventually closed Adair Realty. Since Sharp-Boylston had been second only to Adair in longevity, I then called Charlie and requested his permission to lay claim to Sharp-Boylston being Georgia's oldest Realtor. He gladly consented, and Sharp-Boylston then became Georgia's oldest Realtor.

In retrospect, I often wonder what would have happened if I had remained at Adams-Cates. Henry Robinson held the position of sales manager for many years after I left. Born in 1892, Mr. Rob served as a 1st Lieutenant of artillery in World War I, and since that war's end had always been prominent in business in Atlanta. He started with Adams-Cates in the year I was born, 1931. On his retirement, Adams-Cates tried many people in his position, but they all seemed to leave to go into business for themselves. I may have been able to hang in for a while in Henry Robinson's shoes, but I doubt that I could have remained after Adams-Cates was gobbled up by Grubb and Ellis. Who knows?

FLASHBACK

How did I get into this wonderful business in the first place? I distinctly remember two events which influenced my decision.

A house had sold, I believe somewhere near my Aunt Louise Flemister, on Darlington Circle. It sold very quickly. I happened to overhear Louise and my mother talking about the sale, and how the broker had made a fast $1,000. Now, $1,000 was a huge sum of money to a college boy who was making 50 cents an hour pumping gas (which then cost 23 cents per gallon) after school. To put that in perspective, I later paid $9 for the suit I was married in. (Actually, it was two for $18 from Steins at the corner of Peachtree Street and Auburn Avenue.)

My counselor at Georgia State (then called Atlanta Division, University of Georgia) was a Mr. Merrill. Shortly after the above house sale incident, Mr. Merrill grabbed me (literally) in the hall one day, and said, "Blackwell, you are almost a senior, and you have not selected your major. You need to do that right away."

With the above house sale in mind, but partly just to get him off my back, I said, "How about real estate?"

"Fine," he answered. "You are now a real estate major. Do you want a part-time job?"

"Why not?" I responded with enthusiasm. Anything would be better than pumping gas and changing tires.

We went to Mr. Merrill's office. He got out his yellow pages and looked under Real Estate. The first company listed was Adair Realty. He called Adair, but everybody was out to lunch. So he called the next listing, Adams-Cates, and everybody was out but one salesman, Bob Cline. Bob said to send me on over, and since Adams-Cates was right across the street from Georgia State, I walked right on over immediately, dressed in blue jeans and a wine-colored corduroy jacket, and needing a shave. I am sure of my appearance because I always looked like that at that particular time.

Bob Cline was an amiable, understanding person, but he had no decision-making authority, so he interviewed me briefly and made arrangements for me to come back later to see Henry Robinson, affectionately known in the real estate community as "Mr. Rob."

I do not know what Mr. Rob saw in me, because I did not have strong feelings about whether I got the job or not, had no resume, and never seriously tried to make a good impression. I had never applied for a job in my life, and really did not know how to go about it. Up to that point my summer jobs had always been with relatives, at my father's Amoco service station located at the corner of Bouldercrest Drive and Flat Shoals Road, Bill Flemister's Fulton Hardware on Peachtree Road, and Harry Barber's "country store" located at the corner of Powers Ferry Road and Mt. Paran Road. Bill and Harry were two of my many uncles.

But Henry Robinson hired me anyhow. I had classes at Georgia State in the morning, worked at Adams-Cates in the afternoons, and then more classes at night after work. My first responsibilities were to clean out the listing files (which had Ansley Park houses for $5,000 and less, some listed back in the 1930's), draw maps, and run errands. Mr. Rob saw to it that I got a license right away.

Unlike the extensive courses required today, there were no real estate licensing classes available at that time. My only preparation was to study a little brown pamphlet, published by the Georgia Real Estate Commission, on my own. One of the Georgia Real Estate Commissioners himself, who turned out to be an old friend of my family, graded the exam for me on the spot as I stood there after turning it in. My score was 96.

My first license was dated August 13, 1952.

I continued that schedule of alternating school and work until I graduated from Georgia State in June 1953. Two weeks after graduating, I was inducted into the Army. As mentioned above, Adams-Cates held my desk for me for the 21 months that I "fought" in the Korean War.

I will always, always, remember and be indebted to Henry Robinson.

CCIM

A fine gentleman, named John Correll, conducted a real estate school at Colony Square. John was very active in the National Association of Realtors (NAR). Occasionally he would ask me to teach one of his classes, which I always enjoyed, and earned a few extra bucks.

At that time, NAR was working on establishing a designation for Realtors, similar to the accountants' CPA, and the appraisers' MAI. Finally, the CCIM designation was created (Certified Commercial-Investment Member), and I was fortunate enough to be appointed one of 365 original CCIM's around the country.

Realtors have to complete a series of one-week courses in order to get the CCIM designation, so I had the privilege of teaching several courses in Washington DC, Boston, Kansas City, St. Petersburg, Fargo, Houston, Indianapolis, Reno, and Seattle. I enjoyed this until NAR started demanding that teachers accept more assignments than I could justify. I did not want to become a part-time Realtor, so I terminated my teaching activities.

A PARK ON THE RIVER

Atlanta Baptist Association owned a "retreat" on the Chattahoochee, a few hundred beautifully wooded acres off Roberts Road with long frontage on the river. It contained a large log building which had in times past been a retreat for former governor Herman Talmadge, and then later the Buckhead Century Club, a private club which served alcoholic beverages when liquor was illegal in the area, with gambling and all sorts of wild goings-on.

My good friend, Jack Baldwin, of Draper-Owens, and I happened to be on the Property Committee of the Atlanta Baptist Association when the National Park Service decided to acquire the property for a park. Jack and I represented the Association, pro bono, in the sale to the park service. This tract is now the Island Ford unit of the Chattahoochee River National Recreation Area. It contains several miles of hiking trails, and the old building is now the headquarters for the office which manages all of the parks along the river. Just as in the Gresham Park transaction, I did not make a commission on the deal but still consider it an important transaction because of the value of the park to the community.

THE ERA OF THE JOINT VENTURES AND ATLANTA REAL ESTATE ASSOCIATES, INC.

Beginning in the early 1960's, and continuing until 1972, Atlanta experienced a real estate phenomenon which we lovingly referred to as the "land boom." There was a feeding-frenzy among Atlanta investors to buy land. Any land, anywhere. People called us daily wanting to put $10,000 or $100,000 (a LOT of money back then) into a land investment.

Since a $10,000 land investment was hard to find, we would organize eight or ten of these investors into Joint Ventures, in which they became partners, with Sharp-Boylston as the manager. A typical investment might be ten people with $10,000 each investing in a tract of land in Morgan County which cost $500,000, and on which the seller would take back a purchase money mortgage of $400,000.

Joint ventures were much easier to organize then than now, because there was much less legal scrutiny then. We had a printed joint-venture form which we used. The only variables from one joint venture to another were the list of investors and the description of the land. The only paperwork involved in putting together one of these partnerships was to add a legal description of the property, and add a list of partners with their individual percentage interests. Attorneys were not involved in the organization phase, only in the closing phase.

At any given time, Sharp-Boylston would be managing 30 or 40 joint ventures actively holding land, with others in various stages of buying and selling.

The joint ventures were excellent investment vehicles, but they were inflexible. We encountered many investors with $3,000 to $5,000, as well as larger investors with several hundred thousand to spend. We hated to deny them an opportunity to invest in land, but it was difficult to work them into a joint venture. Occasionally an investor would need his money before the property sold, but the individual interests were not liquid, which could present another problem. A demand for a more flexible form of ownership was evident.

The answer was to organize a real estate investment corporation. Atlanta Real Estate Associates, Inc., which we called AREA, a good acronym, operated cleanly and profitably for many years. The corporate form of ownership gave us the flexibility of selling stock in any amount the investor wanted, and gave the investor the right to offer his stock for sale at any time. It also offered diversification, since AREA eventually owned over 20 properties all around the metro area, consisting of commercial lots, apartment sites, and outlying acreage, valued at several million dollars. Our largest stockholder was C & S Bank, along with its president, Mills B. Lane.

All booms eventually bust, and this one busted with an explosion heard around I-285. All of our properties were highly leveraged. I sensed the bust coming and began restricting the formation of new joint ventures and disposing of AREA's properties as quickly as I could. However, we still got caught with too much land and too little money to make loan payments, and had to deed two tracts, one in Newton County and one in Hall, back to the former owners. The value of the land had declined below the amount of the mortgage. Each joint venture would be dissolved as soon as its investment was sold, and AREA spent the last several years of its existence managing its properties and selling them off one at a time until all were gone.

THE WASHBURN FARM

The primary significance of the Washburn Farm was its size, over 1,000 acres. This Morgan County tract was the Washburn family home place, and was a beautiful tract of gently rolling farm land with long frontage on Hard Labor Creek. Over half was open land, either pasture or cultivated, and the rest was heavily wooded. Atlanta Real Estate Associates acquired this land in a transaction which involved issuing a large block of AREA stock to the Washburns, along with some cash and a note.

AREA held the tract for a few years and sold it to a partnership which had been organized by a local law firm. In this sale, AREA took back a large mortgage as part of the price. This mortgage went into default after a couple of years because of a recession and declining values, so we re-claimed the property by foreclosure. Going through the foreclosure process was a real educational experience for me, culminating with my standing on the courthouse steps in Madison, asking for bids from non-existent bidders, and in effect buying the property back for AREA.

AREA sold it again shortly thereafter, and I hope the buyer did well with it. Counting the foreclosure, we sold those 1,000 acres four times.

(It was on this property that I experienced my first attack by a small pack of wild dogs. My son, Tommy, and I had hauled our trail bikes down there for a ride on the Morgan County dirt roads, and thru the woods. When we returned to load the bikes on the trailer, the dogs attacked as a team. They wanted us for lunch. I had to shoot two of them to protect our lives).

THE RUTLEDGE INTERCHANGE

Another interesting tract in Morgan County was the Rutledge Interchange. Even though it was a long way from Atlanta, I was fascinated by this opportunity to control all four corners of an I-20 interchange. Rutledge and Newborn are small communities near I-20, and I assume that the interchange was built to serve Rutledge, Newborn, and Hard Labor Creek State Park, which is one of the largest state parks in Georgia. The land had long frontage on four other good roads in addition to I-20. The main road crossing I-20 is Rutledge-Newborn Road.

Atlanta Real Estate Associates acquired the property by becoming the managing partner in a joint venture, bringing in several partners, assuming an existing loan, and issuing a large block of stock to the seller for part of the price. The brokers even took stock for their commissions. AREA used no cash for this purchase. This transaction epitomized the flexibility of a real estate investment corporation.

Our objective was not to re-sell the property intact, but to divide it into several parcels. We envisioned service stations and motels on each corner, but that never happened while we owned it. However, we did profitably dispose of the tract through five separate sales over a period of several years, the final sale being to my old friend and former associate, Charles Cobb.

THE C & S LISTINGS

C & S Bank was possibly the most active bank in Atlanta in financing real estate investments and development. They had a very fine real estate department, but when the bust was at its worst, they were foreclosing on land faster than the properties could be assimilated into the department. They did not have enough time or people to really know what they had.

Once they thought they had foreclosed on 20 acres in Monroe, but on our inspection, it turned out to be seven acres.

On another tract in Roswell, we found that they had foreclosed on only a 1/2 interest in the property, and had a partner they did not even know existed. They depended on brokers to dispose of the properties, but since the bank did not know much about the properties, they could not provide adequate information to brokers.

Without good information, it is tough to make a sale. Without exclusive listings, brokers were reluctant to do the research necessary to properly market the properties. So the properties were not selling as rapidly as C & S would like, and kept piling up in the real estate department. Numerous brokers requested exclusive listings, but the bank refused them all.

Despite that all of our competing Realtors were being shot down, I would have been negligent if I had not given it a try for Sharp-Boylston. But my efforts would certainly have been futile if my presentation did not have something which the competitors lacked.

The typical listing presentation enumerates all the many things a good Realtor does – advertising, brochures, information packages, signs, and a lot of hard work. My presentation differed in one way – I promised NOT to put up any signs. The implications of this were immediately obvious to the C & S officials. Sharp-Boylston would not be able to put up a bunch of signs and then just sit back and wait for people to call. We would have to get out and work if we wanted to make sales.

They liked that, and gave us more exclusive listings than I can remember. At one time, we had 21 C & S listings on foreclosed land. This arrangement worked extremely well for C & S and Sharp-Boylston for many years, until the market turned up again and all the properties were sold.

BUYING SHARP-BOYLSTON

In my ninth year at Sharp-Boylston, the president of the company, Cone Maddox, Jr., died suddenly.

His partner, Willie Cox, became full owner of the company. He immediately offered Cone's 50% to me and a few other salesmen. Willie even worked out 100% financing for us at First National Bank.

A couple of years later, Willie saw that we could run the company satisfactorily, and sold us his remaining 50%. From this point on, company administrative duties, plus my sales management responsibilities, cut deeply into the amount of time available for personal production.

THE 21-YEAR EXCLUSIVE LISTING

One soon learns in the real estate business that things don't always work out as we expect them to.

Jonesboro-McDonough Associates was a joint venture which I helped organize to acquire 78 acres on Jonesboro Street in McDonough, at a Southern Railroad crossing. It was two blocks from downtown McDonough, was zoned industrial, had a big old white-columned "colonial" home on it which produced some rent, and seemed to have all the requisites of a good investment. Since I was the managing partner, I was also the exclusive agent responsible for its sale. We bought it in 1971, just before the bust, then struggled through a very inactive land speculation market and 15 years of mortgage payments, eventually holding it for 21 years until its sale in 1992.

For the record, I would like to emphasize here that most of my listings sold much quicker than 21 years.

CANTERBURY LANE-- SALE #1

Since my administrative and sales management duties did allow much time for personal production, I decided to work on land sales and apartment complexes. Activity in the apartment market eventually led me to Steve Vasen.

After representing Steve in a couple of satisfactory apartment transactions, he asked me to investigate the availability of a particular complex on Cobb Parkway. Several months of intensive negotiations came to naught, and it became apparent that we would not be able to acquire that property. However, working with him had given me a very good idea of what he wanted, so I immediately began investigating other properties on Cobb Parkway near Marietta.

This led me to Pine Forest, a 500-unit complex near the intersection of Cobb Parkway and Roswell Street – just south of and across from the Big Chicken. The one story apartments had been built in the 1940's to house employees at Bell Bomber Plant, now Lockheed.

Pine Forest was owned by a Los Angeles investment group, and was managed by some of their Atlanta associates. I always prefer face-to-face contact over using the telephone, so I dropped in their office on the site and asked if they would consider selling. The local people said that it was not for sale, but they would contact the L.A. headquarters, and let me know. They called me a few days later and asked me to come back to see them.

They then proceeded to give me more information than I had hoped for on income and expenses, along with a very useful aerial photograph. Then they gave me a price which I thought was too far out of line to put us within negotiating distance. Steve thought so, too, but he was interested enough to make an offer anyhow.

He prepared an offer which was a long way from the quoted price. Then he asked me to take – not mail – it to Los Angeles personally to submit it. If it had been closer to the quoted price, I would have been glad to go, but considering the wide spread between the two figures, I much preferred to mail it. Steve strongly encouraged me to go in person and offered to pay my way, so I went.

The offer was better received than I anticipated, and I came back with a pretty good counter offer. We went back and forth a few times, and Steve eventually bought Pine Forest for a little over $8,000,000. That was a huge sale back then.

Steve Vasen turned out to be one of the most knowledgeable, honorable, and dependable people I ever met. We worked together on numerous transactions until I started slowing down and got out of the apartment brokerage business. An important lesson I learned from Steve was that there would be a point in each transaction at which the most valuable service I could render would be to get out of his way and let him run with it. I did that many times with no worry whatsoever about the commission.

PRESIDENT OF ATLANTA BOARD OF REALTORS

Being president of the Board in 1972 was not a transaction, but was a big decision, and required a considerable commitment of my time and energy. I had never sought any position at the Board, but had first been elected Treasurer, and then Vice President. I suspect that Cone Maddox had been working behind the scenes on my behalf. When informed that I had been nominated to be president, I instinctively did what I learned later was always done by all presidential nominees, that is, be sure that Tommie Jackson would be there.

Tommie literally "ran" the board. There is no way that a busy Realtor could have taken on that responsibility without her. It was a very rewarding experience and I shall forever be indebted to Tommie for her guidance, and to my fellow Realtors who nominated and worked with me through 1972.

The year 1971, while Emerson Holleman was president, was spent defending the Board from litigation by the federal government claiming that we were guilty of price-fixing by having a recommended schedule of commissions. They were right, but we did it with good intentions. My first official action as 1972 president was to sign the consent decree with the feds, on which Emerson had toiled for a full year. From that day on, commissions became negotiable, each company setting its own schedule without any input from the Board or from other Realtors.

Every Board president has some crisis during his administration. Mine involved a practice called "blockbusting" and Governor Jimmy Carter.

In 1972, Atlanta's residential neighborhoods were very strictly segregated racially. Several individuals of questionable business scruples developed the practice called "blockbusting," in which they would go into a particular neighborhood, buy one house for investment purposes, and then rent it to a family which was not racially harmonious with the other residents. This would then usually cause panic selling, and prices would plummet, thereby enabling the investor to buy several more houses at greatly reduced prices.

When the Atlanta news media picked up on this, they condemned the investors as "realtors." "Realtor" is a term which can be used only by members of a Board of Realtors, such as the Atlanta Commercial Board of Realtors, and technically should be spelled REALTORS, all caps. Governor Carter quickly jumped on the bandwagon, condemning those dastardly "realtors." We were beginning to look pretty bad in the public's eye.

As president and spokesman for the board, it was my responsibility to implement damage control and defuse the embarrassing situation. I dashed off a letter to the Atlanta Journal and Constitution, explaining that they and Jimmy Carter were using the term incorrectly, and that the blockbusters were not Realtors, but instead were individual investors. They obligingly published my letter, which caused the local television stations to contact me for information. I was interviewed on the sidewalk in front of Sharp-Boylston's office and appeared on the afternoon local television news shows. Soon thereafter, Governor Carter also issued a statement recognizing the difference between Realtors and the blockbusters.

A second crisis arose when the Georgia House of Representatives introduced legislation which would make it illegal for a real estate broker to draw up, or negotiate changes in a contract for the sale of real estate. Only attorneys would have been authorized to perform this service. This legislation had already been passed in some other states. Board Past-President Ed Isaacson, founder and president of Northside Realty and father of our Senator Johnny Isaacson, was a close friend of Lt. Governor Lester Maddox, so Ed, Executive Vice President Tommie Jackson, several other members of the Board, and I went down to see Lt. Governor Maddox and enlist his aid in killing the bill. We met with him on the floor of the House while it was in session, and he agreed to help. Shortly thereafter, the legislation was killed.

Any broker who complains about his Board of Realtors dues should remember this and thank the Board that he does not have to retain a lawyer every time he prepares or changes a contract. I understand that this legislation was subsequently repealed in the other states which had already adopted it.

THE CASH REAL ESTATE FUNDS

The bust in the land investment market which started in 1972-73 soon spread to all other types of real estate. Office buildings, retail buildings, industrial buildings, houses, and apartments were all grossly overbuilt. Bankruptcies and foreclosures ran rampant. The situation was exacerbated by a coinciding general economic recession.

Most of our joint ventures mentioned in the "land boom" discussion owed large mortgages. All of these were loans taken back by the sellers as part of the price. Payments on these loans were usually made on an annual basis. The manager would contact all of his partners before the due date and collect from each his proportionate share of the mortgage payment. This worked well for many years, until the bust came.

If a joint venture manager had 10 or 15 partners and one of those partners could not or would not make his payment, then the manager had the extremely unpleasant chore of either finding the money somewhere else or re-negotiating the loan payment terms.

As property values declined, sometimes to a point less than the mortgages, and as business conditions worsened, delinquent partners became more and more common. Since I had organized and managed several joint ventures, I spent a very large amount of my time correcting these situations for several years, from 1973 until about 1980. Also, as some Sharp-Boylston associates would leave the real estate business for greener fields during those hard times, I inherited many of their problem properties. I received no pay for this unexpected responsibility, except a commission when the property eventually sold. It was just a part of the manager's job, but a part which we had not anticipated. With business in the doldrums, I needed to spend as much time as possible with my sales management and administrative duties at Sharp-Boylston, and in working on new transactions, not correcting old mistakes and chasing down delinquent partners.

Just as alcohol and gunpowder do not mix, I decided that there are two other things which do not mix – partners and mortgages, particularly when the investment is vacant land with no income. I vowed never again to set up a joint venture in which the partners would have to be called on to contribute to the mortgage payment. This virtually eliminated me from the joint venture part of the real estate investment field for a few years, and since I had also taken an active part as a principal in most of the partnerships, it also curtailed my activities as an investor.

But business got better. I started seeing more opportunities to invest in land. Investors started coming to me, wanting me to include them in any partnership I might set up, and I became eager to resume my own investment program. I began giving serious thought to a new form of investment group which could have some advantages which would offset the loss of leverage. The answer was the four groups which came to be known as Cash Real Estate Funds 1, 2, 3, and 4, Ltd.

Legal work in setting up the Funds was handled by Jim Ney and his very competent crew at Holt, Ney, Zatcoff, and Wasserman. They also provided some of the investors. Partnership law had become too complicated to use our old standard forms.

We raised enough money from 20 or 30 investors so that each fund could pay cash for two or three properties. Owning more than one property provided diversification which the old joint ventures did not have. Furthermore, we were able to buy properties at much lower prices because we paid cash and closed quickly – often as quickly as 10 or 20 days. When the investment was ultimately sold, the profit would be distributed to the partners, and the original principal would be reinvested in another tract of land. This way, in its lifetime each Fund would buy and sell eight or ten properties, but would never own over three at one time.

All four Cash Real Estate Funds have run their courses and have been dissolved. When CREF 4 sold its last property, eight acres on Maxham Road in Cobb County, we had to take back a mortgage as part of the price. In less than a year, this mortgage went into default, so we foreclosed to get the property back, but we picked up some cash in the process. The Maxham Road tract immediately re-sold at a higher price, with no financing involved. This was my last sale as a broker. Coincidentally, both buyers were churches.

These four partnerships were organized in 1981 through 1985. When I suspected that business would slow down considerably in the late 1980's, I stopped organizing and started concentrating on liquidating their holdings until all were sold.

CANTERBURY LANE—SALE #2

Steve Vasen held Pine Forest for several years, and changed the name to Canterbury Lane. He is a good property manager, and the 502 units thrived under his control. But Cobb County was growing so fast that the demographics finally began to indicate that there may be a better use for the land than apartments.

Warren Chilton had been working on other transactions with another broker who was trying to find sites in the area for Wal-Mart and Sams. Warren showed them the merits of the Canterbury site, and they became interested.

We finally worked out a sale of 400 of the 502 units, taking all of the Cobb Parkway frontage, for a price in excess of $20,000,000.

The closing began at 10:00 one morning and ended at 4:30 the next morning. It was held in a large conference room of a law firm in the Rhodes-Haverty Building (now condominiums). At one time, Steve and I stepped out of the room to stretch our legs, and, looking back, counted 23 people still in the closing room, 14 of whom were lawyers.

SALE OF SHARP-BOYLSTON

Around 1984, I began to see indications that the real estate business was changing significantly. We were having more and more difficulties in competing with the large national firms which were moving into Atlanta. Once when I had made a presentation to represent a large industrial concern, I was told, "No thank you. We are a big company, and we want to do business with big companies."

Again, when we were trying to get an exclusive listing on a property owned by a company with headquarters in Los Angeles, we were aced out by Coldwell-Banker because they sent a person from their Los Angeles office to, in effect, walk over to the company's headquarters and make a personal presentation to get the listing. Coldwell-Banker was new in Atlanta, but they had well established branches all over the country.

I was also beginning to feel burned out and worn out after 25 years of hiring, firing, training, coordinating, and trying to motivate a sales force of 15 to 20 salespeople.

Warren Chilton and I had discussed selling the company off and on for several months. At this time, Warren and I had bought out all the other stockholders and owned 50% each. Finally, in 1986, we agreed that the time was right. We figured out what we thought Sharp-Boylston was worth, made a list of four possible buyers, and the first person we offered it to, Richard Felker, bought it.

Richard was a very active apartment owner, syndicator, and manager. For several years I had made numerous attempts to sell something to him or for him, all to no avail. The only transaction I ever made with Richard was to sell him Sharp-Boylston Co. I have often regretted that it did not work out as well as he had hoped. At this writing, that fine old company, established in 1881, is no longer active in the brokerage business.

FREDDIE MAC

The real estate market was in another recession when I left Sharp-Boylston in 1990. Land sales had dried up, and the vast majority of apartment sales were on the courthouse steps. Vacancies had risen to the point that very few apartment complexes were producing enough income to pay the mortgage. Investors who admitted to being "vultures" soon swarmed in to pick up distressed properties.

The largest owner of distressed properties in Atlanta soon became Federal Home Loan Mortgage Corporation, better known as Freddie Mac. At one point in the early '90's Freddie Mac had acquired, by foreclosure, 80 complexes containing 10,000 units. As C & S had found in the 1970's, Freddie Mac was taking back properties so fast that they did not know what they had.

Their favorite broker was Coldwell-Banker, the "bigness loves bigness" syndrome. C-B got dozens of listings while the rest of us were left begging at the door. Nevertheless, I continued to try to represent Freddie Mac, which had become Atlanta's largest apartment owner. Fellow Realtor Tom Body had an office around the corner from mine in the Atlanta Board of Realtors building, and had also been trying to get some Freddie Mac business. Meanwhile, another friend and former associate at Sharp-Boylston, Ernie Eden, had gone to work for Freddie Mac. Ernie tipped me off one day that FM may be reconsidering its stand on listings, and that maybe I should make another approach. Feeling that Tom Body and I as a team may make a better impression, we made a joint presentation, and were awarded several FM listings.

Some of these listings were nice properties in good areas, but most were so bad that I would not enter them un-armed, and preferred to be in a group. A few really bad complexes had only 10% to 20% of their units occupied. In spite of roof leaks, vandalized units, drug busts, sewage back-ups, rotten carpets, and termite destruction, we sold them.

Tom Body once got caught in the middle of a drug bust while showing a Freddy Mac complex in southwest Atlanta, complete with running suspects, screaming sirens, and police cars skidding into the parking lot from all directions.

I once had to ask a group of prospects to leave a building on Martin Luther King Jr. Drive when I realized that it was in such bad shape due to termite damage that it might collapse at any moment.

Before the market improved and FM got out of the apartment ownership business, I was involved in the sale of 17 of their complexes, totaling 1,656 units. (Thanks, Ernie)

Cox and Hippensteel Tracts

These two land transactions are significant only because of their size, over $1,000,000 each. (Not much now, but a really big sale back then).

From 1964 to 1980, my family lived on Broadland Court in Buckhead. During most of these years, a gentleman named Cox, who called himself our egg man, would come by once a week and leave us several dozen good, fresh eggs. Four kids eat a lot of eggs. These eggs came from Mr. Cox's own chickens on his farm in north Fulton County. He would also frequently bring us sausage and fresh vegetables. After selling that house and moving to Vinings, I lost track of Mr. Cox.

One day in 1994, I received a phone call from a gentleman who said, "Marion, this is Ernest Cox. Do you remember me?" I didn't. He reminded me, "I used to be your egg man." Right away, I remembered him well.

Ernest Cox went on to tell about a tract of land he and his wife, Mildred, owned on Jones Bridge Road outside Alpharetta. He asked if I would be interested in selling it for him. Of course, I definitely was very interested. We went on to enter into the first of a long chain of exclusive listing agreements which stretched through an extended period of very slow development and sewer moratoriums in north Fulton. Ernest and Mildred eventually passed away and I continued to work with their son, Dr. Jerry Cox, until finding a buyer for the land.

Why did Ernest Cox call me after 14 years and why did he and his family allow me to represent them for several years until the property was sold? It was because my great grandfather, Rev. Sanford Blackwell, of what was then Boiling Springs Baptist Church, performed the ceremony when Ernest and Mildred were married in the early 1900's.

This property is now covered with one-story apartments for seniors.

Ms. Bobbie Hippensteel is a charming lady who owned a tract of land on Hickory Grove Road in Cobb County, near Acworth. This was a very desirable tract with long frontage on two roads, and on the CSX railroad. It was zoned industrial.

One of the Cash Real Estate Funds had bought and sold a nearby tract located at the corner of Hickory Grove Road and Baker Road. I had a for sale sign on the property during the marketing period. Ms. Hippensteel saw my name and number on the sign and in 1990 called me about selling her land. This was an attractive, interesting tract, but Ms. Hippensteel did not want to grant an exclusive listing, and I would not work on an open listing, so we just kept in touch with each other for several years. Finally, we reached an agreement and I began working seriously on the property in 1996.

I had numerous inquiries from developers who wanted a residential tract, but the price was too high for residential use. Without neglecting residential developers, I tried to concentrate my marketing on industrial and commercial users.

Several offers and contracts did not work out because of a variety of reasons, including zoning and market fluctuations.

In 2000, we finally found a buyer who appreciated all of the good points of the property and closed the sale.

While working as a real estate sales manager, I would often learn from my salesmen as much as I taught them. From two of our top producers at Sharp-Boylston, Warren Chilton and John Binns, I learned this very productive method: find a good property, develop a close relationship with the owner, and then just hang in there until it sells, no matter how long it takes.

5800 Maxham Road, Austell

This transaction is significant because it was my last listing. The property was 8.4 acres, zoned commercial. However, commercial was not its highest and best use. Demographic changes and several zoning denials caused us to have to hold this tract entirely too long. It was bought by Cash Real Estate Fund 4 in 1989 and finally sold to a church on Nov. 30, 2004. Unfortunately, the church had made a bad business decision and could not keep up the loan payments. After trying to help them every way we could, we finally had to foreclose in March, 2006. I resold it to another church in June, 2006, this time for cash. We collected rent on the property for almost its entire holding period, and made a reasonable profit on the sale. This transaction ended my brokerage career.

MISCELLANEOUS MEMORIES, LESSONS LEARNED, AND INTERESTING CHARACTERS

Late one hot afternoon at Adams-Cates, I received a phone call from a man who wanted to see a 227-acre farm on Redwine Road in south Fulton. Since I lived in south DeKalb at that time, I was not very interested in going in the opposite direction late in the day, and the caller had such a strong, almost back-woods accent that I doubted that he could afford 227 acres. But I agreed to meet him anyhow, and as soon as I drove up to the meeting place in Ben Hill, I saw the error of my ways.

He was in a chauffeur driven, black Cadillac limousine. He was Charlie Bales from Alabama, whose business was organizing and selling life insurance companies. He had the first car phone I ever saw, and used it to buy an airplane while we were driving along. He also bought the farm. Lesson: qualify, but don't pre-judge, your prospects. Incidentally, he bought the farm to use as a private orphanage.

* * *

Ewell Pope entered the real estate business with Adams-Cates shortly before I returned from the Army, after he had recovered from serious wounds received in Korea. A well-known Georgia Tech football star with a great brain and a winning personality, he hit the ground running and was an immediate success. We worked together several months selling foreclosed houses in Chamblee. They had been sitting open and neglected so long that their floors were very badly warped. Once I asked him, "What are we going to say to people about these floors?" He quickly replied, "Notice the modern wavy effect of the floors."

Ewell later went into business with Frank Carter and eventually left brokerage for development, building shopping centers and office buildings from Atlanta to Hong Kong, a far cry from selling $8,000 houses in Chamblee.

* * *

Ms. Smith was a tall, attractive, very well constructed woman of about 35, who wore her long black hair down to her waist. She owned one of those fine big old houses that used to line Ponce de Leon Avenue, a relic of the early 1900's. She called me one day at Adams-Cates about a small commercial building I was offering for sale. I showed her that building but it did not fit her needs, so I watched out for other properties which would suit her better. Another building came up which I thought might fit, so I called her and made an appointment to pick her up at her house.

I arrived at the appointed hour and her housekeeper answered the door, then directed me down the hall to the first room on the right, which I assumed would be her office. Wrong. There I found Ms. Smith waiting for me in bed, dressed in a skin-tight leopard skin leotard-like outfit. I think she could tell by my startled expression that she had gotten her appointments mixed up.

"Oh," she exclaimed, "I'll be ready in just a minute."

Soon she met me in the living room, properly dressed for looking at real estate. "How are you, Ms. Smith," I asked as if nothing unusual had happened.

"My name is Taylor now," she replied. "I got married over the weekend."

"Well, then, how are you, Ms. Taylor?"

"You can still call me Ms. Smith," she answered offhandedly. "I don't think it's going to last."

I never did make a deal, of any kind, with Ms. Smith-Taylor.

* * *

Tromping around over land listings involved certain hazards. Wild dogs are a serious problem in the outer areas of Atlanta. Two Sharp-Boylston salesmen were once set upon by a pack of about 20 dogs while walking land, and barely made it back to their car. I have personally been attacked three times by wild dogs, and once got away only by shooting the dogs. I always carry a pistol when walking in the woods, and in vacant buildings.

* * *

At one time we controlled so much land that the only efficient way to keep up with it was to ride over it frequently on my motorcycle, usually with my favorite riding companion, my son, Tommy. On a nice clear summer day, it was easy to convince myself that this was real estate work.

* * *

Frank Gordy was the founder and owner of the Varsity. While showing him some land once, with Charles Cobb, he made a statement which I will always remember and which shaped a lot of my financial planning: "One good investment is worth a lifetime of work."

* * *

AGREE, Association of Georgia Real Estate Exchangers, has always been an important source of business. While AGREE's objective is to encourage exchanges, sales probably outnumber exchanges by 10 to one. When I had a lot of listings, which was usually the case, I felt that I could not afford to miss an AGREE meeting.

* * *

The best part of my career was the period at Sharp-Boylston while I was sales manager, before I took over the responsibilities of president. I made more money and enjoyed the work more then than any other period. When I became president, I think I was a good example of the "Peter Principle," that is, I had risen to a level at which I was not competent. I was a very good sales manager, but a mediocre president.

* * *

Crucial to the success of any person or organization is a capable and understanding office staff. These are people whom you can depend on to be there every day, who understand the pressures of real estate, and don't take it personally when you are not polite, and who cover up your many errors without making a big deal of it. Georgia Campbell at Adams-Cates handled the whole sales department single handed – and that was in the days of carbon paper and no copying machines. I inherited two of the finest, Doris Duke and Trinette Hite, when I joined Sharp-Boylston, but neither of these two wonderful ladies ever worked directly for me. Polly Archer was one of my first personal secretaries. She had known me since I was six years old, and knew me so well that she anticipated almost everything I wanted or needed (like Radar on *M*A*S*H*). Glenease Sutton and Helen Williamson were the epitome of dependability, and

Debbie Spicer brought sunshine into the office every time she walked in the door.

* * *

One of the most satisfying transactions I ever worked out came as a direct result of having an office in the Atlanta Board of Realtors Building on Lake Forrest Drive in Sandy Springs.

After losing my wife, Virginia, to cancer in 1996, I became very depressed and lonesome. Dating assorted ladies was not for me – since I had been so happy with Virginia. I wanted to settle down again with someone in a permanent relationship.

Kevin Latty is a stock broker who also had an office in the Atlanta Board of Realtors Building, right around the corner from mine. I had known Kevin since he was a kid, and enjoyed renewing our old friendship.

One day I dropped in Kevin's office and asked, "Kevin, I'm lonesome as hell. Don't you know some nice lady you can introduce me to?"

"I just might" was his thoughtful answer.

Kevin and his wife, Ann, then introduced me to an old friend of theirs from Florida, Terry Hunter. Terry was a magazine editor for the Atlanta Journal-Constitution while she worked on her master's degree at Georgia State. She and I immediately became very close friends, and were married the next year. This was the best deal of all!

...and in conclusion...

I don't know anything I would have rather been over 54 years than a real estate salesman and administrator, for two primary reasons. First, I made more money than I ever dreamed I would make. This enabled me to raise my family in a style which we never thought possible, and has provided me with a certain degree of security as I step into another career as a writer. Even though I have preached setting goals all my life, my earnings for the first several years so amazed me that I became afraid to limit myself with a goal, and stopped goal setting after about 10 years.

The second reason is the freedom and flexibility afforded by a sales position in which you are your own boss. I enjoyed doing what I was in the mood to do, such as work late or take off early, get on the phone or get out and make personal contacts, take off for a tennis match or ride trail bikes with my son, Tommy, and schedule vacations without having to ask a boss.

I have never considered myself a good salesman, but have felt that I was more a problem solver. True, sales techniques often entered into it, but it was usually just to get a person to do what was best for him anyhow (Yes! I like that).

It was a great 54 years, but would not have been so great without all you family members, friends, associates, office staff, fellow Realtors, clients, and attorneys.

* * *

Most of the above was written from memory and from my personal files, with a minimum of research. Some readers may note slight errors in amounts or dates. They would certainly note a lot more errors in grammar, spelling, and syntax if it were not for my excellent in-house editor, my dear wife Terry, who encouraged me to write this.

END

TAKE A HIKE

Walking in the woods is one of my greatest outdoor pleasures. A favorite walk is about 4.75 miles on the trails in Palisades East, which is one of the Chattahoochee River parks. Every time I take this walk, I marvel at the fact that such an interesting, natural, almost pristine tract of land is only 9.5 miles from the center of Atlanta, and fifteen minutes from my home. On a walk there last spring, wildflowers and dogwood were blooming, birds were singing, and it was a great day to be in the woods. I crossed several little creeks which feed into the river, and followed the river itself for much of the hike. Saw two king snake babies, and a bamboo grove with plants five inches in diameter and twenty or thirty feet tall. One winter I even came upon a herd of five or six deer, just barely outside the Atlanta city limit.

Here are a few suggestions to make your walks in the woods easy and pleasant. This refers to day hiking, as opposed to camping out. I can spend all day in the woods, but when night comes I want a nice bed and a bathroom, and a bug-proof and bear-proof shelter.

PREPARATION

Let's start at the bottom – your feet. No matter how great the scenery, aching feet will spoil any good hike (done that). Your regular street socks won't do. Get good hiking socks or tennis socks. Then choose the right shoes. Tennis shoes or walking shoes will work well on paved trails such as Silver Comet, but you need more traction and tougher soles for a good walk in the woods. Hiking boots will keep you from turning your ankle on roots and rocks, provide more traction on steep or slick trails, and keep your feet dry if you ford a creek, or get caught in a shower. These boots will be your only expensive investment, but a good pair will last several years.

Carefully trim your toenails. A rough or long toenail can make an adjoining toe very painful after a few hours of rubbing.

Be sure you take enough equipment to handle any situation if you are going to be in the woods for several hours. Equipment varies with the individual and the length of time on the trail. I carry plenty of water, food, a stout stick, map, cell phone, band aids, mole skin, petroleum jelly, compass, magnifying glass, poncho, toilet paper, heart pills, knee braces (2), loud whistle, camera, and sometimes a pistol. The shorter the hike, the less stuff you may need. The only item on this list which I have never used is the whistle.

A good staff is extremely important, and gets more important with age. My staff is useful for discouraging aggressive dogs or people, keeping my balance while crossing creeks on rocks, support on steep hills and very rough trails, and beating back briars when I leave the trail to explore something interesting.

I made this staff myself – well, God made it, I cut and carved it. It is four feet, two inches long, one inch thick, and strong as steel. It was a young maple tree on some woods I owned in Rabun County.

I have never been lost, but a good map will help decide which trail to take at intersections, and can be a big help in a strange area.

A cell phone would be useful in an emergency, such as an ankle sprain. I sometimes call home when I am at a particularly beautiful spot which I want to share with Terry, my wife. I don't mind getting calls in the woods, I like to tell the callers where I am. Of course, many wooded areas are out of range of a cell phone tower.

I occasionally have problems with my knees, especially after walking downhill for a long distance. Once I was up on a ridge on Black Rock Mountain in Rabun County when both knees became extremely painful, and I had a very unpleasant experience coming down off that ridge. Ever since then, I pack two elastic strap-on knee braces.

The compass is just to help orient a map, and occasionally to be sure I am going in the right direction. I seldom use it, but you never know. The sun is also a good direction indicator, except around noon.

Wildflowers can be tiny, so a magnifying glass helps you appreciate them, and helps study rocks for fossils.

Ponchos are useful in an unexpected shower, and can be used as a ground cover when you stop for a break – keeps chiggers off.

The whistle is another item used only in emergencies. If you are injured or lost and need help, you can yell just so long and then your voice will give out, but you could whistle for hours. Get a loud one, available at sporting goods stores.

A camera adds a lot of weight, but every time I go off without one I see something worth photographing. A cell phone camera may be a good substitute.

Most of you would rather not go anywhere if a pistol might be needed, but every now and then I get so far out away from civilization that I take it, just in case. There are lots of wild dogs in the woods when you get out in the fringe counties. I have been attacked by wild dogs three times, but only had to use the piston twice, and only had to shoot once. Packs of wild dogs have actually attacked and killed people in Georgia.

City people take unwanted pets out to the "country" and turn them loose. Their atavistic nature takes over, and they learn to hunt and kill, or go hungry.

We have all seen news about unlucky hikers who encountered predator people on the trail. I will not let predators scare me out of the woods.

I hate to say, "I told you so," but for several years now I have been warning people about coyotes. As they invade more areas and get more accustomed to people, their fear of people will wane. In the Atlanta Journal-Constitution of Oct. 29, 2009, there was an article about coyotes in eastern Canada attacking and killing a lady hiker.

Bears are scarce and will usually run from people. I have had four bear "encounters." On Stonewall Creek in Rabun I came upon a bear skeleton, which only confirmed that there were bears in the area. In the same general area I was startled once when something dashed across the trail about 200 feet ahead of me. I confirmed that it was a bear by its hand-sized tracks in the trail. On the same trail, I once discovered that a bear and I were eating from the same huckleberry patch. He stood up about 30 feet from me and just stared. I stared back, even though I know that staring is rude. I considered introducing myself, but decided against it. Finally, I turned at a right angle so as not to provoke an attack, and he quickly bolted into the woods.

The fourth encounter was on a ridge near the town of Blue Ridge. I came upon a large pile of bear poop right in the middle of the trail. It was still warm, so I just "bearly" missed the pooper.

If you decide to take a pistol on your hikes, be sure you know how to use it, get a license, and be mentally prepared to pull the trigger if you need to, which I hope you never do.

I have recently switched from bottled water to a plastic water bag which is stored in my back-pack. A tube runs from the bag to a clip which holds the tube just over my shoulder. It is much easier to get to than a water bottle, and encourages you to sip water as you walk along. Also, I often lost my water bottles when climbing cliffs or crawling through mountain laurel thickets.

Think about whether you like to walk alone or with one or more companions. It's interesting, and sometimes safer, to be with other people, but then you have the burden or organizing a trip that fits everyone. I like solitude when I'm in the woods. Then I can start, eat, think, admire, rest, answer nature's calls, and quit whenever I want to.

Don't underestimate the amount of time it will take to get in and out of the woods. You don't want to be trying to find your way back to the car in the dark (done that). Dense woods get dark quickly, sometimes when there is still plenty of light outside.

Summer or winter, both have advantages. In winter, you don't have to worry about ticks, chiggers, poison ivy, gnats, or poisonous snakes. When the undergrowth dies out it is easier to leave the trails and follow creeks or just strike out through the woods. In summer, you have more color, more daylight time, and more foliage for shade and to screen you when nature calls. Be sure to use and carry a good insect spray with deet. Apply it to your hat as well as your body. Avoid brushing any leaves – they may harbor ticks or chiggers, or may be poison ivy. Don't sit down on a pine log for the same reason (done that). In late summer and early fall you can enjoy blackberries, huckleberries, persimmons, and muscadines – yum!

Dress for the weather. Layered clothing is always best. My backpack always has room for things I take off as the day warms up.

Make a pre-hike check list to be sure you have packed everything you may need on the trail.

SOME GOOD HIKES

Hike a lot of different trails to see new and different scenery. There are many good trails in Georgia and in the Atlanta area. Some of my favorites are the parks on the Chattahoochee, all part of the Chattahoochee River National Recreation Area, which is one of the best things the federal government ever did for us. My favorites are Palisades East and Palisades West, Gold Branch, Vickery Creek, Cochran Shoals, and the connecting Sope Creek. Maps of trails in the Chattahoochee River National Recreation Area are available at park headquarters at Island Ford, or at www. nps.gov/chat.

My over-all favorite park for convenience, variety, and beauty is Sweetwater Creek State Park near Austell. This park has more good trails than I can walk in a day, plus the ruins of the old New Manchester factory, which was burned by federal cavalry in the Civil War, and a nice Visitor Center-Museum. Scant evidence of the old mill village can also be found in the woods uphill from the factory.

Ruins of the old factory on Sweetwater Creek

Chicopee Woods, in Hall County, has 12 miles of trails, several nice creeks, a lake, and Elachee Nature Center. Spring brings hundreds of trillium, wild iris, and more other wild flowers than I can identify. Wildlife is abundant year-round.

An unusual hike is Arabia Mountain, located south of Lithonia. It is a granite outcropping somewhat like Stone Mountain, but lower and flatter. I discovered it in a book entitled *60 Hikes in 60 Miles,* which I bought at Elachee Nature Center. Arabia Mountain is actually two granite peaks which offer a wide variety of scenery and flora, plus over fifteen miles of trails, some paved. These trails are complex, so pick up a map at the Visitor Center. There is a very pretty lake, rocky creeks, and old granite quarries. Stone remnants of several old buildings are scattered through the woods.

There are several good books on trails, similar to the book mentioned above. For each hike they tell you how to get there, how long and difficult it is, describe what you will see, and provide maps of the trails. Two others are *Hiking Georgia* and *50 Hikes in the North Georgia Mountains.*

Some of my favorite hikes are in Rabun County, such as Panther Creek, Black Rock Mountain, The Chattooga River, a 9 to 11 mile loop on Saga Mountain, Ellicott's Rock, and sections of the Appalachian Trail, which are not in Rabun but are nearby. Tallulah Falls has a variety of trails, from ¼ mile to 10 miles, with one paved trail following an old railroad line.

If you seek trails which are really unusual, which show both the destructive power of nature as well as the ability of nature to restore itself, try the many trails on Mt. St. Helens in Washington. In 1980, the mountain exploded in one of the most violent volcanic eruptions in modern USA. Since then, creeks and rivers have cut new courses and timber has recovered enough to harvest, offering a broad variety of trails around the base, as well as up near the crater.

Mt. Hood in Oregon has mountain-side trails for day and long-range hiking, but it is best to catch them in warm weather. It is hard to follow a mountain-side trail when it's covered with snow.

Back in Georgia, Pickett's Mill State Park, near Dallas, combines beautiful woods and a rocky, winding creek with very interesting Civil War history. One of the few Confederate victories was here, known as The Battle of Pickett's Mill, where a Confederate force turned back a Federal attempt to flank the main line of battle. Here you can enjoy several miles of wooded trails, follow Pickett's Mill (or Pumpkinvine) Creek, and explore old trenches and gun emplacements.

Alabama re-enactors loading their muskets at Pickett's Mill

McIntosh Reserve is a Carroll County park located on the Chattahoochee between Newnan and Carrollton, near Whitesburg. It has over 15 miles of trails plus extensive picnic facilities and playgrounds. At one point the trail stays right on the river bank for about a mile. The river makes a sharp bend here and flows through about a quarter of a mile of rugged shoals. There are more cooters (or sliders, or turtles?) out sunning on the rocks than I have ever seen anywhere else. This stretch is one of the most beautiful parts of the Chattahoochee. On weekdays you may have the whole park to yourself.

The map you can pick up at the check-in station is not a very good map, but it helps.

This land also has historic significance. It was once the home and farm of William McIntosh, a half-breed Creek who helped white people fight against a war-like band of Creeks, the Red Sticks. They eventually murdered McIntosh here in revenge, and for his part in selling Creek land to the United States. An old log tavern, similar to the McIntosh home and tavern, has been re-erected here. McIntosh also farmed and operated a ferry across the Chattahoochee.

Red Top Mountain State Park, on Lake Allatoona, has two good trails, Iron Hill Trail and Homestead Trail.

Homestead is a six-mile loop. The last time I walked it, the trees were their brightest green of spring, the lake was dark blue, and the sky was light blue, making a wonderful combination of colors. The trail follows creeks and the lake shore part-way, then turns up into heavily wooded hills. Watch for the two old home sites which give the trail its name.

The other Red Top trail, Iron Hill, is more level, and is on the lake edge almost all the way. It is shorter than Homestead, but there are several side trails which make it an adequate hike. A gravel surface for bikers detracts somewhat from its desirability. Huge man-made ravines and hills offer evidence of the old iron-ore mining days. There are lots of deer.

Azalea Ridge trail is near the Lake Lanier dam. It follows the Chattahoochee for a while, loops through the woods, and follows the shore line of Lake Lanier. In winter, there are several opportunities to extend the four mile loop by taking side trails farther on down the river or along the lake's shore line. The riverside trail is too overgrown in summer, but good walking in winter. You will almost certainly see deer here.

Kennesaw Mountain has many miles of good trails, but also a few too many runners and hikers. The historic significance of the park adds interest for those of us who like history. During my last hike there, a seven mile loop near Cheatham Hill, I had dropped my car keys on the trail and walked off without knowing it. A runner saw them, then stopped to ask me if I had lost my keys. I found that I had, so he turned around and ran back to pick them up and bring them to me. That's one runner who turned out to be a guardian angel. Since then I always carry an extra set of keys in my backpack.

Two consecutive hikes on the Silver Comet Trail were both very interesting. This paved trail is on an old railroad right-of-way and is almost flat.

The first hike was from Coot's Lake to Rockmart and back, about 8.4 miles. The concrete trail was hot, so I ended up with blisters on both feet. This can be avoided by walking on the dirt edges of the trail as much as possible, and by lubricating your feet and socks with petroleum jelly. In spite of the blisters, it was still a very interesting hike.

The next week I walked from Coots Lake eastward to the Seaboard Air Line Railroad tunnel, and thru the tunnel. Then, climbed the steep bank and walked around in the woods. I did not get blisters because I stayed off the concrete as much as possible and lubricated my feet. This was also about eight miles.

The worse thing about walking on paved trails (such as Silver Comet and parts of Arabia Mountain) is the way bikers come up behind you and whiz by without a warning. Many bikers have absolutely no consideration for hikers. Someday I am going to poke my staff through their spokes.

I have walked Silver Comet all the way from Smyrna to Rockmart, in sections. West of Rockmart the trail runs alongside a busy, noisy four-lane highway, and is not pleasant to walk. Take care for your safety around Mableton where robbers have been known to assault hikers. At Smyrna, be sure to take the detour trail down to see the well preserved ruins of Ruff's Mill.

Providence Canyon State Park, about an hour south of Columbus, has several miles of very interesting trails along the bottom of the canyons and through the woods near the rim.

Alcovy River grows from a sometimes sluggish creek in Gwinnett County to a fast-moving white water river when it reaches southern Newton County. The trail I walked is located ten miles south of Covington at the point where Factory Shoals Road crosses the Alcovy. At this point, the river is 100 to 200 feet wide, very rocky to the point that kayakers class it as "dangerous" and suggest that the kayak be portaged.

From the bridge, there are trails going upstream and downstream on both sides of the river. I walked all of them. The trails are part of a recreation center which is back off the river a few hundred feet. This center has pavilions, plenty of parking, camping, game areas, and other facilities. The trail will probably be well used on weekends, but there was no one there when I was there.

Creeks and marshes are bridged with board-walks. I found the ruins of an old water mill, but am still searching for the factory of Factory Shoals.

WILDLIFE

In addition to bears, dogs, and coyotes, there are lots of harmless critters to enjoy.

On Stonewall Creek trail, a large doe bounced out of some thick brush and landed in the trail not fifteen feet in front of me. I froze. She picked up my scent and started trying to find me, but did not look back far enough for several seconds. When she finally spotted me, she took one spring and just disappeared into the woods. It always amazes me how deer can run through woods without a sound.

A fawn not two feet high almost ran into me on a section of the Bartram Trail in Rabun County.

In Palisades East, I saw one of the largest snakes I have ever seen anywhere, including zoos. This black snake (king snake, I think) had to be six or seven feet long and five or six inches in diameter. It was stalking its lunch and refused to move a muscle even when I tossed a twig at it. It fit the description of an Indigo snake except for the shape of its head.

Again at Palisades East, I was walking down a narrow trail and could hear a large group of chattering wildlife (females) approaching from my front. Finally a line of about 40 little girls, first graders, came around a bend with their guides, all 40 talking and giggling at the same time. I stepped back out of their way and let them pass, enjoying their smiles and waves and hellos. One little twosome studied me carefully. "I thought he was a statue," said one. "No," said the other, "it's a very old man."

At Red Top Mountain and Sweetwater Creek you can see deer in herds.

The deer at Red Top are almost tame, and are very curious. Very early one morning I walked into the middle of a group of a dozen does and fawns, all scratching through the leaves for treats. Again, I froze. They finally decided that I was harmless, and I was treated to about ten minutes of very close observation. Finally, a big buck came up and did not like his harem being so close to a human, so he ran them off over a hill.

I have also seen deer in herds at Palisades East and Sweetwater Creek.

In Washington, a mountain trail in Olympic National Park has a big sign at the trail head which warns the hiker to beware of cougars, bears, and swarming bees, and to yield the trail to "pack animals." What would pack animals be doing back in these woods? After following a beautiful, swift, rocky, river for a couple of miles, I then completed a very long and arduous ascent and had stopped to rest on a log bench at a trail intersection. Soon, I heard something approaching up another trail, but could not see it for the thick undergrowth. Finally, through a small opening in the bushes, I saw a little old lady approaching with what looked like a large animal head on her shoulder. That's exactly what it was – a little old lady with a llama which was resting its head on her shoulder, followed by a train of eight more pack llamas.

We chatted for a while, and she explained that she had a contract with the park to supply food to rangers in fire towers which were so isolated that no road could reach them. She commented on being very tired, and said that she and her llamas had worked 360 straight days. "You lead the llamas in and out every day?" I asked in surprise. "Every day," she answered. Then I realized that I had met the daily llamas. True story.

At Providence Canyon, I could hear the rustling of something stalking me, just off the trail, for about 30 minutes. Then finally I spotted the culprit – an armadillo which was as curious about me as I was about him.

The same unusual behavior also happened on Cumberland Island. This particular armadillo finally dashed across the trail in front of me. I suspect that armadillos are related to 'possums because of the way they like to dash out in front of people or cars.

Don't fear snakes. Respect them, but don't fear them. I have been walking in the wood for 70 years and have come upon only two poisonous snakes. I see non-poisonous snakes on almost every walk in summer, but they are usually trying to get as far from me as they can as quickly as they can. Snakes are not aggressive to people, but will strike if they feel threatened. In summer it is best to stay on trails where you can see around your feet. Scan carefully in front of your feet if you have to leave the trail.

Last summer, on Stonewall Creek in Rabun, I spotted a good-sized copperhead on the trail's edge about ten feet in front of me. I tossed a small stick at him, but just like the black snake at Palisades East, he did not budge. I decided that the safest thing to do would be to turn back and find another trail. After all, he was there first.

Walking in the woods is good for your physical and mental health. The advantages of physical exercise are obvious. Mentally, I like to compare it to meditation. You can let your mind run through any problem or situations you need to think about, or sometimes just let it go almost blank. Great ideas on almost anything can pop into your head at any time. I carry a light tape recorder for this very reason.

Walking can also be a spiritual experience. I always stop at some inspiring place, like a grove of tall poplars, or a rocky creek, and thank God for allowing me to enjoy the natural beauty of His handiwork.

Have fun!

END

Twenty-One Months In the U. S. Army

Or

How I Won the Korean War

The Korean war was not a popular war. There were no patriotic slogans, no Andrews Sisters singing "Boogie Woogie Bugle boy of Company B," no big bands playing "Over There." We were told that if we did not stop the Chinese and North Korean communists from invading Korea, the next line of defense might be the Mississippi River. Thousands of young American men were convinced that they must put their lives on the line to stop the Communist hoards short of the Mississippi. I was not one of them.

Any young man not in college was eligible to be drafted. The news was full of horrible stories of combat in Korea, fighting hoards of Chinese and Koreans, and freezing in trenches, so those of us in college at that time made a special effort to stay in college. Just in case the war was still going on when I graduated, I signed up for ROTC at Georgia State University, knowing that an officer's life would be more challenging and bearable than an enlisted man's. But, after a year of ROTC they discovered that I was somewhat color blind, which would prevent my receiving a commission as an officer. So I dropped out of ROTC with a helpless feeling, knowing that I would be drafted as soon as I graduated. There was nothing to do but wait for the draft notice to come.

And come it did, just a few days before graduation. It gave me just two weeks to get all my personal affairs, which included a new wife, in order before reporting for induction. At that time, this was the most stressful period of my life.

INDUCTION

The draft notice provided that I would report to the Induction Center at Chamblee, Georgia, which was Camp Gordon in World War I, Atlanta Naval Air Station in World War II, and is now Peachtree-DeKalb Airport. The last few precious days before I marched off to war were spent with my bride and my parents. Many tears were shed by all. Then on the final day they drove me out to deposit me at the Induction Center gate. A small bag contained all my personal possessions which the army would allow, consisting of shaving equipment, tooth brush, and a comb. After many hugs and kisses and tears, they drove away, leaving me alone to face my fate.

A large group of draftees, about 50, had reported that morning. The day was spent in testing, both mental and physical. The requirements were not very high. At one point we were herded into a large room, told to stand back against the wall, and strip. This was a new experience for me, 50 men of all sizes, shapes, and colors, standing naked around in a big circle, trying not to stare, and hoping that no one else was staring. Then a doctor came around and listened to our hearts with a stethoscope, looked down our throats with a tongue depressor, checked our testicles for hernia, and our penises for venereal disease, and that was it.

We had not expected to see our loved ones for many months. Some felt that we would never see them again. Then, toward the end of the day, they told us, "Go home. We are not through. Come back tomorrow."

This was embarrassing. I called home, was picked up at the gate, spent the night at home, and was once again delivered to the gate. More hugs, kisses, and tears, but not as many as yesterday. Warmed-over good-byes are uncomfortable.

After a short time I officially became a private in the U. S. Army, was assigned serial number US53192658, then put on a bus and whisked away to beautiful Fort Jackson, South Carolina.

FORT JACKSON

Herded from the bus, we were shouted at and bullied by a bunch of loud, tough looking guys in stiffly starched uniforms. First stop was the barber shop where our heads were shaved. I liked the look. Then we stumbled into a warehouse where we were issued a duffel bag into which we crammed all the military clothing we would need for the next two years. Then we were shoved into a barrack and assigned a bunk and were told to watch the bulletin board regularly until they decided what to do with us.

I was called back twice to an office where they tried to convince me to sign up for special training to enter the CID, Criminal Investigation Division. This would have meant an immediate promotion to sergeant with all the privileges pertaining thereto, and more money. But it would also mean an extension of my enlistment from 24 months to 36 months. Eager to get this military service behind me and get on with my real life as quickly as possible, I declined.

For one week I awaited assignment, crammed into a steaming hot barrack with hundreds of sweating, screaming men from all walks of life, with nothing to do but watch the bulletin board or wait to be called. This was the nearest thing to hell which I have ever experienced. My discomfort was exacerbated by having to spend the first anniversary of our wedding in this hell hole.

Finally, the call came and a group of us was marched off to begin a 16-week training cycle, after which we were to go straight to Korea as a combat unit.

"A" Battery, 45th Field Artillery Battalion

We were marched (or at that stage of our military training "herded" is still a better term) across the post and finally became a unit – "A" Battery of the 45th Field Artillery Battalion, 81st Infantry Division, 3rd United States Army. I was in 1st squad, 1st platoon, and because of my ROTC training, was made acting squad leader. Being squad leader entailed a certain amount of responsibility, but with practically no authority to back it up. The authority came later.

An artillery battery is equivalent to a company in an infantry organization, except our missions are different. "A" Battery was a "heavy weapons" company, and our duty was to support the infantry with machine guns, cannons, mortars, and other weapons which the average infantryman does not carry or know how to operate or maintain.

There were four barracks in the battery. Each barrack, two-story wooden buildings, housed a platoon. Each platoon consisted of four squads of nine men each. Including Non-Commissioned Officers (NCO's), cooks, and a few others assigned to the battery for special purposes, the barrack housed 40 to 45 men. Privacy was a luxury which the Army did not offer.

Of the 160+ trainees in A Battery, the average education level was 5th grade. Several were completely illiterate, could only sign their name. Some seemed almost animal-like to me. I did not know that people like that existed. Only five had been to college, and I was one of two who had graduated. About half of the 160 were black and half white.

Each platoon had a platoon sergeant who lived in the barrack with his platoon, and who was the immediate person in charge of the whole platoon. Our platoon sergeant was a National Guard sergeant who did not have the slightest idea what he was supposed to do. He was a totally helpless, useless person. As soon as the trainees recognized this, he no longer could control the platoon. So he abdicated his responsibility to me, an acting corporal. My only power over the platoon was the right to allocate weekend passes.

Every Saturday morning we would have a parade, which would usually conclude with us marching back to the barracks at about noon. Then we were "off duty" until midnight Sunday, a precious day and a half. I could give passes to half the platoon each weekend, so there was fierce competition for these passes. I kept the platoon in line by offering passes for accomplishment, or withholding passes for failure to cooperate.

Those weekend passes were "50 Mile Passes," that is, we were not supposed to go over 50 miles from the post. If we did we were AWOL, which was a serious offense. That presented a problem since Atlanta was about 150 miles from Fort Jackson, but not an insurmountable problem. It was worth taking a risk to get home to see our loved ones every weekend, so we did it. I could hitch-hike to Atlanta and be there by late Saturday afternoon, enjoy being home until Sunday afternoon, then hitch-hike back to Jackson.

No one questioned the fact that I got a pass every weekend. The sergeant kept in his room. We rarely saw him except during inspections.

We slept in double-decker bunks with sprung springs and thin mattresses. They were more like hammocks than beds, but I never had trouble sleeping, even when surrounded by a cacophony of radios playing country and western, rock, spirituals, and blues – all at the same time. And often a crap game would be going on within 20 feet.

Arguments and fights were common in such close quarters, so Acting Corporal-Squad Leader and Acting Platoon Leader Blackwell did the best he could to keep the peace.

CLOSE ORDER DRILL

Since I had a little Close Order Drill (marching) in 10th grade ROTC at Atlanta Boys High School and again at Georgia State University, I knew how to do the basic maneuvers, knew left from right, and was therefore several steps ahead of most recruits. Many of my comrades had a hard time remembering whether to start with their left foot or right foot, couldn't keep in step, and never mastered the oblique movements. My main concern was a natural inclination to bounce as I walked. Several times I was shocked by a drill sergeant screaming at me, "Blackwell, stop bouncing." I didn't even know I was bouncing, so I never mastered the bounceless march.

THE GARAND M-1

We were soon issued our permanent weapon, a Garand M-1 rifle, one of the best all-round weapons ever used by our armed forces. It was extremely accurate and easy to maintain. You could drop it in the mud, take it apart in your lap, clean each piece, re-assemble, and be ready to fire again in two or three minutes. After Korea it was replaced by assault rifles.

After learning how to clean, maintain, and fire it from a variety of positions, each soldier had to "qualify." That is, we had to fire from three different positions at three different distances and score a certain number of points in order to qualify.

The three required positions were prone, sitting, and standing. We fired a full clip, eight rounds, using each of the three positions at 100 (the length of a football field), 200, and 300 yards. That totals 72 shots at a target as big as a bed, but the bull's-eye looked like a dime at 300 yards.

A huge scoreboard was erected to keep up with the points scored by each man. Bull's-eyes scored 10, the next ring nine, and so on. Scores were recorded as each man fired. Since very few of my buddies could add, subtract, multiply, or (heaven forbid) divide, I was detailed to keep the scoreboard for the whole battery.

There were several firing ranges in a row, separated by berms of dirt as high as a house. Our battery occupied one range, the other firing ranges being occupied by other units. Each range had 20 firing positions, and 20 targets. 20 men at a time would fire from all three positions at 100 yards, then move back to 200 yards, then back to 300, then turn in their score to me. Ten bull's-eyes from 72 shots would give a perfect score of 720. However, some of the guys could not even hit the target, much less the bull's-eye, so most scores were in the 200-500 range.

When A Battery had finished firing and all the scores were in, some instructor asked if everyone had fired, and I replied that I had not because I had been keeping score all day. He told me to hurry up and go through the whole procedure by myself while the rest of the battery watched. Instead of 20 people firing at one time, I was the whole show.

With my trusty M-1 and a bag of clips I walked down to the 100 yard marker, assumed the prone position, and hit eight bull's-eyes. I have always enjoyed firing guns and was always a good shot, but I did not expect what followed. From the sitting position I hit eight more 10's, then again from the standing position. 24 bull's-eyes so far.

By this time the whole battery had noticed what was happening and was lined up behind me watching my performance.

The next station was 200 yards, where I again hit 24 10's. But at that distance the target looked smaller and the pressure was building.

At 300 yards word had spread to the adjoining firing ranges and they stopped firing to watch me. I could see people sitting on top of the berms between the ranges, watching me shoot. This unwelcome audience added to the tension of firing at a tiny target from 300 yards.

The prone position was the easiest because you could rest your elbows on the ground. I was surprised but very pleased to put the whole clip into the bull's-eye. In the sitting position you leaned forward and supported the rifle by resting your arms on your legs. Once again, eight 10's.

When I stood up for the final eight shots at a tiny target 300 yards away, I felt both shock and disbelief that I could be doing this. I knew that I was a good shot, but not that good. Eight shots, the clip sprang out, and I saw the score – seven bull's-eyes and one hole in the nine ring for a total of 719 points out of a possible 720. Well, nobody's perfect.

I was immediately surrounded by people with congratulations and slaps on the back. At that point, for the only time in my life, I lost complete control of myself. Collapsing on my knees I started bawling like a baby and could not stop. I have no idea why, but it could have been a combination of a sudden release of tension which had been building up during the firing procedure, fatigue from the full day of score keeping for 160 men, combined with the 100+ degrees temperature.

They moved me into some shade (offered by the billboard sized score board), gave me some water, and after a few minutes I was over it, other than feeling embarrassed.

I still think of that day often. I am proud of my qualifying record, proud of my shooting, but wish it had not ended as it did. With all the soldiers who qualified with the M-1, certainly someone at some time has fired a perfect 720, but on that day in 1953, I was the best shot at Fort Jackson.

MACHINE GUNS

After mastering the M-1, we then started our education on every weapon which a soldier can carry personally or in a jeep. These included three types of machine guns, two mortars, rocket launchers (bazookas), two recoilless rifles, the carbine, Colt .45 semi-automatic pistol, Browning automatic rifle (BAR), and .45 sub-machinegun, called the "grease gun" because of its appearance. We not only learned to fire each one but also how to dismantle, clean, and re-assemble each weapon.

Cleaning and oiling had to be done carefully and meticulously. On more than one occasion the whole battery would be up until three or four in the morning cleaning some killing device until it suited the cadre.

The three machine guns we learned were .30 caliber water cooled, .30 air cooled, and .50 caliber air cooled. The .50 air cooled was an awesome weapon. Its slug was ½ inch in diameter and the entire cartridge was about six inches long. Tracers were inserted in the belt at intervals, which enabled a gunner to follow and control the trajectory of his shots without aiming, just as you do with a water hose. This weapon was so powerful that we would cut down trees with it, and in one case, started a forest fire with the tracers.

RECOILLESS RIFLES

Any weapon with a rifled barrel can be called a rifle. This includes cannons. Recoilless rifles were cannons which had no recoil. We trained with 75mm and 105mm recoilless rifles. The 75 fired a shell which was three inches in diameter and about a foot and a half long, the 105 was four inches in diameter and a little longer. 75's were fired from tripods, about like machine gun tripods, but the 105 was much heavier and was fired from jeeps or other vehicles.

Because of the back blast, one does not stand behind a recoilless rifle. This was carefully explained to us, but as with a lot of explanations, it went in one ear and out the other. Then they demonstrated by firing a 75 with a pile of wooden ammo boxes 20 feet high behind it. The back blast tore the pile to splinters and set some on fire. This got our attention.

75s had an effective range of one or two miles. It was fun to sit on a hill top and blow up old trucks and tanks on another hill a mile away.

ROCKET LAUNCHER

Commonly known as "bazooka," the rocket launcher was an anti-tank and anti-fortification weapon. Like the recoilless rifle, the bazooka was fired by a two-man team, but was fired from the shoulder rather than a tripod. The rocket was ignited by a battery which was attached to the rocket by a small wire. We were cautioned that if the wire were not properly attached it would whip back and slash the gunner across the back of the neck.

Two instructors demonstrated. The gunner held the launcher on his shoulder, the loader carefully inserted the rocket, attached the wire, tapped the gunner on the head, the gunner pulled the trigger, the rocket fired, the wire whipped back and slashed the gunner across the back of his neck, and he was hauled off in one of the ambulances which seemed to hover around us like vultures.

Next was our turn to learn to fire. I immediately began looking for something else to do.

The rockets came in cans. The cans had to be opened. I immediately volunteered to organize a detail to open the cans and keep a good supply of rockets ready for the other guys to fire. Finding a good shade tree to work under, we opened cans all day and never had to fire a rocket launcher.

MORTARS

Mortars are simple weapons fired by a complex team. Essentially, a mortar is nothing but a metal tube and a base plate. The base plate lies on the ground. The tube attaches to the base plate and points upward. The projectile is dropped down the barrel and fires when it hits the bottom of the tube, and the base plate stops any recoil.

The complication arises because the firing team can very rarely see the target. Mortars have a very high trajectory, often firing at an enemy on the far side of a hill, or obscured by a fortification. Therefore, there are three components of a mortar team, forward observer, fire control, and fire team.

Forward observers sneak several hundred yards in front of the mortar to spot the target. The exact location of the target is radioed to fire control, using map coordinates. Fire control then radios aiming instructions to the fire team. Fire team sets the mortar according to instructions and drops a round down the barrel, and it fires. Forward observers watch the strike and radio back to fire control with information such as, "50 yards short, 40 yards right." Fire control mathematically calculated how the mortar would have to be adjusted to hit the target, radios the fire team, and another round is on the way. As soon as the strikes are close enough, the forward observers radio "fire for effect," and get the hell out of there.

Because I knew a little math I was in fire control. We operated far behind the "lines" in a nice, cool tent, with all the cold cantaloupe we could eat, while the observers and the fire team were out crawling around in the 100 degree heat. I found mortars fascinating.

OTHER STUFF

We did a lot of other stuff…

Learned how to use topographic maps and how to orient ourselves using a compass. (Later, these maps were extremely useful in the real estate business, and I still use them when I plan a hike).

Ran through a canyon firing our M-1's from the hip at red and white figures which popped up mechanically. I would have had a perfect score here, but no one told me not to shoot the white figures.

Calisthenics.

Blackened our faces and stayed up all night learning commando tactics. Our African-American soldiers laughed about enjoying a distinct advantage as night fighters.

Studied weapons used by the Koreans and Chinese, which included spears and cross-bows in addition to modern Russian weapons.

More calisthenics.

Ran obstacle courses: walked logs, climbed ladders and fences, swung on ropes, crawled with our rifles.

Learned how to charge with a bayonet, hand-to-hand combat, and knife fighting.

Lots more calisthenics.

Pulled KP (Kitchen Police). Somehow I managed to avoid KP at Jackson except for one assignment, and all I can recall about it is washing garbage cans.

Dug fox holes.

Threw hand grenades – the one part of training in which I was so terrified that I could barely function. When the pin was pulled, the safety grip has to be held down until you want the timer to start. When the grenade is thrown, the grip flies off and the timer starts, then the grenade explodes. IF you drop the grenade, the grip flies off and you get blown up.

CHOW

Army chow was not bad at all, and there was always all you could eat. Even our field meals, C-rations, were not too bad, but I would hate to have to live on them for a long time.

C-rations came in a box which included several items. The entrée was a can of something which resembled a congealed vegetable soup with mystery meat. Each box also contained a pack of cigarettes and a piece of chocolate. I always traded my cigarettes for chocolate.

SOFTBALL

Occasionally we had time and energy for recreation, usually softball.

We had trained all day, returned and had chow, and still had a few hours of daylight left when someone suggested softball. Almost but not quite exhausted, we could not resist the temptation for some recreation. Those who were interested marched to the softball field and had a wonderful game.

Darkness fell, and now completely exhausted, we were ready to return home. There was a loud and obnoxious sergeant in charge of the 3rd platoon who was the ranking NCO. He called for us to fall in to be marched back. Now, since marching in step is much more strenuous than walking, there was a lot of moaning and bitching from the group, so I started arguing with the sergeant about how we were too tired to march, and he should just let us walk, to which he replied, "Blackwell, you damned educated son of a bitch, shut up and fall in." I did.

BUDDY

Buddy was a sad case. I suspect that he was mentally incapable of functioning on his own. He never learned to make up his bunk, and never learned anyone's name, but called everyone "Buddy." So, everybody called him Buddy, too.

Our First Sergeant, Sergeant Crymes, would get mad at him and chew him out for having a poorly made bunk, so I started making it up for him, since he was in my squad and I did not want my squad to look bad. Then, one day Buddy was gone. We assumed that he was discharged as unfit for military service. While he was a harmless person, I would hate to have to go into combat with him because he could not carry his share of responsibilities, and someone would have gotten hurt looking after him.

But on the other hand, maybe Buddy was the smartest of us all.

JAMES BROWN

I can remember a lot of the guys in 1st Platoon. There was Alexander, Blalock, Bazemore, Ballard, Bates, and 31 others. We almost never used first names. The only soldier who was called by his first and last names was James Brown.

James Brown was a tall, light skinned, good looking black person. He was smart, strong, athletic, and a constant trouble maker. His weakness was gambling – all he wanted to do was shoot craps. He would walk around with a pair of dice in his hand, rattling them in other peoples' ears until he could get up a game. Craps was a very common pastime, but unfortunately, James Brown's games always ended up in a fight. Once, exhibiting a severe lapse of judgment, I helped take a bayonet away from him as he was going after another gambler with it. On other occasions, I was among those who took other weapons away from him – pocket knives, shovels, hatchets, anything he could find.

We were resting in the shade on a machine gun range, having a box lunch, when suddenly a soldier came running through our midst as hard as he could go, obviously terrified, with James Brown right behind him, slashing at him with a knife. They were gone before we could do anything. I never saw James Brown again. I assumed that he was either arrested or discharged.

BLALOCK

Blalock was a big, raw-boned country boy from Mississippi. One night in the barracks he started jawing at me over something, and finally decided to test my authority physically. He came at me slowly with both hands open, not with his fists, which was a big relief to me since I have always avoided having to hit someone on his fist with my nose.

We squared off and locked our fingers. I had no idea what he was going to try, so I tried to keep both hands firmly locked with a good pressure on him, and watch his feet for any sudden move. Then I saw that all he wanted to do was force me down with his hands. We stayed locked for several minutes, each putting as much pressure as he could on the other. "Fights" were always of great interest, so the whole platoon gathered around. Slowly, much to my surprise, his arms began to bend back, his knees began to bend, and he sank to the floor. When I released him, he shook his head, grinned, and walked away. We were always on good terms after that, and he was one of my best supporters when I needed help with the platoon. No one challenged me again.

ALABAMA

Alabama was a good old, hard-working, semi-literate farm boy who did what he was told and never created problems. His squad leader was another good, helpful guy named Jesse Bates. We were taking a break after a particularly grueling day of sweating and crawling through the mud, and probably looked like we had been run over by a tank. While "taking 10," Bates surveyed his squad and said authoritatively, "As soon as we get back, you will change your uniforms," to which Alabama replied, "Who you want us to change with, Jesse?"

One day I saw Alabama sitting on his bunk with a letter in his hand, crying. When I asked him what was wrong, he explained that he lived on a small farm with his parents. He had done most of the farm work until he was drafted. His father had gotten sick and could not handle it by himself and his mother did not know what to do. Someone overheard and commented that he might qualify for a hardship discharge. We sent him to the battery headquarters, and in a rare example of benevolent efficiency, Alabama was on his way home the next day.

A KICK IN THE PANTS

I was standing in line to practice with a .45 Colt Semi-Automatic pistol. With a pistol, the safe position was to hold it pointing straight up. Evidently I had relaxed too much so that it was pointing not up but back behind me.

Suddenly, I received a swift kick in the seat from an instructor who had taken offense at walking behind me and finding himself looking down the barrel of a .45. I instinctively whirled on him with the .45 in my hand. His terrified expression showed that he realized that it might not be a good idea to kick someone who had a pistol in his hand. He gulped, said "Keep the barrel pointing up, Blackwell," and walked away.

JOB WANTED

After 12 weeks of training, with four weeks still to go, two situations developed which caused me to seriously reconsider my position as a trainee in a combat unit.

First, the next two events on our training schedule were two weeks of bivouac in the great outdoors, living in pup tents, sleeping on the ground, enduring 100 degree heat and plenty of mud and gnats. Then, more mud – we were to crawl under barbed wire through a muddy field while machine guns fired a few inches over our heads and mortar rounds exploded around us. I like shooting, but I don't like being shot at.

Second, becoming a trained killer would not be much use with peace coming up, and we were hearing news and rumors that a truce was imminent, and that we would not be going to Korea after all. I felt that I had other talents which would be more useful to the Army.

Considering all of this, I decided on a course of action which was extremely unconventional.

Our First Sergeant, Master Sergeant Crymes, was a tough but fair veteran of many years' service. The Army was his home and primary interest.

One morning as the platoon lined up to march out into the hot Fort Jackson training grounds, I got his attention and asked to fall out and talk to him for a few minutes. He was surprised, but agreed, and as the platoon marched away, Sergeant. Crymes and I stepped aside and my presentation went something like this: "Sergeant Crymes, the war is almost over and I think I can be much more valuable to the Army doing something other than continuing training for combat. I ask your permission to try to find other employment on the post which will benefit the Army more than combat training." Notice I said, "benefit the Army," not benefit me.

Sergeant Crymes was obviously taken aback by this unheard of request, but he immediately saw that it made sense. "Go ahead," he said, and I was gone in a flash. I changed from fatigues to my dress khakis. Then, with no definite plan, I started walking around the huge post looking for offices. I would knock on a door, ask to see the officer in charge of whatever they were doing, and then explain that I had a good education and had been relieved from basic training, and was eager to find a position in which my skills could be beneficially utilized.

My first four or five calls produced nothing, but with the next one I finally got lucky. I met a very friendly Captain who seemed interested in my quest. He called a friend at Post Finance, and the friend said to send me right on over for an interview.

The interview was brief and I was informed that orders would be cut (Army talk for "written") that day relieving me from training and assigning me to Post Finance. I could not believe how fast it happened, and neither could Sergeant Crymes, but the next day the orders came and I bid goodbye to dear old A Battery, packed all my worldly possessions into my duffel bag, turned in my M-1, to which I had become attached and hated to see it go, watched my buddies march away for the last time, and happily walked across the post to my new assignment.

POST FINANCE

At Post Finance I calculated military payrolls and kept payroll records. This was not as exciting as combat training, but I was glad to be there.

The only interesting event during my short tenure at Post Finance related to the responsibilities of guard duty. There are very strict rules covering guard duty. Each soldier is required to memorize them. Every night, soldiers with guard duty assignments would be patrolling their posts. One of the strict rules was that you did not leave your post until formally relieved by the Corporal of the Guard, who was usually a lieutenant (officer of the guard?).

Guard duty was important, but since many soldiers walking guard duty were still trainees, they were not trusted with fully loaded weapons. Guards carried M-1's, unloaded, but with one bullet in their shirt pocket. Yes, just like Barney Fife.

One morning we arrived for work at Post Finance to find that the guard was still on duty. For some unknown reason, he had not been relieved. The guard stood at the main entrance and would not allow us to enter, since his instructions were to protect the building until relieved. We protested, "Come on, man, we've got work to do." He stood his ground. The crowd grew larger and more vociferous. Sergeants and officers arrived and started chewing him out, threatening to remove him physically if he did not get out of the way. In response, he calmly took his one bullet out of his pocket and loaded his M-1.

The crowd quickly drew back, having decided that the safest course of action was to wait for the guard to be properly relieved. In a few minutes, the Corporal of the Guard arrived with his relief formation, the guard was formally relieved, and the relief formation marched away. We entered the building and started work.

FORT McPHERSON

Now that I was out of basic training, my next step was to try to get transferred to Fort McPherson, back home in Atlanta. (Fort McPherson, by the way, is named after General John B. McPherson, who was killed near my home in East Atlanta, during the Civil War).

Fort McPherson was 3rd Army Headquarters, which put them in command of all military operations in the southeastern United States, including Fort Jackson. A message from Fort McPherson to Fort Jackson was treated like a commandment from God. Any kind of duty at Fort McPherson would be better than any other Army post. Also, my whole family was within easy driving distance from Fort Mac.

My good friend and mentor, Charles Rowland, being a few months ahead of me in his military career, had already learned that soldiers in the U. S. Army have more control over their destiny than they realize. Charles had already arranged his transfer to Fort Mac and was stationed at the Post Comptroller's office.

I was still coming home most weekends, so one weekend I arranged to leave early and meet Charles at his office at Fort Mac. Everyone at Post Comptroller was very busy watching the World Series. Charles introduced me to a major who tore himself away from the television long enough to take me downstairs and introduce me to a lady Warrant Officer, who interviewed me for a job. She indicated that they could possibly use me at Post Comptroller (I had two courses in accounting at Georgia State), and that I might be hearing from them soon. Nothing definite.

Being hopefully optimistic, I drove my car back to Fort Jackson rather than hitch-hike, so that I could be ready to leave for Fort Mac at a moment's notice. A couple of days later, I was working at my desk, calculating payrolls, when a sergeant walked up with a paper in his hand, and looking at me in a strange way. "Blackwell," he said, "I don't know who you know, but you have been transferred to Fort McPherson. You are dismissed from Post Finance immediately, and are to report to Fort Mac in two days." Hallelujah!

Trying to be cool, I calmly waved good-by to my co-workers, none of whom I had gotten to know yet, walked out of Finance and over to my barracks, packed my duffel bag as quickly as possible, and headed for HOME!

POST COMPTROLLER, FORT MCPHERSON

When I showed up for work on the appointed day, I was assigned to an office with two other GI's, both corporals who had been there many months and who had definite responsibilities. I quickly discovered that there was absolutely nothing for me to do, and I began to worry about the security of my position. Just to look busy, I requisitioned and received a typewriter and adding machine. First thing each day, I would add up phone numbers from the telephone book until my adding machine tape was an impressive yard long, then just mess around with the typewriter the rest of the day.

Finally, I was given an important assignment worthy of my talents and abilities. The major in charge asked if I had time to take on keeping records for the post Cub Scout den. I agreed to try to work it in.

The den mother was the wife of a Colonel who lived on the post. Once or twice a month I would drop by her quarters and pick up a little metal box which contained all of her financial records. The income (sometimes as much a $5 or $10) would be counted and recorded, expenses tabulated, and the metal box returned to the Colonel's wife. This took no more than an hour. That was all I had to do and I was really getting bored.

Charles Rowland came to the rescue again. He was an auditor, and one of his responsibilities was to audit the Officers' Club. He informed me of an upcoming vacancy in their accounting office, so I applied for a transfer and got it.

The Fort McPherson Officers' Club was a large operation, primarily because there were a lot of officers on the post, including more Generals and Colonels than I thought existed. They had a restaurant as large and capable as any quality restaurant in Atlanta, and were often hosting parties and shows. I was one of three men working in the accounting office. My responsibility was accounts receivable, and collecting football pool bets and cards for our CO, a Colonel who, as I had been told, fronted for a national gambling syndicate. We drew overtime pay and wore casual civilian clothes, both very unusual for the U. S. Army. I had been living at home ever since being transferred.

After I had served 21 months of a 24 month term, the Army announced a program of early discharge for going back to school. I enrolled in the Masters program at Georgia State, and my military career terminated in March, 1955.

In Retrospect...

So, were these 21 months of my life wasted? Not at all. I learned a lot about people, and saw a lot of types of people which I didn't even know existed. My self-confidence was greatly improved by the combat training, and by the realization of how much control I had over my own destiny.

My first child, Danny, was born at Fort Mac Hospital for a cost of less than $9.00. My first home was bought with a 100% GI Loan at 4% interest. And I think I gained a lot of maturity which helped me tremendously when I returned to Adams-Cates Company, which had held my desk for me for the entire 21 months, thanks to the consideration and generosity of my sales manager, Henry Robinson. One thing I learned in the Army which helped me tremendously in the real estate business was how to read Coast and Geodetic Quadrangles. These maps showed topography, roads, and other terrain features. They were invaluable in the land business. All things considered, it was a valuable 21 months.

I did not really win the Korean War. That was just to get your attention.

End

A Few Ideas on Investing, Money Management, and Recessions

• A collection of financial axioms and personal observations.

• "A fool and his money are soon parted."

• "There's a fool born every minute."

• Don't be a fool. Learn to manage your money wisely.

• "One good investment is worth a lifetime of work." Frank Gordy, founder of the Varsity.

• Never, NEVER, pay interest or fees on a credit card. Never. Work hard to get caught up just one time, then never get behind again. Credit card interest and fees are killers. If you are tempted to spend and get behind again, don't. Just do without.

• Old axiom: "There is no such thing as a free lunch." Likewise, there is no such thing as an interest-free purchase, or terms with 0% interest. Think about it. 0%, or any abnormally low rate, is always made up by a high price.

• How much you earn is important. How much you keep is even more important.

• If you invest, don't be greedy. You will never go broke taking a profit.

• Don't pay too much attention to the "pundits" or famous economists or experts on investing. If one says "things are getting worse," there is always another who says "things are getting better." One will say buy, while another says sell. Bone up on economics so that you can make your own decisions. Who was it – Harry Truman? – who said that what we need is more one-armed economists, so that they could not say, "…but on the other hand…."

• If someone has to say, "You can trust me," don't.

• One good way to make time pass quickly is to sign a 90-day note.

• The Law of Risk and Rewards: high risk, high rewards; low risk, low rewards. It's your choice. Choose wisely.

• Don't borrow to invest unless the investment will pay the debt service, or unless you are absolutely sure where the money for the debt service is coming from. And on any debt, don't have unrealistic hopes as to where the debt service will come from.

• "Land is the basis of all wealth." Adam Smith. Land, as used here, refers to all types of real estate, including your home, offices, shopping centers, apartments, etc. My favorite was just land.

• Bankruptcy is theft, with very few exceptions.

• If you don't buy things, then you don't need Consumers Report. If you do buy things, Consumers Report will save you many times the subscription price every year.

• You don't get paid unless you show up for work (I think Mike Mescon said that).

• Don't be a fad buyer. Exercise self-control in spending. You don't have to have every new gadget that comes out. As Mark Twain said, "Denial ain't just a river in Egypt." Big companies spend billion $ on advertising to control your mind – don't let them do it.

• You cannot time the stock market. Learn to use "dollar cost averaging" if you are a periodic investor.

• Diversify.

• Success is the progressive realization of a worthy goal. Nightingale.

• It is often estimated that 20% of the people own 80% of the wealth. If all the wealth in the world were equally divided among all the people in the world, within six months 20% of the people would probably once again have 80% of the wealth. How would you do?

• This 80-20 ratio exists in a lot of groups. In most sales forces, including ours at Sharp-Boylston, 20% of the salesmen usually made 80% of the sales. It is possible to move up from one group to the other with hard, intelligent work.

• If someone wants to sell you a "hot deal"—run. Fast.

• Some of us need the advice of investment brokers and advisors, some don't, but you must take the time to study and understand financial matters.

• Unless you already have a successful record of picking good stock investments, then stick with mutual funds and ETF's and let the experts do the stock picking.

• Read Think and Grow Rich by Napoleon Hill. It will change your life forever, for the better.

• Selling investments to meet living expenses is like eating your seed corn.

• Avoid automobile loans. Their interest rates are exorbitant. Keep a car until you get it paid off, then start a monthly savings account equal to what your car payments used to be. When you accumulate enough cash in the savings account, buy your new car for all cash plus your free-and-clear trade in. Then start a new savings account for your next car. Also, you can negotiate much better deals when you pay cash. And, it's wonderful not to have to make that monthly payment to someone else. And, you earn interest instead of paying the huge interest rates they charge.

• Don't mix religion and financial matters. If a person starts telling you about how righteous he is, starts quoting the Bible, and wants you to pray with him, put your hand on your money and back away.

• You are not going to want to work all your life. Start NOW – invest and save for the fun and leisure of maturity. Who is going to take care of you when you are too old to be productive? Don't be a burden on your children, or on society. Start NOW.

• Adjustable rate mortgages can be good and bad. In times of increasing interest rates, your adjustable rate can be bumped up sometimes by as much as two or three percentage points. This can cause a whopping big increase in your mortgage payment. Don't fool yourself by thinking that your low rate will stay low. Enjoy the low rates, but be financially prepared for the increases which are sure to come.

• Your home can be a source of great pleasure as well as an excellent investment, but not if you lose it to foreclosure. If you have a variable rate mortgage, learn how mortgage interest is calculated, and figure out what your payment would be if the interest rate is increased by two or three points. $100,000 at 4.5% for 20 years = $640 per month. At 7.5% = $817 per month. Big difference. Also factor in an increase in your property taxes, which can go up 3% to 5% annually.

• I've been poor and I've been rich. Rich is better. Beatrice Kaufman

ON RECESSIONS

• It has happened before. It will happen again.

• I was born in 1931, during the so-called "Great Depression." I recall putting cardboard in my shoes when we could not afford to have them half-soled, and eating a lot of cornbread and buttermilk for a meal. I always liked cornbread and buttermilk.

• I can distinctly recall working thru recessions in the 1960's, 1970's, 1980's, and 1990's. Some were severe, some just a little dip. I made a lot of money during the recessions of the 1970's and 1990's by adapting to the changes, and by not changing jobs, but by changing the way I worked.

• There are a lot of things you can do to soften the blow next time it hits, such as:

• Control your debt when times are good – don't wait until hard times to start trying to control debt.

• Don't lease or finance your cars. If you cannot pay cash, just drive an old jalopy until you can.

• Pay off credit cards every month. If you can't, just don't buy things. Learn to do without. It's better to learn to do without expensive gadgets and clothes than without food or shelter. 54% of credit card users pay in full every month (Consumer's Report). They are the smart ones.

• Use things until they wear out, not just until a slightly better or prettier model comes along.

• Don't mortgage any real estate you can't do without, with the possible exception of a conservative mortgage on your home.

• Create a cash reserve. Invest wisely. In addition to real estate, invest in liquid assets, such as stocks and bonds. I learned a long time ago that I am not a good stock picker, so my preference is mutual funds and exchange traded funds.

• Consider making your own decisions, but only if you are confident in your financial education and your judgment in financial matters. There is a wealth of reference and research material available free at companies like Charles Schwab. You can do it all on your computer.

• Assume that your income drops to $0 and stays there for a long time, maybe a year. Keep a cash reserve large enough to pay ALL of your expenses for at least a year. This includes, food, clothing, mortgage payments, car payments (if any, which there should not be), school expenses, and medical expenses.

• When the recession comes and your investment account shrinks, all you have to do is... nothing. Just sit back and wait.

It will come back up. Don't panic, be patient. That old saying is not, "Buy High, Sell Low."

• I do not like "margin" investing. If the market drops, you may have to liquidate to pay the debt. In real estate we called it "leverage." It can be very good at times, but a real killer at other times.

• A good investment account will not only help you through recessions, but will also greatly improve the quality of your retirement. You don't want to work all your life. I am living right now on investments made over the last 50 years.

• I've heard that the definition of an idiot is someone who does the same thing over and over again, but expects different results. Sometimes changing the WAY you work can make a big difference. (This does not mean that you should change vocations. Do what you enjoy and what pays best, but change the methods you use.)

• The summary of all this is simply to be conservative, and persevere, unless you have some mystical ability to predict a recession and recovery.

• And remember, it has happened before, it will happen again.

END

Revised 11-24-07, 2-2-09, 2-9-09, 5-24-09, 2-13-10, 3-30-10, 12-1-10, 3-27-11. The author is ready to discuss or defend any of these precepts at any time. The author is also ready to be proved wrong.

THE VENT

As published in Atlanta Journal-Constitution.
Vents are on page 2 of Metro Section, and at ajc.com/vent.

The US does not need 18 military bases in Germany nor 69 military bases in Japan. That war has been over for 55 years. Bring those boys home and put them on the Mexican border. (Published 3-4-11)

If I didn't live in Vinings, I would like to live in Austell. Good leadership, good people. (3-4-11)

Pre-K was unknown to my generation, and we seem to have done very well. In fact, even kindergarten was unknown to me, and I am now financially independent and leading a very happy life. (3-2-11)

Chambliss will never get another vote from me if he continues to waste more lives in Afghanistan. (11-28-09)

(In mid 2009 the AJC stopped accepting email Vents and started internet submissions. The quality of vents plummeted. Spelling and grammar errors were common, editing became non-existent, and thoughts expressed were primitive. So I decreased submissions. However, I enjoyed sending in these Vents while it lasted).

It's good to pray for health, wealth, or anything else, but don't rely on it. (10-20-09)

Life is more important than time... so stop driving so fast. (9-12-09)

Be patient with us older drivers. Our reflexes have slowed down, and we may be saving your life by driving carefully. You'll be here someday, if you're careful too. (7-4-09)

If you break into my home, you are fair game. (6-09)

To environmental activists: What do you have against poor people? Where would we be without efficient retailers like Target, Home Depot, and Wal-Mart? (5-29-09)

Those "new light bulbs" you complain about will earn your affection when you get your electric bill (5-27-09)

Remember this about the recession: It has happened before. It will happen again. (5-16-09)

President Obama is just like Bush in one respect – both thought that a president had to have a big war in order to be considered "great." Bush's was Iraq, Obama's is Afghanistan. Both waste American lives and money. (5-15-09)

In World War II, we used convoys to help fight off German submarine and aircraft attacks. Why can't we resort to convoys to fight Somalian pirates? (4-23-09)

One thing I liked about growing up in Atlanta in the '40s was that I could ride my bicycle from East Atlanta to Grant Park, lay it down, play around all day, and when I got ready to ride home, the bike would still be right where I left it. (4-17-09)

Talk radio is much more entertaining than music, even if you disagree with the talker. Neal Boortz drives me crazy, but he also makes me think. I guess maturity makes you realize that there are several sides to important issues. (4-17-09)

I'm not as proud of Atlanta as I used to be. (4-17-09)

If more of you people out there don't start agreeing with me, I'm going to stop telling you how to run your lives. (3-21-09)

A great idea – take the energy and talent and money which we are currently expending on high school sports and divert it to educating our children. (3-15-09)

President Obama wants to help balance the budget by cutting back in Iraq. That's wonderful, but it will not help if he increases spending in Afghanistan. (2-28-09)

The time has come for the United States to stop being the world's caretaker and start concentrating on taking care of ourselves. (2-19-08)

The basics of home financing should be taught in high school. (2-18-09)

Real estate people, take heart. The Empire State Building took 17 years to become profitable, and 19 years to reach 100% occupancy. This has happened before. It will happen again. (2-15-09)

Bankruptcy should not be an escape hatch for deadbeats and "shop 'til you drop" spenders. (2-9-09)

So now the U. S. Postal Service is having problems, and is considering cutting back to five day service. Their problems could be solved if they would charge a higher rate for junk and trash mail. (1-30-09)

The Bulldogs would have a great team if they would just learn to shoot, dribble, rebound and pass. (Sports, 1-25-09)

The best tax is a sales tax. People who spend the money should pay the taxes. (1-23-09)

My home county is the only large jurisdiction not to raise its millage rate, dip into financial reserves, cut staff or reduce services. Thank you, Cobb County officials, for doing a great job. (1-16-09)

To Emory: Can't you find some useful project in the U. S. to spend Gates' $14 million on instead of fighting smoking in China? (1-15-09)

I had to explain to my children and grandchildren that I must discontinue my monthly contribution to their investment accounts. No complaints! They're a good bunch. (1-10-09)

When the fast-food person hands me my chocolate shake, and I say "Thank you," I don't understand why the fast food person always says, "Not a problem." If it had been a problem, I would not have ordered the chocolate shake in the first place. (1-7-09. This vent was submitted on Dec. 31, 2005!)

Every time someone rides a MARTA train or bus, that is one less car on the streets, meaning less traffic and less pollution. We all have an obligation to support MARTA because we all benefit. Increased sales tax and increased fares are essential. (1-3-09)

My first Delta flight was on a DC-6 from Dallas in 1959. Since then 90 percent of my flying has been on Delta. I have never had an impolite attendant or a bad flight. Delta even rescued me when another airline cancelled my flight at the gate. Delta has always been, and I hope always will be, an important part of Atlanta's economy. (12-20-08)

Just because we have elected a more sensible president does not mean that we can let up on anti-war activities. Let's get out of Iran and Afghanistan
Now! (12-16-08)

There is nothing more disgusting than an eating contest…unless, of course, it's chocolate. (11-11-08)

Here are four magic words that will make you look better, feel better, and live longer: exercise more, eat less. (11-5-08)

How not to lose your job: Make yourself so valuable to your employer that he cannot afford to fire you. (11-4-08)

If you had ever done business with Washington Mutual, then you will not be surprised at their failure. I am surprised that they lasted as long as they did. (10-1-08)

(Someone sent in a vent complaining about having to be careful about germs, and asked if that was not what our immune systems were for, to which I replied):
Yes, God gave us an immune system. He also gave us common sense. So, go wash your hands. (9-20-08)

I'm all for increasing the sales tax. People who spend the money should pay the taxes.

(In response to a derogatory vent about "rednecks):
There's nothing wrong with being a "redneck." My father was a redneck, and I'm a redneck. I am also a college graduate and retired president of a very successful real estate company.

I'm beginning to lean toward the Democrats, except that their strong stand for labor unions scares me. If it were not for the labor unions, we would all be driving high-quality Fords and Chevrolets instead of Toyotas and Hondas.

To the male who enjoyed watching TV without female interruption, from another male: Your problem is you never had the right female offering the right interruptions. (9-3-08)

I am proud to be in the minority on most issues. (6-14-08)

Politicians should be able to change their minds without being accused of "flip-flopping" on an issue. As situations change, and as we get more information on a subject, there is nothing wrong with changing our minds. (7-11-08)

McCain says that he wants to reduce injuries in Iraq. A good way to do that would be to bring everyone home. (7-08)

The governments of Japan, China, India, and South Korea are funding research to improve plug-in technology for hybrid autos. That will never happen here as long as the oil men are in power. (7-08)

The venter who called the stock market a "gambling casino for wealthy people" is wrong. I am retired, have no pension, and am far from wealthy, but my careful investments in the stock market are now providing a very comfortable lifestyle, and will for the rest of my life. (6-26-08)

In the best interest of the citizens of the city of Atlanta, the entire Atlanta government, from the mayor on down, should resign. (5-08)

There's a book out entitled "Strong Women, Wild Horses." It would probably sell better if you reversed the adjectives.

I used to go grocery shopping with my money in my pocket and bring my groceries home in a bag. Now I take the money in a bag and bring my groceries home in my pocket. (5-24-08)

"Misspoke" is a euphemism for a bald-faced lie.

The term "popular music" is a misnomer. A better name would be "temporary music."

An individual should have a firearm to protect himself and his family. However, it is my opinion that the "right to bear arms" in the U.S. Constitution clearly refers to militia and not necessarily to individuals. Therefore, we should further amend the Constitution.

It's sad that Georgia legislators have lost all of what little respect they ever had. Why do people keep electing such dumb representatives?

That lady who loves her DVR better than any man has never known me.

People should have the right to get fat and eat themselves to death if they want to.

$1.6 Billion for the new international terminal? My bet is $4 Billion after the usual cronyism, graft, and corruption. (3-1-08)

We've carried this grudge too long. Let's open our doors to Cuba and welcome Cuba as a valuable trading partner and interesting tourist destination.

Why should we be worried about a billion people dying from smoking? The world is too crowded, anyhow. Let them choose.

The health care crisis is not caused by too few doctors. It's caused by too many sick people.

In Iraq: 150,000 people dead and billions of dollars in property destruction since we moved in. They would have been much better off with Saddam still in power. (1-14-08)

The way Bush avoids impeachment is by having a vice-president who would be even worse.

Anybody who opposes the Fair Tax does not fully understand it. Before you speak out against it, take time to read the book.

Is Lake Lanier half-full or half-empty?

Life begins when the kids move out and the dog dies.

When you consider Iraq, Iran, illegal immigrants, Venezuela, terrorism, and the cost of maintaining military bases all over the world, isolationism does not seem like such a bad idea.

What's a "sista girl"?

A generous rich guy who cheats on his wife is called a philandering philanthropist. (to which someone replied the next day, that if he were also a stamp collector he would be a philandering philanthropist philatelist).

To the venter who fled Saddam: if life is so much better in Iraq under U. S. rule, why did you flee to the United States?

Thank you for covering the Shih Tzu saga. It's good to read something interesting and entertaining instead of all the stories about people killing and maiming and stealing from each other.

A surge of forces to Iraq will do nothing but offer more targets to the insurgents. (OK, I was wrong on this one).

We don't need expensive scientific studies to tell us that teenage brains are not fully developed. All we need to do is watch them drive. (11-8-06)

The Clayton County teacher who took her class of 10-year-old boys to the Atlanta History Center should have used a chain, not just a rope. Invaluable artifacts were at risk.

I love it when you jealous venters try to drag down Cobb County. It proves most Atlantans don't know an honest and efficient government when they see one.

North Korea dares to be so bold because they know we will not fight three wars simultaneously.

Poker is fun, but it's not a sport.

Yes, I am obsessed with obeying the laws, and believe me, it is a magnificent obsession.

We are already paying thousands of soldiers in Germany, Italy, and Japan who we don't need there, since World War II ended sixty years ago. Bring them home and put them on the Mexican borders. (5-31-06)

Why do some cooks want to ruin a good mess of collards or an otherwise good corn muffin by adding sugar? They may think it's Southern, but it's not. (7-26-06)

What happens to the brain to make one prefer talk radio to music? Maturity makes you realize there are several sides to important issues, and understanding these viewpoints is more important than dumbing down to numbing rhythm and infantile lyrics. (5-12-06)

The best vanity plate I ever saw was "EIEIO." I'm betting the owner is an old farmer named McDonald.(5-29-06)

It is a blessing for an individual to be bilingual. However, it is a curse for a country to be bilingual. (5-16-06)

Women are better conversationalists than men because women don't have to breathe when they talk. (3-24-06)

Cobb schools buy 63,000 new laptops while Atlanta schools are embroiled in a fraud investigation. So, shut up about Cobb schools. (2-14-05)

We have too many soldiers fighting overseas or based in foreign countries and not enough of them protecting our borders.

GM car sales down two percent. Ford down 20 percent. Toyota, Honda, and Nissan are all up. What does that tell us about American cars? (10-6-05)

There are far too many idiots driving cars. An IQ test should be a part of the driver's license test. (4-12-07)

Taxes: Of life's two certainties, it's the only one for which you can get an automatic extension.

It took an hour and a half yesterday to drive from Vinings to Duluth. I can drive to Columbus or Chattanooga quicker than that.

A nation that tries to tax itself into prosperity is like a person standing in a bucket and trying to lift himself up by the handle.

I renewed my firearms license in Cobb County and came to two significant conclusions. First, Cobb County employees are always a pleasure to deal with. Second, I am still ready and willing to shoot anyone who tries to rob or harm any member of my family. (6-5-08)

Note: altogether I have had over 80 vents published. Many were published before I started counting and saving, some when out of town. Here are some which may have been published or should have been published.

Pull our troops out of Iraq, South Korea, Japan, and Europe and put them on the Mexican border. The drug cartels are the biggest threat to our country's stability.

I hope my home, or anyone else's, never catches on fire, but if it does, I am thankful that I am not in Fulton County. In fact, I am thankful that I am not in Fulton County for a lot of reasons.

Stopping (and blocking traffic) for a funeral procession was a fine old custom, showing respect and sympathy. However, it is no longer appropriate with our heavy traffic and four-lane roads.

Let's hope that the economy of India grows to the point that, someday, an Indian computer user will call technical assistance and hear,"Y'all need some he'p?"

Yes, casualties are a fair price to pay for liberty, but it is much too high if it's our casualties and their liberty.

A cyclist tried to pass me on my right side on a narrow street with no curbs, just as I turned right. I watched him fume as he tried to straighten his wheel and handlebars. My car? Not a scratch.

Aid to Africa is nothing but tribute to warlords.

The most efficient, gas saving, money saving speed is 55 MPH. Now would be a good time to save money and lives.

The United Auto Workers, having successfully destroyed the automobile industry in the United States, is now working on Mitsubishi and other foreign auto manufacturers. I wonder how much a car would cost if union-related expenses were not included in the price? And I wonder how much more quality we would get if union workers were not protected from discipline when their work is sub-standard?

To all you poor souls who panic when a cat gets stranded in a tree. FYI, a cat can climb down from anything it can climb up. All it needs is motivation, like hunger. You waste taxpayers' money when you call the fire department for a stranded cat.

Business executives – We hope you have learned this important lesson: don't give credit to people who don't pay their debts.

The people who clamor that we should ignore racial differences are the same ones who make race an issue when it fills their needs.

The world would be a far, far better place if everyone would just follow my suggestions.

END

POETRY AND DOGERTRY

This begins the poetry section. I call it "Poetry and Dogertry."
Dogertry is something that is not quite good poetry, but better than
doggerel. I made it up. M.B.

RETURN TO CHICKAMAUGA

Mounted on his charger, rearing,
Neither God nor mortal fearing,
Resplendent in his uniform of gray and gold,
Bravely with his saber pointing
As if he were knights anointing,
Rode the Colonel, in his stirrups standing bold.

"There they are, lads,
Cringing in those woods across this field.
Don't let them spoil
This sacred soil of Georgia.
Now here we go, lads! Regiment, forward! For home, for God,
For country… give 'em hell!"
Forward they surged with one magnificent yell.

Knee high grass, wildflowers blooming yellow and blue.
The meadow glistened green in summer sun.
Contested ground, deceiving in its tranquility.
A soldier gazed across and cocked his gun.

In the darkness of the trees,
Waiting, quiet, on their knees,
Boys in blue, with muskets ready,
As their leaders whisper, "Steady,
Steady, hold your fire.
One good volley, then retire."

Through grass and flowers brightly gleaming,
With their colors bravely streaming,
Rapidly the Colonel's men advanced across the glade.
Their heads held high and muskets lowered,
As a unit, forward, forward,
In their midst the Colonel led with naked blade.

Some heard from the woods, the one word
"FIRE!"

A brief rattle of muskets.
Followed quickly by thunder and flame.
A six gun battery of Napoleons, loaded with canister,
And the entire blue line
Sent a blizzard of lead and iron
To meet the Regiment.

Blue and yellow flowers glowing,
Nourished now by life-blood flowing
From the fallen forms of brave men who will charge no more.
Sprawling, crawling, ghastly mangled
Once a unit, now entangled
Men and horses stained the meadow with their gore.

* * * * * *

The Colonel's hair is silver now.
His dark blue suit has an empty sleeve.
The arm which held the saber was left upon the field.
Where his regiment once charged, a farmer now hoes corn.
The farmer mops his brow and says,
"All my neighbors wonder why
My corn grows so green and high."
The Colonel turns and goes.
He knows.

This poem was submitted for publication in an anthology of Georgia writers, entitled O Georgia. The editor-publisher said that he liked the story, but wanted me to convert it to a short story instead of a poem. The short story version was then published in O Georgia and again in the magazine Georgia Backroads, and is included in the short story section of this book.

MY GIRLS

Sunburned nose
and bandaged knee,
Trike to bike
then gone from me.
Little girls
so sudden grown,
Molding memories
of your own.
Now you've found
another man
To dry your tears
and hold your hand.
But time nor vows
can take from me
My little girls
of memory. End.

My Girls are, of course, my two daughters, Suzanne and Julie. Suzanne's son, Zac, has a son of his own, so Suzanne is now a grandmother. Julie has twin daughters, Natalie and Lyndsey.

A MOTHERS' DAY POEM*

For the Ladies in My Life
(Lucky Me)

Something tells me that I oughters
Write a message to my daughters
To commemorate upcoming Mothers' Day.
And I'd have to move to Tuscon
If the girls who wed my two sons
Were excluded from these words I have to say.

And you'd surely have to carry
Me away if I left Terry
Out of this expression of my love.
Even though she's not my mother,
Heaven knows I dearly lov'er
And she really is a gift sent from above.

As to many I've confessed,
I am very, very blessed
To have all you lovely ladies in my life.
Kids and husbands love you dearly,
You're the greatest, we see clearly,
Each is proud to introduce you as his wife.

Running families and houses,
Keeping up with kids and spouses,
Cooking, teaching, driving, chopping liver.
I love you and admire you,
With this poem I aspire to
Wish this Mothers' Day will be your greatest ever.

*Actually, I consider this to be "doggertry." It's a little better than doggerel, but not quite good poetry. Anyhow, it's the thought that counts. These lovely ladies include my wife, Terry, my two daughters, Suzanne and Julie, and my two sons' wives, Melinda and Maria. Well, "liver" and "ever" do rhyme, sort of.

THE POEM?

It is possible
To write a good poem
Without rhyme or meter,
But so far in my 79 years
I have seen only one.
So, keep trying.
It gives you something to do,
Keeps you out of mischief.
That one good one?
This is it.

EARTH AND MAN IN CONFLICT

An old woman in central city
coughs and wheezes as her crippled lungs struggle
to cope with the contamination we call air.

The clear cool creek rushes over rocks,
and when it pools,
collects plastic bottles, beer cans, old tennis balls,
and broken lawn furniture.

The doe was hit by a garbage truck
and smeared over the asphalt.
Her terrified, confused fawn waited by its mother's carcass
until it, too, was smeared over the asphalt.

The rolling green hills,
through the smoke of the factory
look gray-green.
A thousand acres of giants are toppled and crushed
to make toilet paper.

A glorious scenic panorama unfolds before me,
but I can not see it
 for the crowd.

A family of mallards,
a school of bass,
and a lone surviving cooter were finally choked out of the pond
by silt from surrounding subdivisions.

Earth strains to support life

until life overwhelms earth,
and abuses it,
then Earth fights back
with plagues, storms, quakes, floods, famine, and wars as weapons.

PRAYER

What are you doing?

I am praying.

To whom do you pray?

To anyone who may be listening.

What do you call this potential listener?

God.

Why God? Why not Allah, or Christ, or Zoroaster, or one of the many names which men have used to identify something which they do not understand?

If I am the one praying, then I get to choose the name of the object of my prayer. Anyhow, I do not think that a name which man may give him is important to God.

What if there is no one listening?

That is a chance I am willing to take.

If there is no one listening, wouldn't that be a waste of time?
Not if it makes me feel better, which it does.

Others kneel or prostrate themselves when they pray. Why do you pray from whatever position suits you?

What right does anyone have to tell me what position to pray from? How could anyone know a "proper" position for prayer?

Position is not important.

What do you pray for?

I start my prayers with thanks for health, prosperity, and all the many blessings which God has poured upon me, and primarily for Terry and my family. Then I pray that God intervene in any distressing situation, such as a loved one who may be ill, and for my own health, and for those who become victims of situations beyond their control.

Does it help to be "in the house of God" when you pray?

No. If there is a God, then by my definition He is omniscient and omnipresent. So-called "houses of God," or churches, are man-made, and do not enclose God. I feel closer to God when I am in a God-made environment, such as a forest, or the arms of a loved one.

There's that "if" again.

Yes. If it is important to God that I accept Him as truly existing, then I think He will do something which man cannot do.

Maybe He has. Maybe this is it. Maybe this is as close to understanding God as I will ever get. Maybe not. I hope not. I hope for a "revelation" which will give me better understanding. I often pray for such a revelation when I am "in church," that is, in the woods.

"The Bible says…"

The Bible is a wonderful piece of literature, it was written by man, re-written by man many times, interpreted and re-interpreted by man through many language changes. Men make errors, and sometime have vivid imagination which they confuse with reality. If God did have anything to do with the original Bible, then how can we know how many errors man has infused over the last few thousand years? How can we assume that God guided men through these many changes?

Why are you writing this?

It helps me understand things if I put them down on paper where others may see them.

What makes you think that you are right?

I don't. Neither do I think that I am wrong.

If God did not make you what you are now, then who or what did?

In order of importance: My parents, Terry, my children, Henry Robinson.

A POEM FOR A FATHER?
WHY BOTHER?

I shall not write of roses red,
But 6-packs of good brew instead.

Nor shall I write of violets blue,
But rhymes of cars and cycles, too.

And let's not talk of silk and lace,
But bats, and who's on second base.

But baseball with its boos and hisses
Can't compete with hugs and kisses.

Search not the malls for perfects gifts,
Just hug us and kiss us -- perfect lifts.

Write a poem for a father?
Why bother?

THE WRITER'S REFLECTION

Perfection!

Submission
*

Rejection
Dejection
*

Reflection
Introspection
Correction
*

ACCEPTION!
Elation!
(Completion)

GOOD PLACES TO VISIT

WARWOMAN DELL

NOT JUST ANOTHER PRETTY PLACE

Dell: A small, wooded valley

Before white people settled in the area now known as Rabun County, Georgia, before the city of Clayton was established, and before Rabun County was carved out of northeast Georgia, Warwoman Road was a well-traveled Indian trail, and the little valley now called Warwoman Dell was a well-established meeting place, as it is to this day.

A good, gravel road provides access to the dell, and follows a rocky brook which is one of the headwaters of Warwoman Creek. The road leads to a parking area about three-quarters of a mile away. Picnic tables and grills are scattered through the woods along the creek. A large pavilion with tables, benches, and a stone fireplace are at the end of the road, with portable restroom facilities nearby. Several plaques tell the interesting history of the little vale.

HISTORIC INTERSECTION

In addition to Warwoman Road, two other routes of historic significance intersect here; the Bartram Trail and the proposed right-of-way for the Blue Ridge Railroad, sometimes called the Black Diamond Railroad.

THE BARTRAM TRAIL

A young botanist named William Bartram left Philadelphia in April, 1773, sailed down to Charleston, and from there spent the next five years walking over the Carolinas, Georgia, Florida, and Alabama, primarily to study the flora of the area. He often traveled alone and unarmed. His travels took him through wilderness areas populated by Indians who were always friendly and helpful, and other areas sparsely populated by whites of questionable ethics and morality.

Through all his travels, he very rarely faced real danger. Once he met an Indian who, just a few minutes before, had left an altercation at a local tavern swearing that he would kill the next white man he met, but passed Bartram on the trail without incident. Again, on a small island in a Florida swamp, he had to stay up all night to fend off aggressive alligators by keeping a large fire burning.

In most of his travels, he was so out-of-touch with civilization that he did not know that the American colonies had revolted against England and were in a war for their freedom.

Bartram's notes are copiously detailed. Many people have followed his descriptions to map out the route he followed. Through Rabun County, and possibly through Warwoman Dell, this route is well known by hikers as The Bartram Trail. It can be easily seen and followed today as it leaves the dell, crosses Warwoman Road, and proceeds along Blue Ridge to the top of Rabun Bald. It is clearly indicated on the Rabun Bald quadrangle. However, according to the quadrangle, the original trail may have crossed Warwoman Creek a few hundred feet east of the dell.

THE BLACK DIAMOND RAILROAD

The author was once wandering through the woods between Warwoman Dell and the Chattooga River when he came upon a sturdy culvert made of finely carved granite, with no road or trail of any kind in sight. Why would anyone build such a large culvert in the middle of a forest? This discovery led to the author's quest for information on the Black Diamond, or Blue Ridge Railroad, and was before the helpful plaques were installed.

Cut into the side of the mountain a few feet above the dell's gravel road is the abandoned, unfinished right-of-way of the Black Diamond Railroad. More culverts made from hand-hewn granite are still evident, and appear to be just as strong as when they were built 160 years ago. A small, dark granite building of mysterious use overlooks the creek.

In the 1850's, a group of investors organized a railroad company called the Blue Ridge Railroad. This railroad was primarily intended to haul coal from Tennessee through Georgia, including through Rabun County, to the port of Charleston. A great deal of work was done, including excavation of a long tunnel near Walhalla in South Carolina, and money was spent on construction of the right-of-way, but the company ran out of funds just before the Civil War started. All ideas of building the railroad were abandoned during the war. In 1899, an effort was made to revive the project, but once again it was abandoned because of inability to raise sufficient financing.

An easy walking path now follows the old railroad bed through Warwoman Dell, intersecting the Bartram Trail.

CIVILIAN CONSERVATION CORPS

When Franklin D. Roosevelt took office as President of the United States in 1933, one of his first official acts was to create the Civilian Conservation Corps, better known as the CCC. The nation was in the depths of a great depression – THE great depression. Millions of people were without jobs. Roosevelt realized that at the same time there was a tremendous amount of work which needed to be done to protect our forests and natural resources.

To meet that goal, he matched the jobless with the much needed conservation projects and enabled many formerly unemployed people to once again support their families. We are still enjoying those improvements eighty years later. The gravel road and recreation facilities in Warwoman Dell are among those improvements.

CCC Camp Warwoman was not in the dell itself, but was nearby, off Warwoman Road. The camp quickly grew to 129 workers, who lived in tent-like facilities which they constructed themselves. Their pay was $1.00 per day, plus food and shelter.

Much evidence of their work is still seen today in Warwoman Dell. These include the picnic pavilion with a stone fireplace, parking area, and several smaller picnic shelters.

On the right of the gravel road, not far from the entrance, are two large concrete troughs. These were fish hatching tanks, also built by the CCC, and used to raise speckled trout which were then released into the streams and rivers of Rabun County.

"WARWOMAN"

Warwoman Creek. Warwoman Road. Warwoman Dell. Where did the name "Warwoman" come from? Several stories attempt to provide the answer. You can take your pick from these which follow:

An Indian squaw named Cateeche killed a white man in a battle and was given the name Warwoman.

Three Indians passing through the community kidnapped a white baby. The mother of the baby followed them until they camped for the night. She waited for them to fall asleep, then sneaked into their camp, stole a tomahawk, killed all three, and rescued the baby. The mother was afterwards nicknamed Warwoman.

A similar story relates that Indians captured two white women, who waited until the Indians had gone to sleep by a creek, then stole their weapons and killed them. The women and their neighbors then named the creek Warwoman.

And, as suggested on one of the historical plaques, the Warwoman was a respected Cherokee dignitary who voiced her opinions at tribal councils, particularly on items relating to war and peace. She regularly visited the dell to preside over councils and rituals.

LOCATION

The popular dell is located on Warwoman Road, 2.8 miles east of where that road intersects U. S. Highway 441 in downtown Clayton. It is shown on the Rabun Bald quadrangle at coordinates 3862-285, for those of you who are familiar with that helpful tool. The quadrangle also shows the rugged terrain of the surrounding area.

In addition to the walking trail which follows the old railroad cut, a short, easy trail leaves the pavilion and winds its way along the creek to the end of the dell, where you will find a small waterfall. For more ambitious hikers, another trail leaves the old railroad line near the pavilion and winds its way up through the hills to old roads which can take you to Lake Toccoa or back to Warwoman Road.

QUADRANGLE

This explanation is for readers who are not familiar with this very helpful tool, frequently used by hikers and explorers of Georgia's backroads. Actually, anything with four sides is a quadrangle, but the United States Department of the Interior Geological Survey assigns the name "quadrangle" to its 55,000 topographic maps of the United States, including the 1,095 maps which cover Georgia.

Quadrangles are named after large communities or significant terrain features, such as the Rabun Bald Quadrangle which shows Rabun Bald Mountain as well as Warwoman Dell and part of the city of Dillard.

These topographic maps show how steep and how high a particular trail travels, as well as creeks or rivers you may have to cross. The elevation at Warwoman Dell is 2,000 feet above sea level, and at Rabun Bald it is 4,696 feet. If you hiked from the dell to the peak, you would climb 2,696 feet. Buildings are shown as small black squares, forested areas are green, cleared fields are white.

The author uses quadrangles extensively in planning hikes.

The scale is 1:24,000, which is about 2 and 5/8 inches to a mile, or one inch = 2,000 feet.

Quadrangles can be bought at most local map stores, or ordered from the U. S. Geological Survey.

End

Kolomoki Mounds

A Relatively Undiscovered Historical Gem

Almost in Alabama but altogether in Georgia, Kolomoki Mounds State Park is tucked away in the southwest corner of our state. This 1,293 acre park is actually two parks in one – a fascinating historical area and a very well developed recreational area.

The mounds, of course, are the most prominent feature of the park. Visitors are immediately drawn to mound A, the temple mound, and the largest of the seven mounds. It is 56 feet high, as high as a five story building, and 325 feet by 200 feet at its base. The 325 foot base is longer than a soccer field.

A raised area on top of the southern half of the mound was probably a temple platform. Researchers have estimated that it would have taken over 2,000,000 baskets of earth to build the mound, each basket dug and filled by hand somewhere around the base, and hauled on someone's back to the top. This back-breaking task is believed to have been completed over 700 years ago.

At that time, approximately 2,000 people lived around the mounds in a village of thatched houses. The Kolomoki area was the cultural, ceremonial, and commercial center for the most highly developed group of people in this part of the world. Occupants of the site at various periods of history are referred to as Weeden Island, Kolomoki, and Lamar Indians. The area around Kolomoki Creek was continuously occupied by one or more of these groups for about 650 years. Compare that to Atlanta's 200 years.

Mound A resembles the mounds at Etowah, but the other Kolomoki mounds are smaller and are spread out over a much larger site. Steps lead to the top of mound A, from which visitors enjoy a panoramic view of the entire Kolomoki Archaeological Area.

The other mounds vary in size, some about the size of a golf green. They were all used for different purposes, primarily as ceremonial mounds and burial mounds. In the 1800's, the Mercier family, which farmed the area, actually used mound G for their family burial ground. Of course, this was long before we realized the importance and historical significance of the wide variety of mounds scattered around Georgia.

The most interesting mound is mound E, which appears to be engulfing the Visitor Center. From the Visitor Center, which actually extends into the mound itself, you can walk inside mound E and see the results of archaeological explorations, revealing the common grave of four people, along with 54 pottery items to be used in the afterlife, as well as pearl beads and copper ornaments. Radiocarbon dating estimates that the mound and grave were used around 2,200 years ago.

The original skeletons were re-buried, but realistic plastic skeletons replaced them, giving visitors an excellent idea of the graves just as the archeologists left them. The grave itself strongly resembles an old, hand-dug well. The viewing area is enclosed and air-conditioned. Comfortable seats are available for the sound and light explanation of the mound and its burials. No other "Indian Mound" historical site offers visitors this unique experience of walking inside a mound to experience this intimate part of the lives and deaths of the inhabitants.

The adjoining museum displays numerous items found on the site, including much more pottery, copper and pearl ornaments, tools, weapons, and effigies of birds and animals. Several well done drawings and paintings depict the life style of the early inhabitants.

Evidence found in mound E and other burial mounds indicates that human sacrifice was common in the burial ceremony of important people.

Don't worry about crowds. Only two other couples were in the historical area while the author and his wife were there, but this was mid-week on a school day. This is truly an undiscovered gem of a historical area. Visitors to both the historic and recreation areas total 150,000 annually.

A hand-out available at the Visitor Center outlines a self-guided tour of the mound area, describing the use of each mound. This is a highly recommended, easy walk.

Temple Mound

The recreation area, which straddles Kolomoki Creek, contains seven picnic shelters, playgrounds, miniature golf, two group shelters, a swimming pool, 24 camp sites for recreational vehicles or tents, three nature trails, a ball field, two lakes for fishing and boating, and a group camp. All camp sites have water and electric hook-ups, picnic tables, fire rings, and grills. A sanitary dump station, bath house, and laundry facilities are also available. This recreation area is extensively used, and can be reserved by calling 229-724-2150 or 1-800-864-7275.

This southwest corner of Georgia includes many other interesting attractions, including Providence Canyon, Westville, Lake Seminole, Lake Walter F. George, and Coheelee Creek Covered Bridge, and is not far from the excellent museums in Columbus.

Kolomoki Mounds is a Registered National Historic Landmark. Blakely is the nearest town, located six miles south of Kolomoki State Park. On Georgia Highway 1 (sometimes called U. S. 27) there are plenty of signs directing you to Kolomoki.

END